OUT
OF HER
LEAGUE

Also by Ava Rani

THE BIOTECH BILLIONAIRES SERIES
The Spare
The Heir
The Charmer

Extraordinary Praise for Ava Rani and *Out of Her League*

"An immersive, addicting, and feel-good romance that isn't afraid to dig deep. *Out of Her League* is a must-read, and Ava Rani paints a world I want to live in forever."
—Catherine Cowles, *New York Times* bestselling author of *Secret Haven*

"Just when I think it's impossible to love Ava Rani more, she writes another stunner of a romance! *Out of Her League* had me in a choke hold from the very first page and never let go. Rani weaves together two strong personal journeys with a satisfying, undeniable love story. Isabelle and Austin's connection is smart, sexy, and full of Rani's signature balance between romantic swoon and social commentary. I adored every moment."
—Grace Reilly, *USA Today* bestselling author of *Yes, Chef*

"*Out of Her League* is sparkling and passionate and a pleasure to read. I love Ava's voice and it shines here!"
—Alisha Rai, author of *Partners in Crime*

"A perfect mix of sweet love and hope. Ava Rani excels at complicated romances with payoffs that are realistic and feel earned. I've never rooted for a female lead more than I did with Isa."
—Julie Olivia, *USA Today* bestselling author of *If It Makes You Happy*

"Ava Rani has quickly become one of my favorite authors and I love how she creates the perfect mix of romance and drama!"
—Salma Rafaf, *People*

OUT
OF HER
LEAGUE

A Novel

AVA RANI

AVON

An Imprint of HarperCollinsPublishers

HarperCollins books may be purchased for educational, business, or sales promotional use. For information, please email the Special Markets Department at SPsales@harpercollins.com.

Avon, Avon & logo, and Avon Books & logo are registered trademarks of HarperCollins Publishers in the United States of America and other countries.

hc.com

FIRST EDITION

Interior text design by Diahann Sturge-Campbell

Eiffel Tower illustration © mitay20/Stock.Adobe.com

Library of Congress Cataloging-in-Publication Data has been applied for.

ISBN 978-0-06-341372-6

26 27 28 29 30 LBC 5 4 3 2 1

To women in medicine:
May your accomplishments be loud,
And your call nights, quiet.

Chapter 1

ISABELLE

*S*ome people found balance when they exercised. Other people read. Some people wrote. My best friend, Selena, loved photography.

For me, it was the operating room.

The cool air, bright overhead lights, and my thoughts. A steady stream of information and ever-changing circumstances. Moving with an assassin's dexterity but a sniper's precision. Circumstances changed, I adjusted.

After over a decade of training, there was no place on Earth where I felt more capable than in here.

"Blood pressure one-ten over seventy, tracking up," the anesthesiologist reported from the other side of the patient.

"Almost done here." I glanced up to my attending, Dr. Thomas. The corners of his eyes—the only part of his face I could see with everything else covered by masking and surgical garb—lifted. He nodded encouragingly.

I drew back to get a better look at the surgical planes, going through the mental checklist of all the steps in a compound-fracture repair.

In the OR, I was a maestro leading an entire symphony mud-dled with sounds of bone saw and the occasional cautery. The minutes melted together and, in that time, every single piece of medical information I'd collected up to that point dovetailed into an opus.

"He's ready to close," I called, glancing up at vitals. Heart rate, steady. Blood pressure, normal. Blood loss, minimal. I took a quick, proud breath, and my shoulders relaxed the tini-est bit.

Coming out from the concentration felt like landing after a long flight—the palpable thump as the jet's tires hit the runway telling you that you were no longer floating.

The serene quiet lifted.

"Good job, Dr. Mercado." Dr. Thomas helped guide a younger resident into appropriate closure.

Some people sang. Some people danced. I mended mangled bones.

And I was damn good at it.

I matched into the best orthopedic surgery residency in the country. I was always the attendings' first choice to assist. I was the first resident in my class to complete cases solo. I wrote the most research.

I had a future, a legacy, waiting for me.

Proof that all the sacrifices I'd made for this career were worth it.

I flicked a quick look at the clock and cursed silently to myself.

"I'm going to head to the floor," I told Dr. Thomas. He answered with a nod, and I made my way out of the OR.

All the thoughts I hushed for surgery kicked back on. Without the overhead OR lights to dim it, the reality that the world never paused was glaring.

I turned the corner from the OR anteroom, got changed out of my OR scrubs, and went through my post-op checklist in my head while also trying to time how long it would take me to get to the bridal boutique.

I walked through the hospital on autopilot, the elevator doors opened, and I was met with the physical manifestation of everything I had to do.

"We have seven post-ops, three discharges, and that trauma case you just completed is coming up from PACU in a couple hours," Ami listed off. She was waiting for me the second I got off the elevator.

Dressed in what felt like a uniform—mint scrubs, the fleece pullover all residents seemed to wear, and a mildly agitated smile—Ami was the perfect junior resident. Always prepared, every question *her* juniors had was addressed, and if she didn't know the answer, she'd expend every bit of energy she had to get the answer on her own before bothering a senior resident.

"Great." I threw my fleece over my scrubs, already freezing in the cold hospital air.

"That case you just did, it was the compound fracture, right?" Ami kept in step with me as we made our way down the hall, her question bursting with at least ten more. "It's probably a good one to recall for the—"

"Winthrop fellowship application?" I grinned. Ami reminded

me of myself. When she reached my level of experience in three years, she'd be a force to be reckoned with.

"It was, and Dr. Thomas let me do the whole case."

"Wow." Ami practically mooned over the idea of completing a case start to finish. I was about to start my last year of a six-year residency. And now, I was leading the surgeries. Surgical attendings acted as a watchful eye while I did what came so incredibly naturally to me. "If you pioneer a new procedure, what will we call it, since the Mercado Technique is taken?"

My nerves ticked.

"I'm partial to the Isabelle Maneuver," I joked, but the reminder sent a thorny prickle down my spine. I was the daughter of two surgeons. My father, in particular, had made such a mark on the field that everyone either expected I'd be exactly like him or assumed his *daughter* would fall short.

But I planned to be better. I planned to be the best.

And the prestigious Winthrop Reconstructive Surgery fellowship was how I would do it. It encompassed traumatic, athletic, and pediatric reconstructive orthopedic surgeries. Deeply rooted in research and innovation, the surgeons who left that program had entire methods named after them.

"Lucky." Ami handed me the list of patients, which I gave a quick review as we made our way to the post-op unit. I folded it lengthwise, then tucked it in my back scrub pocket. "I am itching for more OR time," she said.

"It'll be you soon enough."

We walked over to the nursing station.

"Yeah . . . I know," Ami said with a little doubt in her eyes, but nodded. "I'll get the team."

She walked off to the resident workroom at the corner of the unit to alert the rest of the team—the junior residents and a med student that I was ready to round.

That left me a second to think.

It would take a half hour to round, forty minutes if I ran to the boutique. Thirty if I took a cab that got stuck in traffic. The subway would be faster, but it was a hot summer day and sweat-drenched was not how I wanted to look showing up to the Lily Langham atelier.

I looked down at my scrubs. My appearance probably didn't matter given what I'd be wearing.

I loved my work. Lived for it. Some days, the climb to the top was exhilarating. Others, I made the mistake of looking down and realizing all that was left behind. Like today, when I was going to be outrageously late to my best friend's final wedding dress fitting.

The clock hanging over the nurses' station taunted me with the idea of Selena at the boutique waiting for me, her defunct maid of honor.

Again.

I sent a quick apologetic text to her, knowing she was probably expecting it given my record, and sighed.

Ami retightened the ponytail holding her long black hair back and pushed a few stray strands behind her ear. She gave me a nod that everyone was ready to go.

"Okay." I looked at the junior residents waiting for me to start. "Let's begin."

* * *

Sitting neatly behind precisely laid gray stone between a high-end jewelry store and a luxury mid-rise on Fifth Avenue, Lily Langham's Manhattan atelier was closed to the public when they let me in through the storefront's double glass doors.

"The bride-to-be is upstairs." The design associate motioned to the stairwell that led up to the design studio.

I breezed past her and Selena's bodyguard—who stood as solid as the stone facade next to the staircase—with a quick smile. "Thanks."

My best friend since college, Selena, fell in love with the closest thing to Prince Charming to ever exist and Henry Amari proposed to her at the end of a sun-soaked summer in the Hamptons. Now, ten months later, they were making the final preparations for the wedding in a few weeks.

This July at a castle in France.

"I'm sorry." I rushed up the stairs and found Selena standing on a platform in front of trifold mirrors.

"What do you think?" Selena turned immediately when she heard the signature swish of my scrubs as I raced up the stairs.

"Wow!" I almost yelled, startling a few of the designers.

Selena's long brown hair was loose over her shoulders. She was wearing an empire-waisted wedding gown with delicate lace sleeves that stood brilliantly against her warm-sienna skin. The V-neck led to a bead-adorned bodice, then billowed into a skirt that floated elegantly over her figure and trailed behind her. She looked like a romantic heroine from a novel. I took a few disbelieving steps toward her.

Selena was always beautiful—whether it was in the skin-tight jeans we forced ourselves into as college girls or the office-appropriate dresses she opted for these days. But in this wedding dress, she was dazzling.

"You look like a princess." I took her hands in mine and squeezed, having trouble believing she was the same person I met twelve years ago in college. "I'm so sorry I'm late."

"Don't be." Selena squeezed my hands back. "I wasn't alone. Henry's sister was here for a while."

"Oh, that's so nice of her." Guilt weighed on my chest like a lead apron. I was the maid of honor, yet I couldn't be relied on. In my tardiness, Selena's soon-to-be sister-in-law filled in the gaps.

Selena and I had been pretty much a duo since college. After meeting Henry, Selena's social circles had expanded dramatically. His family and close-knit friend group had welcomed Selena in with open arms.

"I'm glad." I ignored the bitter envy, because it was childish to think I was losing my best friend. She finally had the big family she'd always wanted, and who was I to begrudge her when I was so hard to pin down these days? It was a feeling I was getting used to. "The dress is perfect."

And it was completely Selena. A romantic at heart who had locked it away for so long. This dress was the perfect celebration of all her dreams coming true.

Quiet set over the design studio.

She looked down and turned her engagement ring on her finger. "I have to tell you something."

"Yeah?"

"Well . . ." She took a step off the podium and twisted her fingers around the lace along the fitted waist. "Henry's list for the wedding was too short. He only included around seven people, so I had the planner get all the important names for his side from his mom."

"Okay . . ."

The fact that Selena was marrying one of the richest men in the world came with a lot of perks, including hiring one of New York's best wedding planners. Knowing she had a ton of help made me feel slightly less terrible about being such a defunct maid of honor, but right now Selena's tense frame was making me nervous.

"And one of their family friends that's coming is Francesca Cole. She's some New York socialite they've known forever," she continued as one of the seamstresses gently pulled her hand from the delicate fabric and led her into the changing room.

There was a brief pause and some shuffling. A metallic zip from a garment bag filled the silence.

"And Francesca Cole obviously gets a plus-one . . ." Selena called from behind the door. A second later it began to open. She reemerged in a simple blue dress and stilettos.

"Right . . ."

Selena looked around the room for a few seconds, then back to me, her eyes creased with guilt. "Her plus-one is Blake Thompson."

My stomach hollowed. Static filled my ears.

"I asked Henry's mom, and, apparently, he and Francesca are dating. They have been for a while." Selena's voice sounded suddenly muffled in my ears, like I'd just walked out of a loud concert.

"He's in New York?" I choked out when my lungs managed a breath. My mind reeled. Sharp green eyes filled the back of my vision, like my memory was pulling him into existence. "Since when?"

"I don't know," she admitted, her voice jumping up an octave. "I only noticed his name today when the planner gave me the updated list."

I nodded.

My entire world spun, every memory of Blake and me whipping past my vision. The day we met at orientation. Fooling around in the campus library. The promises we made to each other in all the moments in between.

Our breakup, right when I finished medical school.

The one that only felt like a pause. And every time he was in town, we hit play.

My residency took me to New York. A start-up took him to Silicon Valley. But it never felt over. Whenever he visited, it was like no time had passed.

Selena's voice rang through what felt like being submerged in water. She sat down on the plush bench that flanked the dressing podium. "I can uninvite the Coles. Henry won't care."

"Huh?" I took a quick breath, refusing to let my body show my inner reaction. I was in control; my stupid heart would fall in line. "No, of course not. You can't uninvite someone. And it's okay. I'm not holding on to the same stupid ideas twenty-six-year-old Isa had."

It was a lie. Blake and I had always talked about how we'd pick back up once we became adults with fully realized lives, not immature college kids with big dreams. Now I was one fellowship acceptance letter away from that dream and Blake was . . .

My chest tightened.

I tried not to let myself picture the way I'd always imagined he would come back into my life, permanently. He'd move back. We'd go to that little park for ice cream. We'd laze around on the weekends while he watched the Premier League. I'd finally make that paella that was on my list of things to try for years.

He was supposed to be my one. The one that stuck. The one who understood my life, my ambitions. He had his dreams, too, and once we both accomplished them, he'd be back, and we'd be the ultimate power couple together.

"Have you talked to him lately?" Selena asked hesitantly.

"Not for months," I admitted. We saw each other last summer and it went the same as it always did. He took a cab from JFK straight to my place, waiting there until the terrible hour I got back from work. Then we stayed entwined under my sheets for days and swore that we'd never go that many months without seeing each other again.

"You deserve better." Selena took hold of my hand. "I'm sorry."

I could only nod because every single word I could think of got caught in my throat. My heart raced, and with every beat a new question popped into my mind. When did he come back to Manhattan? Why didn't he think to tell me? How long had he been *seeing* someone? Someone important enough to accompany to a wedding?

We weren't officially together, so we'd both had other relationships in the meantime, but not *real* ones. At least, I hadn't.

I didn't have time. I had the occasional hookup because I always assumed one day it would be me and Blake.

"Isa . . ." Selena's hand waved in front of my face; facets of light bounced off her diamond ring. "Say the word and Henry will have him—"

I put my hand up and forced a laugh. Selena was getting way too used to having her rich fiancé's influence at her fingertips.

"You two are slowly becoming the same person," I said lightly. "I'm fine."

"Are you sure?"

"Yes, really." I pulled my hands from hers and stood up. We got our things together and made our way to the door. "This is your wedding. You shouldn't worry about anything, especially not your maid of honor."

"Please. I have an entire team taking care of every wedding detail." She waved it off. "I am the opposite of stressed about this wedding. I care about *you*."

"I'm fine. Really."

I knew she wouldn't believe me.

My apartment was still littered with reminders of him. Of us. The photos of my med school graduation, his business school graduation, my residency match day celebration—all of it. We were living our separate lives until we were the people we wanted to be, but we always intended to come back together.

We were *supposed* to be together.

"You're still going to that children's benefit with me, right?" Selena took the cue to change the subject as we made our way out of the bridal shop. Her bodyguard, Drake, opened the door, did a quick scan of the street, then held it wider for us to exit. "It's an auction."

"Yes, of course." I linked my arm in hers.

The last remnants of the cherry blossom petals whipped past us in the warm early-summer wind. I tried to focus on something about the wedding, to not center myself in what was a huge night for her. The final fitting.

"Isa . . ." Selena yanked on my arm. "Come on. I know that look. Talk to me."

I waited a beat and sighed. "I still have a plus-one to your wedding, right?"

"You can have a plus-fifty." A devious smile slowly skated across her mouth. "Come to brunch if you can, sometime before we all fly out to Paris," Selena insisted. "We can put my future sister-in-law's meddling skills to work and find the perfect make-your-ex-jealous date."

I laughed as the idea cemented into my mind. I could deal with how all of this felt later. For now I was going to deal with how it looked. If Blake had moved on, then maybe I had, too.

I ignored the dull ache in my chest, because I was a woman in surgery. We didn't break. Especially not over a guy.

Chapter 2
AUSTIN

Clouds hung over the weathered red brick that wrapped around a three-story building in Brooklyn. The Mistry Foundation had purchased it over a decade ago, right after I signed a giant contract renewal with Farnham FC in the Premier League.

"There are developers interested in the lot," said Alice, the Mistry Foundation's one-woman coordination team. She took care of all the day-to-day operations at the community sports centers. "And we aren't using it." She looked at me pointedly, as if hoping I'd chime in.

"Yeah . . ." I murmured, the humidity dragging my lungs down in a tired exhale.

Alice's gaze shifted from me to Zoya Mistry, probably hoping she'd be more receptive. "Selling the field gives us the funding to keep the building maintained and thriving for years." She flicked her eyes back to me before tucking her phone back in her pocket. "Think about it."

"Yeah . . ." I murmured again.

She turned on her heels to walk back inside.

The second the heavy metal door shut behind us, Zoya's reply was lightning fast. "You can't sell this field."

"I wasn't planning on it," I assured her. I took a few steps away from the building and gazed into the overgrown field adjacent to it. The grass was longer than it should be to kick a ball around and all the posts were weathered after a couple years without proper maintenance.

"Good, because the kids love it."

I let out another long sigh. "This place was supposed be a lot of things."

It was left in my care and I fumbled it.

"Well, for now it's still doing *exactly* what you and Theo wanted for it fifteen years ago," Zoya reminded me. "The neighborhood's kids have a safe place to occupy their time after school. Some of them come out here and play soccer *even* when the grass isn't mowed."

Theo and I had wanted to do a lot of things together. My best friend since we were kids, he was responsible for making me who I was today. He had practiced soccer with me in the alley behind his family's restaurant in Queens every night. Later, he had made sure scouts paid attention to the talented upstart from the city. Once I had landed a contract and started making actual money, he even helped me start this foundation.

I wondered if he'd be disappointed now. I was injured, no longer playing in the Premier League, and the foundation was struggling to make ends meet. But I was trying to correct course. "Theo would—" I started.

"Would be happy that you're moving along in your life," Zoya cut in. "While we're on the subject, any news on the coaching front?"

"Jesse says there's some interest in coaching B team for a couple clubs in the Premier League and the French league." My agent was emailing me daily, actually, trying to get me to accept an offer. Now that I was seventeen years into my career, it was time to start looking at the next step. Coaching was the obvious choice, but I couldn't move back to Europe until I knew I'd left this place in a good position. Put it back on the path it was on before Theo died.

"Great, *see*? It'll all work out," Zoya said, trying to encourage me the way Theo always used to. "You have your next move lined up, and the foundation has the Amherst auction to look forward to. That'll help."

Zoya and Theo got together around the same time we'd begun the Mistry Foundation. They were perfect for each other. I was away playing in England at the time, so I saw their love story unfold mostly through phone calls and a few visits—that should have been more frequent—during the offseasons. They were the kind of couple that made you believe in love. After he died, Zoya did a commendable job filling Theo's shoes—taking a leadership role at the foundation and looking after me.

"For now." I huffed a long breath, blinking away all the memories. "It needs to go well."

In a few days, the auction would hopefully raise enough funds to keep the sports programs here running a while longer. But while a few hundred thousand dollars was a lot of money, this place needed more than that if I wanted it to become what Theo and I had dreamed up as kids.

"It will. You need to buck up." Zoya walked a few steps forward into the slightly overgrown grass. "And one day, who knows, maybe your and Theo's dream to expand this place will pan out."

We wanted to create a formal way to nurture the next generation of talent. The football clubs in Europe usually had their own version of this, each one scouting and developing talent that would eventually make its way into their teams. We wanted to build something like that.

"Theo always joked it would be so successful that we'd become the avenue into a competitive American league." I smiled, hoping I hadn't demolished our chances by stepping away for so long. "For now, I'll stay in the city and get this place back on stable footing."

It was a lofty idea that required hundreds of moving pieces outside of a charitable organization. A fully staffed training program, scouts, contracts with affiliates, press, external funding, a league partnership to make sure that talent had somewhere to go. And hopefully that somewhere wasn't too far from home.

"It will." Zoya smacked a hand on my shoulder supportively, pulling me from my mental spiral. "And I think *you'll* sell for a lot."

I was already regretting one of my donations to the auction: offering to train a fan for four weeks in the offseason. It reeked of washed-up athlete, but it was for a good cause. "It was better than your original idea."

She barked a laugh. "I still think 'win a date with Austin Cade' would have done well."

The metal door opened and, this time, a tiny mess of black hair and boundless energy ran out.

"Come on, sweetie. Let's go to the kitchen." Zoya held out her hand to her daughter, Joseen.

After Theo died, Zoya sold the startup they'd founded together and made a hard left turn into cooking. She started a catering service and built a demonstration kitchen to run classes in. Through the grief, she poured herself into something new, and I envied her ability to do that.

Because I felt stuck. And all I wanted to do was move in the right direction. Get myself back on the path I'd always intended to be on.

Joseen's lopsided ponytail shook with a vengeance. "I want to go to practice with Uncle Austin."

"You can help me bake some cupcakes," Zoya offered.

Joseen shook her head again.

"How about we read that new book?" I asked, squatting down to look at her eye to eye. My knee, recovered from the surgery but not the same, pulled with a stiffness I couldn't shake. "I got a few new ones for you."

Even though she looked exactly like her mom—big brown eyes, a toothy smile, pin-straight hair—every time I looked at her, I saw Theo.

I saw the scraggly kid that made sure his mom made two lunches because he knew I wouldn't have one. The kid who sat on the playground at school with me until the sun went down, sounding out words and teaching me to read because none of our teachers were equipped to handle a kid with a learning disability.

Her face sagged down. "I don't like it. I'm not good at it."

"You *are* good at it; you have to try," I encouraged.

"Can I come to practice?" she negotiated.

I sighed. Now that my knee was six weeks post-op, I was back—with some regularity—to practices, but something felt *off*. "It's not for a few hours, so two books and you can come."

"Okay," she answered immediately.

I stood and took her hand. "Come on. Books, then practice."

I didn't take too long to think about the fact that I was probably just outmaneuvered by a five-year-old.

* * *

After practice, I left Jo to kick a ball around with some of the other players while I went to the rehab room for physical therapy.

"Stability is more pronounced. You're doing great for six weeks post-op," Dr. Mercado announced from behind the screen, tilting her body to the side so she could see me. "You're not favoring your right side anymore."

She wasn't my usual doctor. I'd seen her a few times working with Dr. Reinhold, but today she was filling in for him. She was much younger than Dr. Reinhold, and prettier, too, I'd noticed. Her curly black hair was pulled back in her signature bun, and the mint-green scrubs contrasted against her sienna skin.

She was just as focused as Dr. Reinhold, though. When I entered the room, she got right to business. Now she stared at the pressure monitor while Trevor, the team physical therapist, instructed me to go through some basic rotation movements.

"So I should be good to play soon?" I already knew the answer, but still I hoped for a different one. If I could play, at least then I could get my mind off the other daunting tasks ahead of me.

An ACL tear was never good, and I'd already healed from one in the past. This time, I probably wouldn't recover as well. In some twisted irony, I played twelve years in the Premier League against some of the best talent in the world, and yet the injury that might actually end my career was one I got here— two years into playing in the American league.

"Technically, I'm not your doctor, so I can't give you a prognosis." Her eyes tracked along the screen again. "As far as playing goes, let's keep focused on the recovery plan first."

"Right, *then* playing," I added.

She glanced up at me, expression unreadable, then back at her notes. "You're in the offseason. *Try* to relax."

"Easier said than done," I mumbled.

For so long, playing soccer was the only way I could feel balanced. It was the only thing that motivated me. At least when I eventually moved to coaching, I didn't have to lose the game, just the play.

"Look." Her voice rose for a second before distilling down to a solemn note. "It could have been a lot worse. You've had two ACL tears in your career. Your knee looks great, but you need to take recovery seriously."

I sat up a little straighter at her show of concern. "I will."

She let out a conciliatory sigh. "And . . . I don't know. Don't let the reporters rile you up."

"You watched that?" I grimaced. It wasn't a great interview.

After weeks of getting my head around a slow recovery, I was finally making moves toward my next step, when some punk with a microphone—one that never played professionally a day in their life—talked about my retirement like it should have happened two years ago. Back when I turned down an extension to my Premier League contract to play for the American league.

"It was on in the hospital waiting room," Dr. Mercado said dismissively, then turned her attention back to her notes. Her fingers tapped along the keyboard, then she looked back up at me. Her manner shifted a bit, her lips moving from a straight line to curved at the edges, like she was *trying* her best to be nice. "You used to be great with the press—charming, even."

My interest spiked. "Soccer fan, Dr. Mercado?"

"*God* no." The statement popped out of her mouth and her eyes widened at the unintended honesty.

I chuckled. "Tell me how you *really* feel."

"Well . . ." The corners of her mouth tipped up. "It's just not my thing. It takes such a long time to kick a ball back and forth, and nothing really happens."

"And what sport *do* you like to watch?" I nudged a little sarcastically, feeling a bizarre fizz wondering what she'd say next.

"Are those baking competitions considered a sport? Because they should be." She typed a few more things into the computer, then looked back at me. "But I will say, the injuries in your sport are far more interesting. And after Dr. Reinhold let me scrub in on your case, I'm a little invested in that knee. So can you please tell the person who owns it not to screw up all our hard work?"

"I'll take it easy." I put my hands up. "On the knee and the reporters."

She smiled. "Good. The injury changes your knee, not *you*."

"You gonna be here awhile?" I found myself wondering. Then I realized I'd said it aloud. I cleared my throat. "With the team?"

"I'm not sure," Dr. Mercado said, which prompted Trevor to laugh.

"Don't be modest!" Trevor said. "This one's destined for big things. She's headed to a big fancy fellowship."

Her shoulders lifted. "Well, that's my hope. Interview invitations go out in a few weeks, and I won't find out if I got it until the fall." The words were modest, but the spark in her eyes exuded confidence.

Trever smiled. "Oh, trust me, you'll get it."

This was a conversation they'd clearly had before, and I suddenly felt very out of the loop.

Like she knew what I was thinking, Dr. Mercado looked back at me. "But to answer your question, I'll be here through the end of the summer to finish my residency. Dr. Reinhold is still your doctor. I'm just filling in today."

I nodded as I slipped off the table. I turned to leave, and then her voice stopped me.

"Austin," she called, looking over her shoulder toward me. "Just give it some time. Things will get better."

I nodded before closing the door behind me.

Staring down the barrel of a career change, it was a hell of a lot easier said than done.

Chapter 3

ISABELLE

$\mathcal{I}$ pinned my cell phone between my chin and shoulder as I pushed open the double doors to the Lightning training faculty, smiling politely at the receptionist.

"I thought you had the day off," Selena's voice admonished through my phone. "I was gonna bring you lunch."

I did have the day off until I got a call from Dr. Reinhold. He was still away and needed someone to cover his follow-ups. With the team's offseason in the summer, these were the last few before training camp in a couple months.

"Don't change the subject on me. What do you *mean* you invited press to your wedding?" I asked. Selena worked in public relations and knew how to manage a crisis, but now that she was marrying into a high-profile family, the press had become a menace for her.

"I'm inviting *one* magazine. The reporter Malcolm Parks is supposed to be pretty good with privacy and discretion. Giving *Voulez Magazine* exclusivity should dry up demand from paps."

"And how exactly did you manage that?"

"Long story. One I was going to tell you because I thought you had the day off!" Selena repeated.

"I did, but . . ." I trailed off, walking down the hall toward the back of the training facility.

Normally routine follow-ups would have been handed off to a physician assistant, but I was happy Dr. Reinhold trusted me with it. And he was writing my recommendation for the Winthrop fellowship, so I couldn't exactly say no.

Even though I was enjoying this sports medicine rotation and the research I'd done in it, I'd never been a fan of soccer. And now all it did was remind me of Blake, because he *loved* it. But this was my way to the Winthrop fellowship, so I'd deal with it.

"I volunteered," I answered and stopped mid-stride when I walked into what seemed to be a heated discussion between two players in the hallway—Blaine and Landon.

Just as I stopped, Blaine's fist connected with Landon's face. Landon hit the ground a second later and, just as he stood with the clear intention to retaliate, Austin Cade burst in from the opposite end of the hallway and pulled them apart. He stood between them, breathing hard and grimacing like an exhausted big brother.

"I gotta go." I hung up and tucked my phone in my pocket.

Blaine pushed Austin out from between them and skulked off. Austin let out a controlled breath, then looked menacingly at Landon, pointing for him to go into one of the exam rooms.

I followed a few steps behind and got situated to make sure Landon wasn't too badly hurt.

Noticing my entrance, Landon sat down on an exam table

and leaned his head toward me, letting me grip his chin firmly as I flashed a penlight at one pupil at time. "You're lucky. An inch to the left and we'd be calling optho for an emergency surgery."

He sat with his arms tightly crossed and a scowl on his face, showing no remorse for his actions. I wasn't around the team all that much since I was only here for research, but I knew that this grumpy midfielder—or whatever his position was— had been in altercations before. Dr. Reinhold had warned me about him.

"I wasn't doing anything wrong," Landon spat out.

I heard an exhausted sigh from Austin behind me.

"When I walked in, I heard you say some . . . interesting things about his girlfriend." I ran the penlight over his eye one last time. "How did you think that would go?"

"I didn't think he'd freak out." Landon rolled his good eye, because the other one was swelling up more with each passing minute.

Something shuffled behind me. I flicked a glance over my shoulder and saw that Austin was about to walk out. "You. Sit."

I turned back to look at Landon's eye but used my left hand to point at the other elevated exam table in the PT room.

"I'm fine," Austin answered.

Blaine had shoved Austin when he got in between the two and I was sure I'd seen him wince when he landed hard on the injured leg. It was probably nothing, but *I* didn't miss anything. And Dr. Reinhold didn't trust many residents to work directly with the team, so I wasn't going to let anything happen on my watch.

"That knee was repaired at the hands of a master. Show some respect and sit down."

He didn't say anything, but I heard another sigh, followed by the crinkle of the plastic covering on the exam table.

"It was a lucky shot," Landon mumbled as I checked his nasal bridge for damage.

"Good aim for a lucky shot," I quipped back with a little more heat in my voice than intended.

I'd already been in a sour mood before the fight broke out. Before Selena called, I was spiraling about Blake again. This time I had tried to rationalize the pain away. I couldn't possibly still love him, right? How could I, if I hadn't seen him in over a year? We'd always said we'd give it a try, a real one, if ever he moved back, but we also agreed to date other people in between. We had both known something like this might happen.

But the more I'd tried dating random people, the more I felt like it was *supposed* to be Blake.

He understood me. He understood what it meant to have sky-high expectations both for yourself and from your family. We didn't need to sacrifice our ambitions for each other. At least, that's what I'd assumed.

"Okay." Turning Landon's chin a couple more times to get a final look at his eye, I confirmed there wasn't any serious damage. "You look fine."

"And so do y—"

"Landon," Austin barked in warning from behind me.

His gruff, protective tone filled my memory with a TV clip

I'd seen right before the Olympics a few years ago. The one that made every American woman collectively swoon.

It showed the American Footballer, Austin Cade, descending the steps of the team jet with an infant in a car seat tucked under his arm, held protectively close to his body, staring down the press like he'd personally vet every molecule of air the baby breathed, daring anyone to get too close.

My body warmed thinking about it.

I clicked the penlight off and dismissed Landon. "Ice, ibuprofen, and a little more self-control next time."

I turned on my heel and walked to the other exam table. My schedule may have been crazy, and residency may have taken up too much of my life, but the actual work had a way of making me forget about all those awful truths.

As Landon slammed the door closed, I said to Austin, "I appreciate the chivalry, but I'm more than capable of defending—"

"My goddaughter is in the building, and you never know when she's in earshot," Austin whispered conspiratorially, bracing both arms on the table as he leaned just slightly forward.

I nodded. The infant from that car seat years ago was now the kid that I'd occasionally see running around here. A little girl with jet-black hair and giant brown eyes who looked at Austin like he brought up the sun every morning.

"So . . . where is she?" I was never great with kids, but even I had to admit it was sweet.

"Joseen is kicking a ball around on the field with her mom."

With that, we went through the same drills Austin probably did on a daily basis with his physical therapist and Dr. Reinhold, checking the joints, muscles, and ligaments for strength and resistance.

I sat down at the small workstation in between the two exam tables and wrote a quick note on both Landon's and Austin's files for Dr. Reinhold. "Well, everything looks fine."

"Sorry for the interruption to your work."

"I don't mind, really." I could spend hours in an OR filled with people, but it was as good as being alone. When I concentrated on my work, everything else went quiet. Best of all, when I started operating, it was like an out-of-body experience. Nothing mattered but the tool in my hand and the task in front of me.

I enjoyed my research, but I found myself enjoying the days I filled in for Dr. Reinhold, too. Once I started the fellowship, I wouldn't be as hands-on with patients, so I was taking it all in while I could.

Austin let out an exhausted laugh. "Landon's a good kid, but he's all fight some days."

I smiled. When I'd first met Austin, he'd seemed a little standoffish, but that was probably just because he was frustrated about his injury. It didn't take much to see he was very much the big brother of the team. Older. More mature. Willing to be patient with people.

"You sound like a coach," I said.

Trevor had told me coaching was probably in Austin's future. He definitely had the patience that coaches tended to have.

He was quiet for a beat, his eyes lost in thought, before he looked up. "Yeah?"

"Yeah . . ." I shrugged. "But I don't like soccer, remember? So

I wouldn't hinge any career decision on my limited knowledge of team sports."

He chuckled and hopped off the exam table. "Thanks, Doc."

I nodded as Austin left and I checked the time. I still had a lot more to do before I could head to Selena's. I'd try to be quick about it and make up for lost time. Just a few more tasks, then I'd go.

Chapter 4
AUSTIN

$\mathcal{I}$ didn't have a problem with fancy parties and I wasn't terrible at mingling. In fact, I used to really enjoy it. Probably because when I was in my twenties as a footballer, these parties always meant beautiful women in London who *loved* my American accent. And I was an idiot who had really enjoyed that type of shallow shit for a long time.

Now, in my mid-thirties, I mostly just wanted to go home. But this auction was too important to miss.

"So have you given my plan any thought?" Jesse, my agent, asked as he typed into his phone, his drink untouched because he'd spent the last five minutes reading off different variations of his future plans for me.

I put my whiskey glass down next to his on the bar behind me and glanced around the entry hallway inside the Great Hall of the Met. The Amherst Initiative's annual New York's Most Worthy charity auction was in full swing. Celebrities and socialites spilled through the wide hallways examining the displays, which featured some of the larger items lined up for the auction later.

"Yeah . . ." I responded tightly because, actually, no, I hadn't been thinking about my next move right now. I'd been thinking, hoping, that tonight went well. The only other thing I'd ever attempted outside of soccer was this foundation, and it was struggling. "But tonight is about the foundation."

Jesse had been handling my career since I was eighteen, when I was promising and got pulled into the European leagues. I landed in the UK and ended up in the Premier League. It was a Cinderella story—if Cinderella had a pushy, fast-talking agent instead of a fairy godmother.

Jesse's mouth stayed a tight, unmoving straight line. "There wouldn't be a foundation without Austin Cade, so he needs to quit sulking and start making a move into coaching while there is interest."

I loved the game and I wasn't sure I was ready to let it go. Coaching seemed like the perfect compromise. A place where I could succeed. And I was tired of feeling like I was failing. I was injured, the foundation was struggling, and I was still making up for lost time with Joseen.

Jesse was right; we *did* need to move fast if I was going to transition to coaching. But I couldn't just hop on a plane and disappear off to Europe again. Not before I'd set things right here.

"I'm not sulking." But like my knee, any will to be charming had been severely battered over the last few months. "I'm just thinking."

The auction started soon. It would take place in three parts, one for each arm of the Amherst Initiative. My foundation, the Mistry Foundation, was part of the first block of the event.

"You *are* sulking and you've been this way the last few months." He clicked the side of his phone and tucked it in his pocket. He took a long sip of whiskey. "I didn't pull that kid off the streets in Queens all those years ago just for you to drive your own career into the ground now."

I bristled. "I'm not doing that."

"And what about bailing on an insane Premier League contract, coming home, and then signing one here to stop any chances of going back?" Jesse huffed. When I went against everyone's advisement and signed with the New York Lightning, Jesse had to bend over backward with the agency's partners to keep representing me instead of passing me off to some assistant. "What would you call that?"

"Grieving," I bit out. I didn't want to *keep* having this same discussion.

What was I supposed to do when the only family I had—the one I put on the back burner for years while I chased a dream and all the frills that came along with it—died? Theo got sick, and a couple years later, he was gone. The *least* I could have done for Theo was to have been around more in those final years. I couldn't make the same mistake with Jo and Zoya, at least not in the immediate aftermath when they needed support. I couldn't go back to the Premier League, but I also couldn't bring myself to stop playing. Besides, that would have only pissed Theo off. The New York team was how I stayed in the game and at home.

"Look." Jesse raked a hand through his hair, apologetic. "I get it, okay? But it's been two years. The world can't wait around for your comeback forever. Now that you've had a pretty bad injury this late in your career, the sooner we move you to a new path, the better."

I let out a conciliatory breath. He was right. "Okay. Let's set up some meetings."

His disposition instantly brightened. "Great, because I talked to FC—"

"Just let me get the foundation on its feet."

I couldn't fuck up the *one* thing Theo left me in charge of.

"Fine. You focus on settling the foundation, so long as you let me line up some meetings in the meantime. If an offer comes, then you can choose."

When I didn't say anything, regret dragged down the corners of his mouth. After two decades of knowing him, we were friends now.

He tapped his foot on the floor. "If it weren't this bad, I wouldn't be this big of an asshole, okay? You only have so long before the interest in you dries up."

"I get it," I said. I tilted my head back and scanned the room, stopping for a moment at each high-top table covered with crisp, white linens and tiny floral arrangements. Then a flash of yellow caught my eye.

Leaning against the bar only a few feet away was someone I knew, but in an entirely different context. Her jet-black hair, usually pulled back into a tight bun, was loose and bouncing in curls along her shoulders. Mint-green scrubs were traded in for an elegant dress with thin straps that left her shoulders almost completely bare. The canary-yellow satin kissed every curve along her skin.

As if she could feel my stare, she turned her head in what felt like slow motion to catch my eye.

Every gear in my brain was riddled with sludge, moving slowly to piece together who I was looking at.

Isabelle.

Dr. Mercado, I corrected myself in my head.

The woman standing beside her leaned close to whisper something. The side of Isabelle's mouth tipped up along her cheek in quiet, teasing acknowledgment. She and her friend picked up their drinks and took a few steps to us.

"I thought you auctioning yourself off *had* to be a misprint in the catalogue," Isabelle said by way of greeting.

I swallowed against a dry throat. "Huh?"

She flicked her wrist up and displayed the packet with all the items up for auction tonight.

"Oh right," I answered, still trying to focus. "It's for a good cause."

"Hi." Her friend's cheerful greeting finally cut through my haze. She stuck out her hand. "Selena Montez."

"You're with Pearson PR," Jesse immediately cut in from behind me, seemingly recognizing the name. "Right?"

"Yes," Selena answered, and Jesse perked up like he hadn't been laying into me five minutes earlier.

With that, Jesse went through a light-speed introduction and took it upon himself to pull Selena away into a conversation. Jesse, always working, knew how to make inroads when

I needed them. And apparently, right now he had designs on Selena's contact list. At least all the irritation he had with me seemed to evaporate.

That left me alone with Isabelle. After an extended moment, I pushed the words out of my mouth. "Are you secretly a socialite, Dr. Mercado?"

I was still trying to figure out why I was so thrown seeing her here. She had a life and friends outside of the few pockets of time that I saw her. But something about seeing her in this setting, confidently moving through a room of Manhattan's biggest donors like she belonged here, was . . . intriguing.

She let out a small, airy laugh. "It's Isabelle. Actually, call me Isa. Dr. Mercado makes me feel like I should still be in scrubs."

I nodded. "Isa."

"And no, I am just the third wheel to my best friend tonight." Isa tipped her chin in the direction of Selena and Jesse, who'd taken a few steps away from us, deep in conversation. "But *your* date seems . . . charming."

I coughed a nervous laugh. "He's my agent. And he's a little annoyed with me."

"Why?"

"Depends on how much you overheard."

"Enough." She winced. "But maybe I was right about the coaching thing . . ."

"You were." I put my drink down on the bar, trying to ignore how her eyes seemed to sparkle under the dim chandelier's light. "Coaching is probably the next thing. I just need to spend some time with the Mistry Foundation before I commit to anything else."

"That's your foundation," she said like she was confirming it to herself.

"Yeah."

"Well . . ." Her tone jumped up like she was trying to lift the mood. She flipped through the catalogue. "Nothing says committed to a cause like *being* an auction item."

"That was a friend's idea," I pointed out.

She opened her mouth, but another voice filled the space between us.

"Oh, Henry's here." Selena had stepped back toward us to put her glass down on the bar. She smiled politely at me and then took Isa's arm in hers. "The auction should be starting soon. It was nice to meet you, Austin."

She pulled Isabelle away, who waved a quick goodbye over her shoulder.

Once again, I was at the bar alone with Jesse but, this time, I wasn't scowling.

Chapter 5
ISABELLE

*W*e passed through the elaborately engraved limestone archway, past the large atrium on our way to the sculpture court, where the auction would start at any moment.

I had never been to any glitzy events like this until my best friend got serious with a guy who was at the center of Manhattan high society. Henry was a regular Prince Charming and Selena enjoyed being part of his world, but she also appreciated having a familiar face nearby, and I dutifully fulfilled the role.

But Selena had grown more confident in these circles now, and these days it felt more like I was the kid-friend to her and her fiancé's couple-parent energy. Still, she kept inviting me and never left me alone.

"So, what are you bidding on?" I flipped through the extensive auction packet. Tonight's offerings included items from across the spectrum of art, media, and sports.

For some reason, my eyes kept wandering back to Austin's listing. My stomach tilted, just like it had when I saw him here.

I was used to seeing that athletic build, wavy brown hair, and marginally annoyed set of cerulean eyes in scuffed-up, grass-stained training gear. But neatly dressed in a well-tailored tuxedo with his hair slicked back, he looked . . . well, it reminded me why he'd made such an impression with the ladies back in his Premiere League days.

"There's a piece by a reclusive photographer coming up for auction later." Selena opened her booklet to the page she had earmarked and showed it to me. It was a landscape of the Alps. I'd barely paid attention to the arts section when I'd flipped through the pamphlet earlier. Selena was the creative one, not me. "Henry's been trying to find this piece for me, and apparently it's being auctioned tonight."

"Sorry to intrude on date night," I said so quietly that it was almost lost under the sounds of our heels clicking against the stone floors and the soft conversation that wisped around the room.

"Don't apologize. I invited you." Selena's eyes moved up and around the stone columns as we settled at a high-top table. The lit-up sculptures that were part of the Met's permanent collection served as meeting points for the guests, each surrounded by a few tables for drinks and conversation. "Besides, I checked your calendar, and you weren't working tonight. I figured this was probably more fun than sitting in your apartment stewing. I'm not even going to ask if you cyberstalked him."

She was right. I'd already found Francesca's social media, and she was so perfect it was painful. Voluminous brown hair, perfectly tousled in every picture. Her outfits were effortlessly put together. There weren't any pictures of her with Blake, though. When I started scrolling deeper to see if she'd ever posted photos with other guys and clicking on the profiles of every friend she'd been tagged with, I realized I was spiraling into a full-blown, Verdejo-fueled cyberstalking spree.

Selena caught my expression and nodded. "And, you're doing me a favor, too. I'm pretty sure Henry ran off to try to get the collector to sell it before it goes up for auction, so I could use the company."

"You can return the favor by buying me a—"

The end of my sentence was cut off by flowing brown hair and a pair of silver-gray eyes. Like it was happening in slow motion, she stopped at the table next to ours, flipping her hair over her shoulder. She took a sip from her wineglass, then let out a perfect, short laugh at something someone said.

My mouth hung slightly open. I tried not to stare directly, but it was *her*.

Francesca Cole.

The heaviness became jagged in my stomach, swelling into something painful.

"What are . . ." Selena looked over her shoulder and followed my line of sight. She paused for a second. "Oh."

After scrolling through so many of her social media photos, I would have thought seeing her in person wouldn't catch me off guard—but it did. Which was ridiculous because I didn't know this woman. But she might have come with a date. My eyes darted around in dread.

"Is Blake here?" Selena whispered and glanced around the room, too. When she turned back to me, my eyes were already fixed on something else. Something sparkling.

The glittering diamond on Francesca Cole's finger.

"Oh . . ." Selena's mouth went wide as her eyes followed mine.

My vision blurred. The room spun.

Disappointment and sheer humiliation compressed around my throat. They were *engaged*, and all this time I thought he was my . . .

The room became muffled under the sound of my heart beating loudly in my ears. Something close to adrenaline ran through my veins, lighting a spark that sent furious heat through my body.

Don't react. Not here.

It hurt. Viscerally.

What if I had followed him to California instead of insisting on the better residency program in New York? What if I had spent more time visiting instead of taking on more research? Maybe then I would have been living out my own version of happily ever after. That ring would have been sparkling on my finger.

Did I choose wrong?

"I'm fine," I choked out, taking a step back. Francesca probably didn't know who I was, but still I hoped she wouldn't see me.

I *couldn't* have chosen wrong. If I had—all these years of working late evenings and weekends, bailing on my social life, and putting my personal life to the side—what was all of this for? What was a life partially lived, alone and tired all the time, in service to?

"Isa . . ." Selena whispered. "Do you want to leave?"

"The bidding starts at twenty thousand," the auctioneer called in the background. I could just barely register it.

The setting crashed back on me at the sound of a gavel slamming against the podium.

I rolled my shoulders back. Being wounded felt weak. And *nobody* was going to see me look weak. "Of course not. Who cares, right?"

The pain hardened into something else, smoothing over the momentary crack in my resolve. Blake was the one who chose wrong, and I was going to make sure he knew it.

"Right." Selena gave my hand a quick squeeze.

Across from us, Francesca's perfectly polished voice suddenly called out, "Twenty thousand!" She lifted her paddle, the ring glinting on her finger.

Selena's eyes narrowed and she mumbled something under her breath. She tapped her paddle against her hip. Her weight shifted between her legs.

"Forty thousand!" Selena raised her paddle, her usually soft expression hardening to steel.

"Selena . . ." I cautioned with surprise. "What are you bidding on?"

I glanced up to the podium, but there wasn't any object on display. We hadn't gotten to the arts portion yet.

Francesca didn't look in our direction before she countered. "Sixty."

"I don't know, but she's not getting it," Selena whisper-shouted to me. "One hundred thousand."

Selena's bid silenced the room.

"One hundred and fifty," Francesca countered a bit louder. For the first time, she glanced to us for a passing second.

A slow, humiliating prickle stung along my skin. I was five feet from a woman I knew more about than I should have. And to her, I was a complete stranger.

"Two hundred," Selena called back.

Every eye in the room volleyed between Selena and Francesca.

"Two hundred and fifty thousand."

My hands shook as I opened the booklet, eyes racing across the numbers to find whatever item could be this competitive.

I'd looked at this page before. It was the sports section.

And the item up for auction was a four-week intensive with the American Footballer himself.

My stomach hollowed. Blake was a huge Premier League fan. Francesca was viciously bidding against Selena *for* Blake. Because of course she would, she was his fiancée and this was something he'd love.

"Put her out of her misery." Henry, Selena's fiancé, reappeared behind us. He handed her a drink, then pressed a kiss on her head as his shoulders rumbled with a silent laugh.

Selena grinned.

"One million," she called casually, like she was ordering a latte.

The room went completely silent aside from Henry's, now audible, chuckle.

"One million." The auctioneer's eyebrows shot up and stayed there. "From the exuberant soon-to-be Mrs. Amari. Do we have one point one million?"

The room stayed silent.

"Sold." The gavel banging against wood drew every eye back to the auctioneer. "A foundation record to paddle number seventeen."

Henry looked down at Selena inquisitively.

"I *really* wanted to win." She casually patted his chest. Then the corners of her eyes dipped as they met mine. "Are you okay?"

No.

"It's not a big deal." I tried to shake off the deep soreness that settled across my chest and shove it into the corner of my heart where I kept everything else I didn't have time for. "I don't care."

When I saw them together at the wedding, I couldn't react like this. I never aspired to be a humble loser and I wasn't about to start now.

* * *

I needed a drink.

While Selena was waiting for the landscape photo to go on auction, I decided that I'd try to make myself invisible at the bar. All I wanted to do was go home, but that felt like admitting defeat, and if I just made it through the night, I'd feel better. But on my walk to the bar, a pair of crystalline eyes, confused more than anything, caught mine.

It was a befuddled Austin Cade.

Under the archway that led to the main bar in the atrium, we passed each other, and he stopped me. Curiosity lined his forehead. I took in a breath to explain, but he beat me to it.

"Jesse just told me your frien—"

"I can explain that." I put my hand up and tried my best not to look as defeated as I felt. "But I *really* need a drink first."

His eyes softened and he tipped his head in the direction of the bar about twenty feet away. That look—one I didn't know well so it took a second to identify—was pity.

God, tonight was mortifying. Not only was the guy I'd stupidly thought I'd end up with, *my* one, engaged to someone else; now I got to explain why my best friend just spent seven figures on four weeks of lessons or something with Austin.

When we got to the bar, I ordered a drink and tapped the cool, polished wood. I had promised an explanation. "So . . ."

"You have a little crush on me?" Austin deadpanned, so seriously I knew he was joking. He was being nice, and that only made me feel even more humiliated. He pitied me and he didn't even know why. "That's why you had your friend buy that?"

A laugh, one I wasn't expecting, popped out from between my lips. I smiled, thankfully, at him. Even though I didn't want to accept his kindness, I sort of had to.

I leaned my side on the bar and faced him. "Selena only bought it so someone else couldn't."

The corner of Austin's mouth tipped up before immediately straightening. He turned and leaned against the bar as well. "Seems a little—"

"Petty?" I cut him off and cocked my head. "I don't know what to tell you. Selena can be petty. And she's getting awfully comfortable with that Black Card."

This close, I could make out every detail of his face. The lines along his forehead deepened for a moment before smoothing out. Then he chuckled lightly. His expression became brighter. He looked more like *that* Austin I'd seen in interviews on TV years ago. I found myself wondering how he went from the American Footballer to the surly man living quietly in Manhattan.

"You're welcome, by the way," I added, chipper. I was going to fake being okay until I actually was and, right now, I needed to think of anything else. Anyone else other than Blake, because in that moment it all felt too heavy. "For helping your foundation."

"Taking credit?" His upbeat tone felt a little forced. Instead of asking why I *needed* a drink, he seemed content with trying to distract me from the reason.

And I was going to let him. "Shouldn't you be charming donors instead of questioning me?"

He blinked a couple times and turned uncomfortably back to the bar. He tapped his hands on it like he was thinking.

"Charming donors is a lot harder when they aren't your best friend," he shot back. "See how easy it is when you don't have that loyalty on your side cutting checks."

I crossed my arms.

"Watch and learn, Cade." I patronizingly tapped his chest, the rich fabric and firm muscle beneath sending static up my arm.

I was smart enough to know I was being baited, but welcomed the distraction. My brain and my heart needed it.

I motioned for him to follow.

Chapter 6
AUSTIN

$\mathcal{I}$sa *looked* the same, canary-yellow silk draped around curves I pretended not to notice, but something knocked the brightness out of her eyes in the hour between seeing her before the auction started and now. At the very least, it seemed like she needed a distraction.

So, for a half hour, with me as a captive spectator, she demonstrated just how easy it was for *her* to charm donors.

She talked to a real estate tycoon about infrastructure investment, then discussed the future of the publishing industry with the head of one of the major publishing houses in the city, all while weaving in the Mistry Foundation, my foundation.

"Well, Dr. Mercado, I hope to see you at the City Health Initiative dinner. Your father attended last year and was incredibly interesting to talk to," Mayor Wilson said jovially at the tail end of a conversation with Isa about the geopolitical implications of another Alders presidency. "A man of many accomplishments, he failed to mention that chief among them is his brilliant daughter."

The comment made Isa's shoulders momentarily slump, but just for a second. "I like to think I'm my own accomplishment."

"You certainly are. And we'll be sure to check in with the Mistry Foundation, see if we can't get more eyes on that cause," his wife added as the mayor walked away with a delight-filled chuckle at an offhanded comment Isa made about the state of politics.

I was never happier to be invisible.

I was terrible at mental math, but thirty minutes of Isa talking to these donors probably raised more for the foundation than I had in a year.

"You know I never actually challenged you to anything," I told her. "Especially not your best impression of a *Jeopardy!* contestant after too many espresso martinis."

Whatever gloominess had been hanging around her earlier at the bar evaporated.

"I'll take 'well-rounded surgeon for five hundred.'" She grinned, clearly only hearing the compliment and nothing else. She took a beat while the rest of that sentence settled in. "My dad taught me if someone leaves a conversation with you anything but impressed, you've failed."

Yikes. That sentence explained *a lot* about her. "That's . . ."

"That's my dad." She shrugged. "But it's served me well."

"And the foundation, thanks. We could use it."

She paused, staring across the room, her tongue tucked to the inside of her cheek.

I waited a few seconds, then waved my hand in front of her face. "Isa?"

Her eyes narrowed; she flicked a look over her shoulder to the auction hall, then back at me. "Your foundation needs funding."

"Yeah . . ."

"Sooner rather than later?"

My brow dipped. "Yes."

She crossed her arms. "This is going to sound insane but keep in mind I am Ivy League educated and every plan I've made for my life has worked so far."

Marginally terrified, but more curious, I took the bait. "Okay . . ."

"My best friend, Selena, is getting married in a few weeks. The Amari wedding is basically a captive audience of the kind of people who could set the Mistry Foundation up for good."

"Okay . . ." I repeated, starting to understand what she was getting at.

"You need rich people with deep pockets? I can do you one better. They'll all be drunk at a wedding. So be my plus-one."

It did make sense. If one evening with Isa shmoozing these donors was this successful, then another could fast-forward all my plans for the foundation. And I could focus on everything else Jesse was lining up for me.

"That's very generous of you," I said, then quirked an eyebrow. "And not *that* insane."

She smiled, though a flicker of embarrassment tugged at the corners of her mouth. "It's not that generous, because I need something, too."

I waited for her to continue, but when she only took a long swig of her drink, I probed, "Yeah?"

She paused a beat, as if mentally calculating, then lifted her chin decidedly. "I need you to pose as my real date."

Of all the things I could have imagined her saying, this was not it. I blinked a few times. "What?"

"It's . . . unorthodox, I'll give you that," she conceded. The look in her eye made it clear that she *needed* this for some reason. I'd known her only a few weeks, but she always presented as strong and unwavering. This look was almost lost. "You're not *my* patient. It'd just be for the wedding. And I'll help you charm all the guests you want. All you have to do is show up and be my date."

Her throat shifted. She looked over her shoulder to the auction space again, then back to me. The straight line of her lips wobbled like it was the only thing holding back tears.

"So, you *do* have a little crush on me," I teased her, mostly because that look on her seemed . . . wrong.

A tiny laugh pushed out from between her lips. Relief flooded through my body.

"No." Her lips quirked up. "But my ex-boyfriend was a fan of yours for years. And this would just destroy him."

"Ah, revenge. Now I understand." This was more on track with the idea I had of her in my head. Vengeful seemed more on brand for her than defeated.

"I know it's petty and childish." She shrugged. "But it'd help both of us. And I happen to have it on good authority you've been instructed not to get on the field through the rest of the offseason, so you're free." She snapped her fingers. "So do we have a deal?"

Outside of the fact that this may be a good idea, I had to

wonder what this ex did to her. Because Isabelle seemed proud. She radiated it. So, whatever he did, it was bad enough that she was willing to put on a skit.

"What did he do that makes you want to exact such brutal revenge?" I had to ask.

Her shoulders tightened. "Nobody wants to be the ex that lost. And if I show up with you, I won't be so . . ." She cut herself off. "Call it what you want, but it's a week and a half and it's in France and—"

"Wait, what?" This thing was in France?

"I'm so sorry. Did you have other plans? Selena did just buy you for the next four weeks." Her shoulders lifted, her pride refilling. "And frankly, I think you could use the vacation. All you've done the past few weeks is broodily haunt the training facilities and yell at reporters."

She was a whirlwind of contradictions—blunt to a fault, a little mean, with the occasional flash of vulnerability. Somehow, all of that landed in the "reasons to go along with this" column in my mind. Her plan was wild, no doubt, but maybe it was exactly what we both needed. And honestly, her company wasn't so bad. It might even be fun.

"Well, when you put it like that."

"So? Do we have a deal?"

I guessed it would be fine. Probably good to get out of the city and clear my head for a few days. "Sure."

A wide smile burst across her face. "Great. Then we can check all those items off the list. Piss off Blake. Make some money for the foundation. Move on."

She ticked each item off with a raised finger like she was

playing mental *Tetris*—fitting blocks of time into a schedule in her mind.

"Hey! I was looking to make sure you were okay." Selena's voice drifted back over to us. "You'll never guess what we were bid—"

"Was it lessons with the American Footballer himself?" Isa drawled sarcastically, gesturing toward me.

Selena realized then that I was there. Her eyes darted between us. "What did I miss?"

"I'll fill you in later." She linked arms with her friend and the two began walking off. Throwing a look over her shoulder, she called out to me. "I'll get you the details."

I stood there, a mix of relieved and confused, but mostly wondering what I'd just signed up for.

Chapter 7
ISABELLE

A few days after the auction, I got a text from my parents. They were in town for a night and all my petty plans for vengeance took a back seat to readying myself for dinner.

I usually had monthly dinners with my parents at their home in the suburbs of DC. They always felt more like business meetings. I gave them updates on work and they let me know of any connections I needed to make or lectures I should attend to help network.

We sat tucked in the corner of one of my mom's favorite places to eat—a high-end bistro in Gramercy Park.

Tables were arranged neatly in the center of the room with luxurious leather-lined booths in the corners and along the walls. The brass fixtures gleamed against the dark polished-hardwood floors, countertops, and tables. We came here every time they were in town.

"Matthew tells me you've been spending quite a bit of time within this sports medicine program." My dad shook his head disapprovingly, the golden glow from the Edison bulbs above us deepening the shadows in the lines that creased in his fore-head and highlighting his year-round scowl. "I'd be concerned you're getting pulled offtrack, but I know you're too smart for that."

The New York Lightning's team orthopedist—Matthew Reinhold—was my mentor in residency. He didn't choose to work with residents on a sports-medicine rotation regularly and *definitely* didn't choose many of them to help with research. But he took me on for both, which was an accomplishment on its own.

"You're not considering forgoing the Winthrop fellowship," my mom chirped up for the first time, her words laced with concern. Up until that point, my dad had spent an hour going over his latest lecture series for surgeons at the University of Oslo. "Are you?"

"No," I corrected immediately. The leather seat sighed beneath me as I shifted in the corner booth. "Of course not."

At the time, I didn't have any *specific* interest in sports-related injuries, but I knew Dr. Reinhold's opinion mattered. It worked out since the latter years of my training opened up my schedule a bit, so I made the time. It would get me closer to Winthrop, so every Thursday, I was looking at data with Trevor at the New York Lightning training facility.

"Oh, good." My mother's shoulders relaxed; she tucked her curly black hair behind her ear. The thin golden bracelets on her wrist clinked as they slid down it. She, being a general surgeon, decided against a fellowship altogether after her initial surgical training.

She and my dad met as kids growing up in Washington

Heights. They were high school sweethearts who broke up for college and then were reunited in medical school. It was their version of a fairy tale, if you chose to end the story there.

My mom was top of their med school class. They wanted a family, and surgery wasn't exactly forgiving for two parents who needed to invest in their careers. So, my mom was the one to forgo the advancement. Of course, that wasn't ever how my mom explained it to me. To this day, she insisted that it was her choice to take a step back and invest in our family while my dad invested in his career. But I couldn't help seeing someone whose wings were clipped. Especially when she pushed so hard for me to pursue the Winthrop fellowship.

"Dr. Reinhold is on the selection committee for the Winthrop fellowship," I continued. This was my way to make my own name. "And I'm first author on the research we're doing with recovery times following minimally invasive meniscus repair."

I ended up enjoying the work. Putting together a shattered knee was a puzzle, and watching the difference I made in real time was more fulfilling than I thought it'd be. It was interesting work that I had never considered until it became a way to get closer to the Winthrop fellowship. But Dr. Reinhold was a great teacher, and the visits to the New York Lightning facility were fun.

There were the surgeons who masterfully executed tried-and-true surgical techniques and there were the surgeons who *created* them. My mom was the former, my dad the latter.

"Strategic alliance." A smile curved up my dad's cheek as he cut into his steak. "That's my girl."

Sometimes I wondered if I was Dr. Felix Mercado's legacy or Dr. Carolina Mercado's redemption. Either way, I was desperate to come out from the shadow of giants, and it was clear that I had one of two lanes I could pick. My dad's or my mom's.

So, I tried to be perfect to make what seemed like my mother's sacrifice worth it. I tried not to have needs, only accomplishments.

I never lost. I was never wrong. Nobody was tougher, nobody had more grit. Nobody would ever tell me that I didn't have what it took, because I had it in spades. I didn't need anyone, so nobody else could ever pin their unhappiness, or forgone dreams, on me.

"Are you in the city for another lecture?" I asked.

From the time I was a kid to now, my dad had been constantly asked to speak at conferences around the world and flown to international hospitals to give lectures and provide care to world leaders and dignitaries.

"Well . . ." He cleared his throat and put the utensils to the side of his plate. "As you know, Senator Fitzgerald Alders is planning his presidential run."

"Yeah . . ." I drawled, wondering how any of that pertained to my dad.

"He's still putting together a campaign team, but his current chief of staff wanted to have lunch to discuss matters that concern the medical community."

Yeah. That was it. Surgeon General.

"Isn't it a little soon to be picking a cabinet? He hasn't even announced the run," I pointed out.

"Plan for opportunity," he reminded me. Easy for him to say;

he had my mom to keep the wheels on in his personal life so he could *plan for opportunity*. "And speaking of preparation for opportunity, what's this I heard about two weeks away?"

"I didn't take my vacation days for the last two years," I defended, putting down my spoon, knowing he'd have something judgmental to say about my missing work for Selena's wedding. My pulse picked up. "This isn't anything above what any other resident normally gets."

"Yes, but two *consecutive* weeks." His tongue clicked. "You'll miss some good cases, I'm sure. The first couple weeks of July are always busy. You're the senior resident. You'd be doing nearly the entire surgery. It would be good experience to talk about for your Winthrop interview."

Summers in the city meant great business for trauma doctors because of unprepared tourists mixed with traffic and dehydration.

"Maybe, but I'll get more unique ones around the time college students file back into the city in the fall," I rebutted.

I'd already given up a lot of my personal life in service to this dream, and my relationship with Selena was the only one to withstand it. My heart hollowed. I took a deep breath and remembered that, in his own way, my dad cared. He always looked out for my future first, encouraging me to take the same successful path he did. Present-day Isa could deal, as long as future Isa benefited.

"Felix," my mom warned gently. "She is Isabelle's friend, of course she's going."

"She's my *best* friend," I corrected. "I'm getting the Winthrop fellowship regardless. I'm not going to litigate the wedding."

I put myself through unending months of work, all so that I could get two uninterrupted weeks as a functioning maid of honor to my best friend, even though every wedding task was handled by her enormous staff.

I was always so quick to exchange my free time for something, anything, to advance my chances at the Winthrop fellowship, and Selena was the only person in my life who stuck around for it. I had to be there for her now.

"Fine." He cleared his throat and pulled the napkin from his lap slowly. Folding it neatly, he placed it at the side of his plate. "But remember that you can speak to me that sternly when *you've* accomplished what I have."

"That's enough, Felix." My mom's second warning was the one that stuck, and my dad's face immediately softened, but he didn't say anything. She reached her hand across the table, warm and steady. "As long as it doesn't affect your work, have fun."

One day I would be as accomplished because, despite how he pushed me forward, a part of me was sure I had to prove it to him. And I would.

After a few minutes he picked up conversation about his plans to meet with the soon-to-be Alders campaign.

Chapter 8
AUSTIN

**THE AMERICAN FOOTBALLER'S
MILLION-DOLLAR FOUNDATION**

Zoya laughed into the morning air after reading the online article on her phone. "You're relevant again, this time in the society section."

I held my hand up to my brow and watched the field. It was freshly cut and the air smelled like grass. "I don't know why you're laughing. Auctioning myself off was *your* idea."

The event was a huge success and the items that the Mistry foundation auctioned off sold for higher than anything else. The foundation made nearly five million dollars altogether after the first item went for a million. I had a few more interested donors and what seemed like a last-ditch effort to keep it alive started to blossom into something bigger.

"It was for the foundation, and I was right." Zoya took a sip of her coffee, looking out into the field ahead of us—the one filled with kids running back and forth, in some degree of order, as they played what was supposed to be a soccer match. "It *did* help. Although, no offense, a million dollars is a little high."

"It's a dumb idea, isn't it?" I said, thinking about the deal I made with Isa a couple nights ago.

"No." Zoya smacked my arm with the back of hers. "You're going to the Amari wedding. Do you realize all the important people that will be there? Getting an invitation to *that* wedding is probably more lucrative to the foundation than anything you've done in the last few years. You know that, right?"

Nope.

It was shit like that that made me sure I needed help with the foundation. My best friend, Theo, was always the one who handled the financing aspects of running a business. The foundation needed money, but it also needed someone with more vision and charm than I possessed.

"You can keep the field, the building, and not worry about it for years," she chirped. "If you want to."

"I know." I smiled, thinking that this was a chance to, at least, keep the dream alive.

It would probably never happen—having a functioning training academy that fed into a vibrant American league—because our best players left the country. But as long as that field was there, a part of me held on to the idea that it could.

"I'm sure Jesse was thrilled," Zoya added.

"He was."

I had already gotten three calls from Jesse. He'd set up two meetings with football clubs for coaching opportunities. One was in Paris, FC Remy slotted in during the wedding week perfectly. The other was Farnham, my old team in London. He wasn't going to waste my trip there.

"It's nice to see you being, I dunno, human again."

"Gee, thanks. I was injured," I drawled sarcastically while watching one of the kids smack the ball with his hands like he was playing volleyball. I yelled out to field, "Hey, what did I say about using your hands?"

I looked back at Zoya, who tapped her fingers along her coffee cup. She gave me a knowing look, with one eyebrow raised. "You've been a little insufferable lately. The last time you got like this, even Theo was worried."

My heart twinged at the memory.

I was always a little lucky. My only other serious injury happened right in the finals seven years ago, so I recovered back home in the offseason. It was when Theo and Zoya got engaged, and I spent the entire summer being a pain in the ass.

But they picked me up because that's what best friends do, and I got back to playing.

"I still can't believe you're going to the Amari wedding," she complained aloud. "You already got a decade of being the American Footballer. Haven't you had your fair share of fun?"

"It wasn't *that* great," I lied. At the time, it was.

Aside from the paps being insane in the UK whenever I went out, that type of fame came with a lot of short-lived thrills.

"Liar." She rolled her eyes. "Why can't I run into a sexy surgeon who needs a plus-one?"

This time I raised an eyebrow. "I didn't say she was sexy."

Isa *was* beautiful. A fact that stuck out in my mind since the auction. Although that's as far as I let any of those thoughts go since this entire plan was giving me a migraine. But being a fake boyfriend for a week would be easy. If anything, I was curious to see the guy that fumbled someone like her. Clearly, Isa wasn't over it, and I wondered who the hell this guy was.

"Oh, come on. You don't need to be a two on the Kinsey scale to know that team doctor is *hot*."

"That's more than I ever wanted to know about you." I grimaced. "And she's not the team doctor."

I was going to take this chance to get the foundation ready to go and my career onto the next stage. That was all. As Zoya pointed out, this was a good opportunity. I wasn't going to waste it.

"But seriously." Her voice distilled to something more serious. "I'm glad you're moving forward with coaching."

"Yeah . . ." I needed to adapt. Move along. I couldn't hide out in the States forever. "Now, you can stop bothering me about it every five minutes, *Mom*."

"See?" She snapped her fingers. "All snippy and insufferable."

I rolled my eyes. "Between you making sure I have an activity scheduled and Jesse trying to push me into different jobs like a real-life career day on steroids, I'm *really* trying to be a little less snippy."

I could see the change in myself over the last few months and I wanted to get back to steady—having some sort of purpose—I just didn't know how.

Before she could say anything, a loud cheer from the field

erupted when one of the kids scored a goal. They weren't actually playing a match, but it was sweet.

"Good job, Jo!" Zoya called from the sideline, and her daughter, Joseen, high-fived the other kids.

One of the nice things about playing in the States, outside of being home, was that nobody cared who I was. Not many people outside of certain spaces even recognized me. Struggling to survive as a kid to being a professional athlete, *this* was a kind of normal I never really had.

The kids began to gather up their things on the sidelines.

"Austin Cade, fancy billionaires, and a surgeon," Zoya mused. "Take pictures."

Chapter 9

ISABELLE

*T*he unfortunate reality about residency was that it was incredibly isolating.

Every year around this time in the early summer, the residency match scattered outgoing medical students across the country. Most graduates ended up hundreds of miles from home in a new city without much in the ways of social connection. Pile that on top of a crazy work schedule, it made forging new bonds pretty difficult.

I sighed and turned my pint of beer around on a coaster.

I wanted to do something social tonight since I'd been working nonstop in preparation for being away for the wedding in a week. But my coresidents were working and, since my work life ate up all the friends I had before residency, I was alone. So, I came here.

Being alone in public felt a little less lonely than being alone in my apartment. The Irish pub on the Lower East Side wasn't too far from the hospital and it was dingy enough that none of the attendings or anyone of consequence would be here.

As I waffled over ordering some fries, a shadow loomed behind me. I glanced over my shoulder.

It was Drake, Selena's bodyguard. A second later, Selena emerged from behind him.

"What are you doing here?" I asked, peeking behind her through the smudged windows. Sunset had long passed, and twilight took over the sky.

"We share location settings," Selena reminded me as she took a seat next to me and picked up the menu. She took a minute to look it over before getting some soda water and fries. "I noticed your pin wasn't at work for the first time in ages, and I had to see it for myself."

"I'm fine," I assured, absentmindedly turning the coaster. I would have called her, but I was *trying* not to always play third wheel to Selena and Henry. "And my schedule has been pretty good this week."

My life as senior resident was less intense than when I was a junior—I got to see the sun these days—but I knew that wasn't what she was talking about.

She moved the soda water between her hands. "I know you held on to his old sweatshirt for a reason. The photos. It's okay to admit that a part of you thoug—"

"I'm fine," I assured her softly.

There were little parts of our past that I had held on to. I assumed he had done the same, too . . . maybe not. Like his old college sweatshirt, the one that was so lived in that it was threadbare and most of the lettering had worn off in the last decade, it felt like a promise I had made to myself. That once all the hard work of my career was done, our lives together would be easy. Finally, something to relax into.

But like all things, this was yet another challenge. And a part of me was exhausted with those.

"If you weren't, though." Selena fiddled with her napkin, turning it on the polished amber-colored bar top. "It's okay. I mean, I know you and Blake officially weren't together anymore, but I figured that, eventually, you would be again."

"But we weren't," I repeated pointedly in agreement. "So he did nothing wrong. I'm not upset."

She swiveled around in her chair to face me. "If you were, there's no shame in being hurt."

"I'm not hurt." The words propelled out of my mouth so fast, Selena noticeably flinched, and Drake's usually undaunted body shifted. "Sorry."

I didn't need to ask for help; I fixed my own problems. I needed a date, I got one. I needed to get past whatever it was that weighed my muscles all week, and I would.

"Okay, well, that's great." Her voice squeaked and went up an octave. She didn't believe me. "Because I wanted to tell you something." She paused and chewed on her lower lip for a second. "I've never met Francesca, but I've met the other Davenports. They're nice." She began slowly like she was walking toward fire. "From what I hear, Francesca is, too."

Envy burned at the sides of my throat. Not because of Blake, but Selena was *my* best friend. It was one thing to feel like I'd lost everything else, but I hated feeling like I was losing her, too. Not that I was, and certainly not to Francesca, but logic was fighting for its life in my brain.

I pushed all the clamor in my head down and tried to sound perfectly okay with all of this.

"Maybe I'll make a friend," I added dryly.

I hated that I was jealous. I wasn't exactly sure of what, maybe that he found happiness with someone else while none of my relationships after him ever became serious because I always assumed he'd be the one I'd end up with. That fact cracked fractures along my resolve.

Having serious relationships wasn't exactly easy in residency either, but that didn't matter because, in my mind, I'd always had Blake. The eventuality I had pinned those romantic hopes on while I achieved my dreams.

"I'll hate her if you want me to." She reached a hand out and took mine for a second, giving it a gentle squeeze.

"Don't." Thankfully the fries arrived, and I could start eating my feelings. "She's doing me a favor, right? Clean breaks heal faster."

Selena would protect me with everything she had if she had to, but she was also sensible. She was trying to make the next steps forward easier, get me used to the idea that whatever pain I was feeling now would probably get worse when I saw them together.

"Exactly. It wasn't meant to be. Better a bruised heart now than a divorce filing in a few years," Selena agreed. She took a long sip from her glass of soda water. "And I happen to love your idea to bring Austin."

Selena swiveled her seat back to the bar.

"Oh yeah?" I plucked a perfectly golden fry from the center of the basket.

"Imagine the look on Blake's face when he and Francesca see you on the arm of the American Footballer."

"Yeah . . ." At least I'd have some decent company. He'd lived a compelling life, born in the States, playing at the highest level in the Premier League. He probably had great stories. Not that he got much press these days. "And I sort of promised we would use your invite list as a way to find patrons for his foundation."

Selena gave me the exact reaction I was expecting.

"Have at it. That's what all the rich people do at these things anyway." Selena dipped a few fries in hot sauce. "The founders of a venture capital firm are coming; start there."

I nodded.

"And . . ." She chewed and took a long sip of water. "I talked to his agent, Jesse."

"Really?"

"He called me after the auction last week. He's setting up meetings for Austin, I guess for coaching or something. I sent him the itinerary."

Yikes. I didn't know Jesse outside of meeting him at the auction, but he seemed like a pageant mom after too many red-eyes.

"He's already planning all the ways he can use this," Selena continued. "I told him a *Voulez* reporter will be there, and he's trying to—"

"Nobody is stealing *your* thunder at *your* wedding," I interrupted, feeling so defensive I propelled myself a bit forward.

Selena was doing way too much when she should have been handing things off to me. I was already leveraging her wedding for my own childish revenge.

"I don't mind, really." Selena put her hand up. "I was actually hoping I could assign you a maid-of-honor task?"

I felt a little less useless or like an item on her to-do list to fix. I sat up straighter. "Of course."

"I told you I gave *Voulez Magazine* an exclusive on our wedding for a reason." Selena grabbed another fry. "They're owned by the same media company that owns most of the European tabloids."

My brow crinkled as I put it together, remembering what she'd mentioned on the phone. "Right. You give *Voulez* this, and it'll dry up the demand for pap photos?"

"It's a win-win. They don't need to outcompete themselves." A smile stretched across her cheeks. "And I get a nice, relatively quiet wedding."

"Selena Montez, mastermind." I nudged her shoulder playfully with my own. "So, what do you need? Seems like you have it all figured out."

"Do me a favor and keep Malcolm *distracted*. Pictures of some statues and women in ballgowns should be more than enough. Everyone has signed NDAs, and this is certainly better than being mobbed by paps, but . . ."

"Done." I put my hand on hers. She didn't have to explain. I knew. There were so many ways I missed out on having a regular life with Selena over the last few years. Not many nights out, vacations, road trips, nothing. But I could do something for her now. "I am his newest shadow."

"And it works for Austin, too. He can get some press for his foundation."

"You know I didn't hire you, right?" I asked Selena playfully, hoping if my tone lifted, my spirits would, too. If Jesse hadn't called her, I was sure she would have done it, because she was never going to let me hurt in all of this.

"Isa." She laughed and leaned her head on my shoulder. "With a resident's salary? You couldn't afford me."

A bleak night turned brighter with her laugh, a beer, and a basket of fries.

* * *

After stress eating a few more baskets of fries with Selena, I headed home.

I threw my keys onto the countertop under the dim pendant lights' glow and walked straight to my fridge. I needed some ice-cold water and some sleep and I'd feel better.

My exhausted muscles pulled me forward and, just as I opened the fridge, I looked at all the vegetables that had gone bad waiting for me to use them.

The tomatoes had turned a brown color with a fuzzy gray mold growing around one side of them. They gave way to gentle pressure from my fingers. The sentiment decayed in my heart, making it heavy.

I looked up from the fridge and my absent-minded scan of the room stopped on the counter.

Sitting in the corner was the oversize college sweatshirt— Blake's college sweatshirt. It was threadbare after a decade of washes. I knew I needed to throw it out. But it was comfortable and throwing it away felt like losing something.

My mind flooded with memories of him.

And in that second, the fatigue, the sadness, the frustration all blended together. A match lit by that stupid sweatshirt burst alive with a determined flame.

I grabbed the sweatshirt in one hand and stomped back to the fridge, piling everything that was definitely past its expiration on top of it. The jalapeños that I had had no idea how to store, next to the milk that had been there for weeks, the eggs that I had bought in hopes I'd make myself a nice breakfast in the morning on occasion.

All of it piled on top.

A few loud cracks on the floor stopped me just as I was turning to close the fridge door. I looked down. The eggs, having teetered off the top of the pile of things in my arms, lay on the floor, pooling at my feet.

And like those fragile shells, it all just broke.

My arms dropped; everything but the sweatshirt joined the eggs on the floor.

The levies that kept my mind in check finally became too overwhelmed. With an anger that had nowhere to go, I let it out.

The emotion that clogged my throat cleared with a furious scream into the sweatshirt. When my throat burned, I finally let the tears loose. They stung as they slipped down my cheeks, and I slid down to the floor.

Each arm fell limp to my sides, and the sweatshirt fell in the mess.

The fog began to clear, and I stared at the sweatshirt, then around my apartment.

I was alone. Me and the mess I made in the kitchen.

Blake had moved on. Selena had moved on. And I was in the same place.

On top of all that, in a couple short weeks, I'd have to see how far moved on they both were and how left behind I was.

In deference to my work, my personal life had stalled out.

But I *had* to be the best. I wasn't going to live in my father's shadow. And after my birth had plucked the wings off my mom, I wasn't going to be anything other than perfect. She'd look at her sacrifices and be proud seeing the career she didn't get to have in me.

I tried to remember that, but tonight, all of that pushed to the back of my mind.

The painful truth I never let myself admit was too hard to ignore—tonight I let myself feel it. There were some things I wasn't going to have.

The tears became a steady stream. My body rocked underneath a quiet sob.

I'd let myself feel whatever this was and pull it together tomorrow.

Chapter 10
AUSTIN

I was too old to be pretending and Isabelle's scheme was a *little* childish, but the numbers didn't lie. The auction a week ago happened to raise more in one night than we had in two years. Now was the perfect time to capitalize on it, especially since Jesse wanted to move on the coaching interest sooner rather than later.

I pushed the button to the elevator.

The pre-war apartment building was beautifully maintained and had a doorman. The crown moldings and antique finishes along the lobby and hallway were clearly restored with care. Growing up poor, I used to imagine the types of people who lived in these buildings. Wealthy with easy lives and no concerns.

With each passing floor ding, I found myself wondering more and more about who Isabelle was. How had she become the always-in-control workaholic surgeon with a vendetta?

I walked past each bronze sconce to the end of the hall-way, apartment number forty-eight. I knocked on the door and heard a few steps that stopped. Then started again.

The door swung open.

"Austin." Isabelle blinked a few times. Her hair was down again, like that night at the auction. The curls bounced around her shoulders. In a pair of shorts and a loose-fitting T-shirt, she looked approachable, casual.

A rogue jitter threaded between my muscles. She looked . . . different. Beautiful, but in a different way this time. I filed that thought away with all the others in the "she's helping you out, so don't make this any more complicated" part of my brain.

"What are you doing here?"

"You told me to come by to figure out the wedding details," I reminded her. After the auction, I got a text with bullet points of what we needed to discuss, an address, and a time. If that wasn't daunting enough, I still wasn't exactly sure what level of "playing pretend" we were doing. "Remember?"

"Oh! Right." She opened the door wider and let me in. "Sorry, I umm . . ."

"Long night?" I took a few steps inside.

It looked like she was cleaning. Her kitchen had a few full trash bags. Next to them were a couple boxes. A crumpled sweatshirt sat on top of them.

Another—open—box sat on her couch with a final one on her kitchen counter that overlooked the entire living area. Each box was partially filled with frames and other random items.

"Something like that." She turned and went back to throwing things into the open boxes.

"So . . ." I rubbed the back of my neck. I didn't know what about all of this made me so uneasy. It was simple. "Should we jump right into your to-do list? We should probably know something about each other if I'm going to pass as your date to a wedding."

"Grew up in DC. Sydney-Wells Academy, Columbia undergrad, Harvard Med, ortho residency," she listed off like I had asked for her academic résumé. If she was expecting mine, it stopped after "grew up in . . ." I just barely finished high school and that was only because Theo would have dragged me across the graduation stage if he'd had to.

"I meant, what exactly do you need from me?" I took a few steps closer to the kitchen island, where a couple of small boxes were lined along the side that overlooked the living area. "I get you want to make your ex jealous, but you don't really seem like the type to be bothered going to a wedding alone."

Even if an ex were there.

She seemed pathologically independent. I assumed she was either seeing someone or didn't want to be seeing anyone. Beautiful, successful, and smart; if she was single, it was her choice to be.

"My ex will be there with his fiancée." She said it casually, but her voice went up an octave. "I felt kind of funny about showing up solo. It's an added bonus if I get to watch the skin melt off his face."

My eyebrows jumped. *Skin melting* seemed like a lot. I wondered what he'd done to deserve it.

"And I'm how you do that?" I asked skeptically, trying to remember all that she said in the whirlwind of thoughts at the auction.

"Performative modesty isn't necessary with me." She rolled her eyes and turned back around and closed the lid on the first box, now filled. "You know you were a big deal for a long time."

"I try not to take myself too seriously." It wasn't a performance; I just didn't like to harp on that time. I didn't *want* to hang on to my glory days. If anything, I was trying to learn from them. The air in the room was tense, and clearly she'd had a rough night, so I tried to diffuse it. "So this has nothing to do with your little crush on me?"

"You're not exactly my type," she snapped, but the razor-sharp reply came with a light, patronizing smile, cutting away whatever weighed on her.

"Noted." I grinned widely; at least it was a little less tense now.

I didn't know if I should be offended or not, but my heart raced in anticipation of something that I couldn't figure out. I glanced into one of the boxes on the island. Was her type scraggly and unremarkable? Because the one thing all the pictures in the box had in common were one guy.

"And this doesn't break any rules for your residency?"

"I am not your doctor," she reminded me again. "I helped Dr. Reinhold out a few times, but I have absolutely no bearing on your surgery, recovery plan, any of it." She placed a few more random items into a box. "Not that it matters. We're not actually dating, so it's not like it crosses any lines anyway."

As she turned around to sort through another stack of items,

I picked a picture out of a box absentmindedly. It was a photo of her with that same guy, his arm slung around her shoulder. It looked relatively recent, maybe in the last year or so. They were in the New York harbor. What did he do? "And you're not trying to make him jealous so you'll get back together?"

An older picture behind that one was just the two of them, each holding out a Harvard pennant from what I assumed was grad school.

He was smart.

Made sense, someone like Isa probably wanted someone who could keep up with her intellectually. *That* was probably what her type was.

Now I *was* a little offended.

She turned around and caught me poking through the box. Lips thinning into a flat line, she gently plucked the picture from my hand and returned it to the box. "I'll settle for making it through the week with my pride intact."

Framed photos, a stuffed giraffe, some cards, all thrown in a box. He meant enough that she was holding on to all of those things. Till now.

I nodded. "Pretty bold move for him. Showing up with a fiancée, knowing this is your best friend's wedding."

"Yeah, well, if he wanted a reaction, I'm not giving him one. All he'll see is that I've moved on, too." She looked at the floor for a second before pulling her gaze to mine. "Thank you, by the way." Her pride competed with sincerity. "For being a good sport about this."

"The foundation hasn't ever been this successful. So, I think we're even."

"The foundation." She took a deep inhale, shut the last box, and released the breath. Taking a final glance, she turned around on her heels and walked further into the apartment and motioned for me to follow. "What's the story?"

"What do you mean?" I asked, stalling. My hands felt a little clammy. I couldn't pitch something. And the idea of having to eloquently tell the smartest person I'd ever met about it felt like more pressure than an important match.

Isa plopped down on the couch. "Well, now you know about my noble quest to make my ex-boyfriend cry." I chuckled and took a seat on the ottoman across from her. Her face brightened. "So, what's the deal with your foundation? I mean, why not run it full-time, since it seems so important to you?" she thought out loud.

"Coaching was always the plan and there's interest now; usually these types of things are all about timing." Coaching felt like a safe place to go.

And I didn't know what the requirements were to run a foundation, but I'd been in multiple meetings with the current director of the Mistry Foundation, who was a recommendation by Theo and Zoya. They all went to the same Ivy League college together. And it seemed like more than I could do on my own.

"Right." She fidgeted like she didn't agree. "I'm only saying, putting yourself up for sale for the sake of a charity seems like it means a lot to you."

"The foundation was actually my best friend's idea," I explained. Theo had also had the idea for the soccer academy.

"Oh." She smiled, sitting up straighter. "Joseen's mom?"

"No, her dad, Theo. We started the foundation while I was still playing in Farnham," I told her. "Although Zoya sort of became the sister I never wanted when they got married."

"I know the feeling." She grinned.

"Theo started it and when he wasn't able to continue it, I took over. Well, the best I could, anyway. Hopefully, if it can keep getting this type of funding, it can get a fully outfitted staff," I clarified. A team that was *qualified* to run a foundation. "It's meant to give kids a place to go when they're not in school. Maybe learn something while they're there."

Like I did when I was a kid. Except that place was usually the alley behind Theo's parents' restaurant. It was where I learned soccer from his grandfather. Where I ate most of my meals, and where Theo taught me how to read because I was the fifth grader who couldn't.

"That's really great, Austin." The genuinely impressed pitch in her voice made my face heat. A compliment from her felt like sitting in the sun. And I didn't know how to react to that.

"Thanks," I said quickly. I glanced around the coffee table and saw a little black notebook. The nerves funneled into doing something with my hands. I picked it up and flipped through it. "What's this?"

"Oh, those are de-identified case logs." Isa craned her neck forward. "I log every case I've ever assisted in into our electronic medical record, and it spits out a list."

Each case had a paragraph or so of different notes written next to each one. Each one's case number was highlighted; it looked like some organization method.

"What are they for?"

"Pink is reconstructive cases, blue are trauma recon, yellow are athletic injury . . ." She rattled off a few more colors while I noticed there were *a lot* of yellow ones. "Some fellowship programs require them in their application process."

"Oh, that fellowship?" I asked mostly to myself.

That book had easily a thousand different surgeries that she'd assisted in or performed. All logged with notes. My brain had trouble wrapping itself around the idea that someone knew all of this.

"It's actually not for the Winthrop fellowship." She took the notebook, closed it, and ran the elastic fastener over the cover. "Winthrop is a prestigious, robotic-assisted reconstructive surgery training program. *This* is for Dr. Reinhold. He has a fellowship that spans over a couple years working on athletic injury from pediatrics all the way up to professional athletes."

I didn't know the difference between them, and I didn't want to sound stupid and ask. But apparently I looked confused, because she went on.

"The Winthrop fellowship takes all sorts of reconstructive cases: traumatic, athletic, pediatric. Dr. Reinhold's sports medicine fellowship is exclusively athletic injury."

"That's cool." There had easily been twice as many yellow highlighted cases in her notebook than any other color. "You gonna throw your name in the running for the sports medicine one, too?"

She laughed. "It's not due till after the Winthrop decision is back, so hopefully no."

I felt marginally disappointed for a reason I couldn't pinpoint, and my mouth twisted. "You're not even considering it?"

"Only a handful of people in the world are ever considered for the Winthrop fellowship. The surgeons that come out of that program are the ones innovating the techniques that everyone else uses." She said it like it was obvious or a forgone conclusion that she *had* to be one and not the other. "I'll deal with a plan B if I have to. But hopefully plan A works out."

I was still waiting for an explanation until I realized that was it. "So, it's for the prestige?"

She pulled a stack of ornately decorated invitations from the pile of mail.

"Is that judgment I hear?" With a teasing tenor, she stood, and I followed suit. "From a man who literally kicks a ball around a field for applause." She tilted her head up like she was thinking. When she looked back down, our eyes caught. "That's a choice."

"Technically I kick it around a field for *goals*."

She rolled her tongue from inside one cheek to the other but didn't reply.

I think I won that round. A flutter moved through my chest.

"You know, you can be a little mean," I said.

"Oh, come on." She grinned. "You've battled through two ACL injuries and months of recovery for each, but a bruised ego's too much? Don't tell me the American Footballer, living legend Austin Cade, can't handle it."

Something sparked along my muscles. Her bluntness lit up that competitive fire again—whatever game this was, I wasn't about to fold. I smothered a smile.

"Anyway, these are all the events for the wedding festivities." She handed me the stack of invitations, unable to concede.

They were navy blue with golden calligraphy that looked like it was hand painted. "We leave in a week. When we land, there's a welcome dinner, then the Mehndi in Paris, the Sangeet at Versailles. Then it's a quick trip to the Vosges mountains for the ceremonies. A Catholic one for Selena in a castle's chapel and then a Hindu ceremony in the vineyard."

Zoya was right; this was like attending a royal wedding.

I rubbed the back of my neck, wondering what I'd gotten myself into. "Got it."

Chapter 11
AUSTIN

*P*rivate jets weren't a new experience but they were never something I felt comfortable in. For a lot of reasons. The primary one being that I hated flying. So far, the flight wasn't bad, but even the slightest bump always reminded me that more could show up out of nowhere.

Selena, the bride-to-be, was asleep in the bedroom, and her groom was in the next section over from us, quietly working on his laptop. It left Isa and me in the lounge part of the plane. Isa spent the entire time reading and rereading the same section of a Word document on her laptop. I couldn't help but lean over to read it, too. It was three paragraphs comparing the long and complicated road to becoming a surgeon to preparing a meal. In this case, paella. A lot of it probably went over my head, but the writing was smooth and oddly moving.

"Is that your application?" I asked, trying to get my mind off the occasional bumps in the air.

"Yeah, my personal statement for the Winthrop fellowship."

Isa stared at her computer screen like she was trying to intimidate it into blinking first. "I submitted it last week."

My face contorted, confused. It was already done? "So now . . . you're trying to scare it?"

"I like knowing I didn't mess up." She read it again.

Her eyes moved along the screen, reading it one last time. She smiled and closed the laptop, like reading it for the seventieth time was the one that convinced her it was perfect. Not that she could change it now.

"Do you cook?" I wondered.

I was never a good writer, probably because I was just as terrible at reading, so I could never really fathom how people could weave words together into something cohesive. Especially not something as, in my opinion, nausea-inducing as surgery into something artistic like cooking.

"No, but it is something I have always wanted to get better at." Isa tucked the laptop away and now pulled out a small notebook, the same one she had on her coffee table when I was at her place a week ago. The one with mostly yellow-highlighted cases. "I've been trying to re-create this paella I had in Spain once."

"No luck?"

"No time." She sighed. Her finger ran down each individual line item and she compared them against a paper tucked inside the notebook. It was the case logs she'd mentioned a few days ago. "I buy the ingredients, I get everything ready, and when I have both the time and energy to actually make it, the ingredients have gone bad."

Another bump startled me. I gripped the armrest again. I

never got used to flying, no matter how often I flew between the States and Europe or around the world. A long silence filled the cabin. I could occasionally hear the sound of a keyboard in back, a reminder that the groom-to-be was there, working.

"So." Isa closed her notebook and tucked it into the handbag next to her. "Is the foundation the reason you decided to leave Farnham?"

My pulse ticked up. "Did you google me?"

"*No*," she said, too fast. She leaned further into her seat. "Maybe I've been taking interest in the sport."

"Have you?" I raised an eyebrow. I specifically remembered her saying she didn't like soccer.

"I have a lot of interests." She looked at her nails. "Well-rounded surgeon, remember?"

"Oh okay." I pretended to believe her. "Hey, how long's a match?"

"That . . ." Her eyes flickered around the cabin. "Depends on . . . penalties." She smiled like she surprised herself.

"Uh-huh." Something competitive sparked in me. It kept happening around her. I crossed my arms. "What's offsides?"

She opened her mouth, then closed it. "Well, if you don't know already, then I think we have an answer as to why the US team lost the last World Cup."

"The attacking player is past the final defender . . ."

"Fine, you win. But I didn't google you." She put her hand up. "You *do* realize you were pretty famous for a while there, right?"

"Vaguely," I drawled sarcastically.

I used to live for that fame. I loved it. I loved the press.

I loved the attention from everyone. Anything a twentysome-thing guy could want, I had. A complicated mess of women, money, notoriety. I got so wrapped up in it that I failed to see what was important. Then Theo got sick. I realized just how much I lost sight of in the flashbulb's glare. If my life hadn't been so littered with distractions, maybe I would have seen Theo more.

I could see clearly now and I wasn't going to make that mis-take again. I had a clear path forward.

I went on. "Just like you'll remember what offsides is if you'd just listen—"

"I can't sit through that explanation."

"I don't see how you have the patience to spend a decade learning how to be a surgeon but cannot sit through learning a simple rule."

"Oh." She smacked my shoulder with the back of her hand. "One of them is interesting."

Another dip brought me right back to the anxiety I had a few minutes ago. My fingers gripped the armrest a little tighter.

Isa's eyes flicked to the armrest and back.

"It's actually very safe," Isabelle explained. "And, generally, turbulence can't take a plane down."

"Can we not talk about planes going down?"

"Those dips that feel like free fall are only around a hundred feet."

"How comforting."

"Well, I know back in *your* day the planes flew a lot closer to the ground," she teased. "But now, in the modern era, we're thirty-five thousand feet up. A few feet don't really seem like much."

"For the record, I'm only like eight years older than you." I swallowed the anxiety. "And do you moonlight as a pilot?"

"No . . ." She looked up in thought. "The prefrontal cortex, when busy executing command-related functions, takes priority over the amygdala's neuronal activity."

I didn't say anything. She had to know that sounded like a foreign language.

"Let me distract you," she translated and leaned forward. Her warm breath swept across my neck. A few curls fell forward, almost brushing against me, and suddenly it was all I could think about.

My heart continued slamming against my sternum, but for another reason. I cleared my throat. "Okay."

"Since we're going to be pretending to be dating for the sake of pissing off my ex . . ." she began offhandedly like she was teaching something. "It should look somewhat serious." She paused like she was putting it all together in her head.

"Right."

"Let's say we've been together six months. That's serious enough to make him crazy but not so serious that anyone is going to be asking questions about the future."

"Okay," I answered curtly. If she wanted to upset him, that probably meant she was stuck on him. That fact coiled around in my head. "Anything else?"

"Well, when in settings for the wedding, we can be affectionate. But not over the top."

I swallowed hard as the plane dipped again. "What's over the top?"

"There's affectionate and then there's *affectionate*."

"You realize those are the same words, right?"

"How about a code word so we know where the line is. Something that would never come up in normal conversation." She went quiet thinking. A little jarring in the cabin seemed to rouse the thought. "Oh." She snapped her fingers. "How about offsides?"

"You will do anything to not learn what that really means."

"I think it's a more interesting use of the word." She leaned forward so that she was only a few inches from me and put a hand on my shoulder. "So, something like this." She removed it and leaned back. "Although hand on a shoulder is a little *friendly*."

Without waiting for me to reply, she pursed her lips and cocked her head to the side like she was performing a medical exam. She put her hand back on my shoulder, then slid her palm flat against where it met my chest. My heart sped up with every inch her palm moved. "That's probably fine, right?"

I swallowed against a dry throat. "Yeah, sure."

"And I guess for you . . ." She poked her tongue into her cheek thoughtfully. She took my hand and put it on her knee. Her skin was soft and lush and the wave of chills that ran up my arm begged me to move my palm up her leg.

A magnetic draw pulled me, and I leaned in an inch.

"This is fine." Isa's unfazed voice snapped me from the daze.

I pulled my hand back like it was burnt. "Is it?"

"Sorry." Her face reddened and she leaned back into her seat. "I didn't mean to disrupt your Regency-era sensibilities. I'll tuck my ankles away now."

"I know how to be affectionate; I don't need lessons."

Before she could answer, the sound of someone clearing their throat interrupted us.

We both pulled back from each other. Isa and I looked toward the back of the plane. Selena's fiancé wasn't more than ten feet from us.

"I can hear you." Henry glanced up at us from behind his laptop screen, an eyebrow raised. "So, can I call offsides?"

Chapter 12
ISABELLE

When we landed, Austin went to unpack, and I went directly to meet some of the wedding-planning staff with Selena. I wasn't tired and I had a complete week to be here and present for my best friend, so I was *going* to be.

"We've checked and double-checked with our staff and local officials. I can assure you there won't be any press." Jean-Luc, the divisional president for the Ritz's European hotels, guided us through the Ritz Paris's different event spaces a few steps ahead. "As an added measure, all guests have been checked in under pseudonyms."

Selena nodded and her planning team took over with questions and details.

"That's him." Selena leaned in and whispered to me. Her heels clicked through the grand marble lobby as we made our way in the direction of the garden. She tipped her head to the side toward a man speaking to one of the hotel staff a few feet from reception. "Malcolm Parks, the *Voulez* reporter."

I stayed in step with her and flicked a glance over my shoulder. Tall and lanky with curly dark brown hair, he wandered into the Ritz like he was lost. He adjusted his rounded glasses and pushed them up the bridge of his nose.

I looked back at Selena as we stepped out into the Ritz Paris's garden's stone patio from inside.

"Got it." I saluted her playfully.

Along the edge of the garden, towering hedges—perfectly manicured—extended up, cloaking the green in privacy. Roses and magnolias perfumed the summer air.

"Wow . . . this is unreal," I added.

The wedding festivities would span over a week's time. All two hundred guests were staying at the Ritz Paris for the first few events: a welcome party, a Mehndi, a couple days for guests to enjoy the city, and then the Sangeet at Versailles.

Then, every single guest would be taken via either jet or private car to the French side of the Vosges mountains for the ceremonies.

A literal fairy tale made real for my best friend.

"I know." Selena's mouth hung open as we walked along the stone path. Just above the hedges' perfectly lined tops, you could see Paris's iconic wrought iron balconies and mansard roofs from the adjacent buildings. "I want next week to get here already."

"Well, try to enjoy it," I reminded her. I wondered what that kind of love felt like. I thought I had had it with Blake, but I had never been as deliriously happy as Selena seemed to be all the time. It gave me a spark of hope. "This is beautiful, Selena."

Tomorrow's welcome reception would be in the Salon

Vendôme and the garden would be lit with twinkling lights so the guests could filter out.

"It is, isn't it?" Selena looked around, disbelievingly. The city was just outside of the leafy walls; it was hidden but not secluded. "A little different from the rooftop garden we had in that horrible place in Brooklyn."

It hadn't been a garden so much as a flower bed next to an unregulated bee colony. The bees hadn't had enough flowers for food and ended up eating syrup at a nearby cherry processing factory.

That place was all Selena could afford at the time, so we had made it our own.

Selena giggled so loudly it was nearly a squeal. "That red honey."

"I can't believe you tried it!"

"It looked like candy." She playfully smacked my shoulder. "And *you* dared me to."

"I didn't think you'd actually do it." I smiled and leaned my head on her shoulder. I was an only child, but Selena was my sister.

"Well, I think the honey here is probably safe to eat," she teased.

I paused for a second and took in the moment with her. We weren't in our tiny apartment in Brooklyn anymore. The shift that was happening in front of me felt like an endless trail of monkey bars. But I was stuck, unable to move forward, and my grip slowly loosened as she passed beside me.

I closed my eyes and, just as I did, I tried to swallow a yawn.

"Isa, go get some rest." Selena gently patted the side of my forehead. "I slept on the plane, but you've got to be exhausted by now."

"Yeah, we can handle this with Selena." The voice belonged to Selena's soon-to-be sister-in-law, Sloan. She walked up from behind us and slung an arm over Selena's shoulder, pulling her into a side hug.

Selena's new family was wonderful. It still yanked at my heart, though.

"The Amaris bought out a bar for dinner and drinks in the city for a little family night tonight, before the rest of the guests start arriving," Selena said, linking her arm in mine. "Why don't you get some sleep beforehand?"

I nodded and unlinked my arm from hers.

I started walking back to the room, but not to sleep. I was the "power through" type of traveler, so I was determined to stay awake until I was on Paris time. But Selena could spend the day with her new family. And maybe I could use that time to get myself together a bit.

* * *

I swung open the door, sure Austin was probably unpacking, but he was nowhere to be found. There was a large living area and a fairy-tale-esque Juliet balcony that overlooked the Seine and the seventh arrondissement on the other side.

I walked into the bedroom. Taking a quick glance in at the French baroque-style furniture, my eyes were drawn to the tufted headboard in between the intricate lattice work that wrapped around the heavy mahogany posts.

One bed.

My pulse ticked up. I forgot about that. Oops.

"Tell me again how you don't have a crush on me?" Austin's warm breath swept down my spine, and a ripple moved through my body. I jumped a bit, not expecting him or whatever that feeling was. I looked over to the side of the room where the bathroom door was open and steam spilled out. "Because one bed seems . . . *convenient*."

I took a quick glance over my shoulder. He had a towel wrapped around his waist, his hair wet with droplets occasionally rolling down his sculpted frame. He walked past just as quickly, over to his suitcase in the corner.

My eyes followed as rivulets tracked down his pecs.

"Says the man in a towel," I shot back, taking a hard swallow and pulling my attention away from his unreasonably solid body. I hoped my face didn't look as warm as it felt. "Put some clothes on."

I ignored the erratic thumping in my chest.

He was hot. So what? Lots of people were hot.

"I didn't know sharing a bed made you so nervous. Oh, that's right." I snapped my fingers. "Your Regency-era sensibilities. Sorry," I cooed patronizingly. He leaned over his suitcase and pulled out a shirt, but instead of putting it on, he put it on the side of the bed, crossed his arms, and looked at me. "Don't worry—"

"You'll be gentle?" His cheek twitched.

"Nope." The anxious buzz became something else, because going shot for shot with him was a little fun. "But if you're scared, I'll put a little pillow wall up for you."

His tongue tucked to the side of his mouth.

"Alright but watch those hands." He walked past me, his shirt and what I could only assume were boxers in hand, with a rolling chuckle.

Deep and heavy, the sound settled at the bottom of my stomach.

"Tonight is a dinner followed by a wine tasting with whoever's here so far." I felt the need to shift my weight between my legs and, at the same time, the reminder that I came up here to rest and maybe get some work done popped into my head. "Will you be clothed for that?"

He stopped at the bathroom door and turned back to me. His grin became blinding. "Where's the fun in that?"

This guy. This version of Austin seemed like the Austin Cade from interviews. The ones I only watched because, while I didn't care for soccer, he was the dream guy for collectively every red-blooded American woman every four years during the World Cup or the Olympics.

"It's going to run a bit late into the night," I added.

"Don't worry. I can keep up." The side of my mouth lifted. Was he being funny or forward? A little of both? I sort of . . . didn't hate it.

"A night out at a bar is a young man's game." I needed to stop baiting him and do what I came up here to do, but the thrill it sent down my body was addicting. "That's all I'm saying."

"It'll be good practice. You know, to pull off the perfect ruse." He waved me off and shut the bathroom door behind him to get dressed.

The reminder stole the warmth in the room.

Blake was going to be here soon. Probably tonight or tomorrow. I hated myself for it, but it made my mind wander to all the reasons Blake chose *her*. Why—while I'd held on to the idea of him—he let go of me.

It was proof that my brand of ambition didn't get the same happy ending that everyone else's did. That my uncompromising, unyielding commitment to my career meant there were some things I got to have and some things I just couldn't. And breaking because of a wounded heart wasn't an option when you were a woman in a male-dominated field. I had to be on top of my game at all hours.

And like an alarm, it pulled all my shields up.

I walked to my suitcase, grabbed my laptop, and tried to put it out of my mind.

Chapter 13
AUSTIN

String lights hung around the towering, exposed beams at the charming restaurant and wine bar a block over from the hotel. It had an entire cellar below and was known for being the place where every renowned sommelier chose their favorite vintages.

I waited for Isa at the bar.

After having to take care of something for Selena, Isa told me she wanted to get a glass of wine from the cellar. On her way back, I watched her stop to talk to everyone within eyeshot. And while that was fine—I wouldn't have minded enjoying the soft French jazz at the bar by myself—I was cornered by the mother of the groom, who proceeded to ask me a slew of pretty personal questions without much thought.

Once the older woman left, I turned my glass of whiskey and took a long sip. Eventually, the familiar lavender scent of Isa's perfume neared. I glanced up to my side. "Were you *making* the wine?"

The soft light skimmed over the silky green fabric of her

dress. It clung to the gentle curves on her chest, the swell and fall around her hips, ending just above her knees. The hypnotic swish of her skirt with each switch of her hips was broken when she stood next to me at the bar.

"I wasn't gone that long."

"Twenty-seven minutes." I blinked away the stare.

"Oh no." Isa cocked her head to the side. "Did you have to make small talk?"

"I did, actually." And I'd never had to lie so many times in a row.

"Well, I promise it was for a good cause." She gave me a cheeky smile and patted my chest patronizingly. "Selena's soon-to-be brother-in-law, Xander Sutton, runs a capital firm. I set you two up on a playdate."

"Playdate?" I grimaced.

"Sorry, *man* date," Isa clarified. "He played soccer in college. Since this group is a captive audience for a while, he and some of the other guests are going to play a friendly game. I told him you'd love to come. Let him win and . . . you know, be nice." She flicked her hand in the air. "The foundation will be set in no time."

Ignoring that I felt a little bit like Joseen in that moment, I smiled. It was progress and we'd only been here a few hours.

"Well, I guess I should hold up my end." I took another sip of the whiskey I'd been nursing while waiting on Isa to return. "Where's the idiot that fumbled Dr. Isabelle Mercado?"

"Not here yet." She tapped her fingers on the polished wood. "But, in the meantime, we have a tiny assignment from the bride."

I lifted an eyebrow.

"That guy over there is Malcolm Parks, the *Voulez* reporter," Isa explained. "I need to keep him entertained and make sure he's playing by the rules. And since you might want to practice some of those social skills, why not do both at once?"

At a small iron-framed table in the corner, Malcolm sipped a glass of red wine, watching his surroundings like a bird perched over a building. His curly brown hair was slicked back a bit, exposing rounded, wire-rimmed glasses. He looked down at his notepad, scribbled some notes, then went back to people watching.

"Yeah . . ." Now I definitely felt like I was Joseen being set up on playdates. "Jesse mentioned he'd be here."

Jesse also said talking to him might be the perfect way to create—what he called—organic interest. Whatever the hell that meant. All I knew was I had to be interesting and strike up conversation. It was easier said than done, but luckily Isa was with me.

I was sure she had memorized the perfect encyclopedia for the occasion.

"Great." Isa put her drink on the bar. "Also, why did Beatrice Amari tell me that four children was the perfect number?"

"She cornered me, asked me a million questions, and honestly, it's your fault." That woman had lured me in with her kind, motherly smile, but her crisp British accent sounded like the Queen's, and she asked me questions with the speed of an Interpol agent.

"My fault?"

"You didn't tell me I'd be interrogated."

"What is so hard about saying, *I'm not sure?*"

"If I was good at thinking on my feet, I wouldn't need you to help me with the foundation," I reminded her. I didn't have an easy grace with everyone like she did. That's why being here was great, but I still sort of needed her to be the charming know-it-all she was at the auction. "Besides, you want us to seem committed and deliriously happy, right?"

"So you thought the best way to show that was turning me into a human gumball machine?"

"*Pretend* human gumball machine."

Her lips stayed in a tight line across her face, but the corners tipped up rebelliously. "No more kid talk."

"I'm sure little David, Marta, Christian, and Alex will understand."

Isa choked on her drink, her brow crinkled. "You named them?"

"She kept looking at me."

"And you happened to have names at the ready?" she said in hushed tone.

"Why does it matter?" I whisper-shouted back. "They're make-believe."

She straightened. "Who said I even want kids?"

"I had a quarter second to give that woman an answer. You're lucky I stopped at four."

"Well, get a handle on your biological clock, Cade. We need to keep Malcolm Parks busy, not create a fictional family."

"Right," I conceded.

"Talk about the foundation," she suggested, hearing the unsure dip in my voice. "Or sports, or, I dunno, anything. Anything else except children."

"You sure?" That stupid flutter moved through my chest again. "One more and we have a band. Few more and we have a starting lineup."

The back of her hand smacked against my chest again. I moved my head in the direction of the reporter, who was gesturing for us to join him on the other side of the restaurant.

"You know, they aren't the kinds of *bones* I work with," Isa warned. "But keep talking and I'll *fix* you myself."

She closed an eye and drew a few smooth curves in the air with her finger. I raised an eyebrow.

I had a feeling she was used to getting the last word. And I was curious as hell as to what happened when someone else did.

"I dunno." I leaned in, feeling a surge of that *something* from earlier. Confidence, nerves, excitement. "I have a feeling you'd change your mind if you got your hands on it."

She stopped, her eyes snapped up to mine—wide—and her mouth hung open just slightly, staying like that for another few seconds, at a complete loss for words.

Shit. Maybe I read that whole thing wrong. "Sor—"

"Well played, but offsides," she warned seriously. But the smile and tiny laugh that floated over each syllable made me believe it landed how I'd intended it to.

Whatever else she planned to say was cut off when we arrived at Malcolm's table, and Isa pointed to the empty seats. "These seats taken?"

He motioned for her to take a seat.

We settled in and Isa quickly dominated the conversation, asking him about what he was doing at the Amari wedding, as if she didn't already know.

"I have to admit, I'm a fan your work," Isa said. "Particularly when they had you on the politics column."

Of course she'd researched him. I found myself spellbound by how easily she could shift to become an expert in anything.

That turned the conversation to Malcolm's early reporting days, when he'd dreamed of doing more *substantive* work. "With all the corporate interests in news media now, fair reporting doesn't really exist," he bemoaned.

Isa leaned on her elbows, hands folded on each other as she focused on him like a boxer waiting for the bell.

"Didn't you write that five-page hatchet job on a singer who happened to be connected to some copyright scandal years ago that amounted to nothing?" Isa mused. "Was *that* fair reporting?"

I coughed into my drink.

Admittedly, I wasn't great with the press, but I had enough media training to know not to antagonize them—not that I always listened to that advice. But a gut reaction to something ridiculous or inflammatory was a lot different than Isa running up to a conversation to simply start a fire.

"Offsides," I whispered into her ear and squeezed her thigh beneath the table. Then lifted my voice in warning. *"Honey."*

"It's fine, truly." Malcolm pushed his black-rimmed glasses back up the bridge of his nose with an intrigued smile. He leaned into the table toward Isa, and looked at her like she was a puzzle. One he wanted to figure out. "This evening is more interesting than I expect this entire wedding to be."

A tiny curve peaked up at the side of Isa's mouth.

Malcolm's eyes shifted between the two of us. "So, how did you two meet?"

Isa tensed.

"Off the record," Isa demanded. That didn't help. It looked like she was guilty of something.

The words feathered like flames across the table.

He laughed, putting his hands up. "A society fluff piece is bad enough; I wouldn't debase myself with tabloid fodder."

"She was doing research with the team doctor. I happened to see her a lot after my injury." I ran my hand down her back, surprised at how easy it felt. Maybe this wouldn't be so hard.

At least not for me. Isa was a different story. She stiffened.

I gave her a confused look. A hand on her back wasn't much, and we were doing this for *her*. Why was she bombing the performance all of a sudden?

"Yeah." She put her hand on my thigh and scrunched her nose at me unconvincingly. Turning back to Malcolm, she began, "So, tell me about the state of . . ."

And they were back at it. Malcolm put down his notepad seconds later.

* * *

Hours into the night, Isa and I ended up back at the bar at the front of the tasting room.

"Well, Malcolm is dealt with." She looked over her shoulder at Malcolm, who was essentially passed out in the small corner booth. Isa may not have been overly believable, but her sometimes domineering conversation style drove him straight into too many glasses of Beaujolais. "For tonight anyway."

"Good thing. I don't know how much longer he could survive your cross-examination."

"I was nice," she defended halfheartedly.

"*That* was not nice."

She waved it off. "Reporters haven't exactly been kind to my best friend. I wanted to see how easy he is to knock down."

"And the verdict?"

She glanced back at him with an upside-down smile. "A stiff breeze is all I need."

My heart raced imagining all the ways Isa could dress down anyone in a matter of minutes. I didn't know why that was so . . . interesting, but it was.

"I'm sure he signed a very restrictive contract before coming here, so maybe try being nicer? It might help with the believability of our relationship, too, because nobody was going to buy that performance." I was sure she was already aware. She turned to lean her back against the wooden bar. "I'm guessing acting lessons weren't on the curriculum in those fancy schools you went to?"

We were supposed to be two things: nice and a couple. Isa couldn't sell either. In *this* setting, being effortlessly charming was difficult.

"He had me a little thrown," she explained. "He kept scribbling on that paper. I didn't want to say anything I couldn't back out of. Facts are easy, but lying is less . . ." She trailed off. "Anyway." She poked me in the chest gently. "Someone had to keep the conversation going. You could have taken advantage of the opportunity to make yourself seem interesting, but you were silent."

"Who can keep up with you dominating the conversation?" I leaned in a little more. "Are you *actually* prepping to be a *Jeopardy!* contestant?"

A smile tempted the corner of her mouth but ultimately lost. "I like to be prepared when I know I'm meeting someone."

She looked around the bar. Some of the guests were still there; most of the family had already cleared out. She nodded her head in the direction of the door. The hotel was only a block away.

We stepped out onto the cobblestone-lined street.

Under the velvety stretch of the Parisian night sky, we meandered down the Champs-Élysées. The City of Lights was just that, dark but alive. A soft hum—a symphony of distant laughter, clinking glasses, and the occasional purr of a luxury car gliding by—made the energy palpable.

"Why?" I asked as the summer night's breeze swept across her curls, making them dance gently. "Isn't that what conversation is for? Getting to know someone?"

"You never know when it'll come in handy." Her steps against the pavement were a little off-balance as she leaned some weight against me. She swayed a bit, occasionally brushing into me. "You know, like when I'm charming the mayor for *your* charity."

"Right," I agreed sarcastically. "And God forbid someone knows something you don't."

She blinked a couple times, surprised by my barb. I was half expecting she might be offended, because it seemed like she didn't like to be caught off guard. She prepared herself so she never would be.

"Doesn't happen often," she assured me, looking straight ahead. The dim glow from the street lanterns skated up the line of her jaw as we walked past.

"You're very smug for someone with the acting skills of a cardboard cutout in a high school play."

This time her smile won out and a laugh burst like a fire-cracker from her full lips. A thousand tiny sparks landed on my skin, popping down my body in a delightful sensation.

Her eyes slid across the street, then over to the grand stone facades of a closed luxury boutique we walked past as we made our way to the hotel entrance. Anywhere to not meet mine. "You're not very good at this either."

On the long list of things I wasn't good at, I was sure act-ing probably made it on there. But this may have been the one thing in the entire world, besides athletics, that I might actu-ally be better at than her. And it seemed like it bothered her. Isa didn't want to lose; it was oddly enticing.

"Still better than you," I challenged as we walked into the Ritz's marble lobby.

"Mm-hmm," she hummed and walked even slower now. Her body leaned against my side, and I was tempted to swing an arm around her. But that was forward, and we didn't need to pretend in front of an empty lobby . . . I couldn't figure it out, but I still wanted to. "At least I'm not the one who needed to create fictional children to convince people we were *dating*."

"No, you're the one who avoided the subject altogether." I chuckled. Beneath the sweep of her dark lashes, a playful smile pulled at her lips. A warm tension stretched between us, nearly collapsing the rest of my thoughts. "I guess I found the one thing that scares you."

She looked back ahead, like she was gaming out what to say. My fingers tingled waiting for her to whip back her response.

"Nothi—" She and her sentence stopped dead in their tracks. Her entire frame, relaxed and leaning a bit against mine a few seconds ago, went completely rigid like a deer caught staring at an oncoming truck.

I looked in the direction that had her frozen and saw a couple walking toward the elevator, in front of an art-lined wall. The woman pushed her brown hair over her shoulder. The man, the one from the pictures in Isa's apartment, the ones she was throwing away, followed a few steps behind the woman. Her ex.

"Blake." The woman took a step closer to him and wrapped an arm around his waist. "Come on. I'm exhausted."

The reminder was a downpour on the breezy night we were having.

Isa turned so her back faced them, inching closer to me, like she was using my body to hide.

They walked into the elevator and the doors shut.

"Isa . . ." I looked into her eyes as she stared blankly at the floor.

For someone who was always ready to pick a fight with anyone, I'd never seen her appear so defeated.

Chapter 14
ISABELLE

I froze.

I never froze.

One of the most important aspects of my job—what made me so great at it—was being able to think on my feet. Assess the damage, make a plan, and execute it in milliseconds.

But there, in the sparkling marble lobby, fifty feet from the elevator bank, I was stuck. Immobilized with the realization that after years of ignoring and suppressing the awful feeling that I was being left behind, my present finally caught up with my past.

Everything hit me at once. A torrent of memories. The spiced smell of his cologne. The flecks of brown that could only be seen in the morning sun inside those mossy-green eyes.

More painful than all of that was the reminder that I couldn't have both—the career I wanted and the guy I'd always fig-ured I'd have—and what I chose meant those memories would never make their way to being a reality again.

"We'll wait for the next one." Austin's deep voice pushed me out of the spiral. Looking forward instead of down at me, he tightened his jaw.

The room went from slow motion back to full speed when I felt a light but steady pressure against my lower back. Austin's hand led me away from the elevators.

I didn't say anything, only moved like I was on autopilot.

The elevator. The hallway. The room.

All of it progressed through my vision in frames, muffled by the sound of blood rushing through my ears.

Finally, the metallic slide of the lock clicking behind me pulled me out of my head.

"Are you okay?" Austin asked again, his voice soft but formal.

"Of course." I took a hard swallow and rolled my shoulders back. The neatly organized living area in front of us was dark aside from the tiny lamp that lit the corner. "I was . . . I was just thinking . . ."

My topsy-turvy gaze finally landed on his. The sharp edges around his face softened. "About?"

I didn't want to talk about it. I wasn't supposed to react like this. I should have done *something*. Anything to prove I was okay no matter how not okay I felt.

"It's a good thing they didn't see us," I admitted out loud. Now that it was out of the way, I could be prepared, not completely disarmed. "I guess I do need to work on my acting game." I swallowed against a sandpaper throat. "I was trying my hardest out there and all I did was freeze."

His lips fell at the corners but recovered with a tiny half smile. His eyebrows drew in.

"Next time, I'll be ready. We'll put on a little show," I added.

I pulled together every part of me that hurt and shoved it down. Walking into the bedroom, I made myself busy by going to the closet and grabbing a few pillows.

"You don't have to do that." He loomed in the doorway, pointing to the pillows with his arms crossed. "I'll sleep on the couch."

"No," I countered. He had a recovering knee and that would have been cruel. "You're injured."

"I'll be just fine."

"It's a giant bed; I won't even know you're there. You'll be safe." I pointed at the pillow wall. "See?"

His eyes watched me, and it was another beat before he said, lips lifting, "You can just admit you want to share a bed with me."

The attempt at humor did little to disguise the look on his face he'd been wearing since we got in the elevator. At first it looked like disappointment, which didn't make any sense.

But now I saw it for what it was. Pity. He was bantering to distract the sad girl from her humiliating circumstances. I hated that I sort of needed that diversion.

"Seriously, it's not a big deal." I pointed to his side of the bed.

He didn't say anything, but he walked into the bedroom and over to his suitcase neatly stacked on a holder in the corner.

We got ready for bed almost wordlessly, finally settling onto our respective sides of the mattress.

The curtains were drawn, and it was nearly pitch-black. I lay awkwardly in bed trying to get to sleep.

"You were really trying your hardest out there?" Austin's voice cascaded over the pillows between us, repeating what I'd said when we got back to the room. "At acting that whole time, I mean."

I wasn't sure how any of this could get more humiliating, but here we were, talking like we were in sleepaway camp through a wall of pillows cutting across the thousand-thread-count sheets.

"Yes, coach. I *know* my acting could use some work." Adjusting my head on my silk pillowcase, for some reason I wanted to remain perfectly still. Maybe I'd disappear if I did. "But don't worry. I'm a quick study. I'll get the hang of it before we're in front of anyone that might be of consequence for the foundation."

He didn't say anything else, and I closed my eyes, hoping that I'd wake up and feel just slightly better.

* * *

I woke up to the sound of the shower turning off, and the pillow wall very much intact.

I didn't get to sleep until late into the night, my mind replaying him—frame by frame.

I chose living up to my full potential and that wasn't something I was ever going to litigate. Blake was a living and breathing reminder of what that meant. A bright career and future that didn't look like the happily ever after we were celebrating for Selena and Henry.

I sat up in bed. I needed to reset, regroup, and focus on what I wanted: petty revenge in the form of watching the skin melt off Blake's face when he saw me again . . . and being a decent maid of honor.

A puff of steam floated out of the bathroom as the door opened, and Austin walked out.

Wrapped in a towel. Again.

"You're up," Austin said, running another towel over his hair.

The water trickled from his wet hair, down his torso's broad expanse, and over every ripple of his washboard abs. My eyes tracked a drop of water like I was staring through a car window on a rainy day. The rivulets glided down the rigid muscles slowly—down his pecs, running over each rippled curve of his abs, and finally disappearing into the towel.

Right at the spot where the V at his hips met the towel, just above . . .

"Tell me again how you don't have a little crush on me?" His voice yanked my eyes to his.

Warmth ran up my face, against the deep warning from my brain reminding me that while I wasn't above a fake boyfriend to piss off an ex, I *was* above getting pity fucked.

Not that he was offering, but still. Standards.

So, I was going to pretend that all of . . . *that* did nothing for me. I was sure the dopamine would wear away quickly anyway.

"You could get dressed in the bathroom." I waggled a finger in the air, trying not to let the memories from last night pull down my voice. Seeing Blake was a shot at my heart that hit dead-on. I took a breath, reset to calm and confident and unbothered. "This is clearly a cry for attention."

The deep notes in his corresponding chuckle clanked against my ribs.

"I have to get to the Stade, the soccer stadium outside the

city," he called as he walked into the small closet where our suitcases had been unpacked a bit. "To meet with FC Remy."

A few minutes later he came out in suit pants with a neatly ironed shirt in his hands.

"Right, you're meeting with that team." I folded my legs beneath me in the bed. His manager had a pretty tight schedule for him to go see teams and be present here.

"Informally." He nodded and paused. "You gonna be okay today?"

"Yeah." I dropped my eyes to the blanket. I began adjusting the pillow wall even though it was remarkably intact. "Selena invited me to wander around Paris. But I was hoping to find some downtime later to do some work."

"Wander around Paris all day or spend it working," he wondered almost playfully.

I wished he'd stop doing that. Teasing me because he could tell I was sad. I didn't want his pity.

My eyes glanced up along that chiseled muscle, when he looked back at me and clocked that I was staring.

I scrambled to find words. "I can do both."

I could at least try.

"I was thinking about going to this place on the Seine after the Stade. We have a few hours before that welcome party thing," he offered. "Want to come along? Maybe it'll get your mind off things."

"No, thanks," I answered before I gave myself a chance to think about it. "If I have some time, I'd really like to get those cases logged."

He paused, threw the shirt over his shoulders, and began to button it up. "The ones that don't actually matter because they're plan B?"

"Everyone needs a plan B." My mind twitched at the idea of not getting the one thing I'd been killing myself for. "Even me."

He nodded, then his expression turned more earnest. "Are you sure you're okay? Last night you—"

"I wasn't expecting to see him at the elevators is all," I excused. "I was jet-lagged and tipsy. I'll be Oscar-worthy next time, promise. I'm over it."

I forced a toothy smile.

"Yeah," he agreed, his voice dropping to a mumble as he walked out of the bedroom, low enough it sounded like he was talking to himself. "Seemed like you were over it."

It was almost inaudible, but I heard.

I didn't know what I was feeling. I was holding on to *something* all this time. Love seemed to be the only explanation as to why I felt so completely turned around. And the humiliation that someone happened to witness me being that weak only made it worse.

I was Isabelle Mercado. If something hurt me, it was because I let it.

I let myself believe that the fairy tale I witnessed happen for Selena could happen for me. Nobody was waiting for me at the end of my long journey to my goals, and that was fine because I wasn't giving up my chance at a legacy for *anyone*.

I was choosing myself, and the world had a way of punishing women for that.

All I had to do was remind myself of my mom and all that

she could have been if it weren't for what held her back. She had all the makings of greatness, but then she became a wife and mother. Only one person could have the crazy schedule because someone had to raise me. So, she did. And my dad got the legacy.

I wasn't ever going to let anyone do that to me.

Chapter 15
AUSTIN

*T*he bustle of the city outside was silent on the pitch at the Stade.

The last time I was here, we lost the men's World Cup semi-final. A surprise to no one because, even though the American men's team was getting more competitive by the year, the talent pipeline was no match for the other global leagues.

A few months later, I didn't extend my contract with Farnham, and after that, I went home and signed with the New York Lightning. Going from the Premier League to an American league was all the proof anyone in the business needed that I was becoming irrelevant.

Honestly, it felt like a relief.

This place was a reminder that nothing lasted forever.

"Checking on ghosts?" a familiar voice called loudly from behind me.

I didn't bother turning around. Before I left Manhattan, Jesse set up this meeting with the team owner, so I knew the word would eventually get to Wes. I'd finished talking to the team management about an hour ago. Since then, I had been sort of stuck here, unwilling to leave the pitch. So, I ditched my suit jacket and kicked the ball around.

"Nah, I'm just wondering how you managed to miss that penalty kick in the first half," I answered. I took a deep inhale. The warm summer breeze swept across the pitch as I ran the tip of my shoe along the top of the ball and popped it up in the air.

A quick swipe with my foot, and the ball skimmed the back of the net seconds later. About three inches to the left of where I expected it to go. My knee wasn't back to where it needed to be.

"See?" I looked over to him—Wes Turner—with my head tilted patronizingly. "Easy."

"*That* goal you managed to make." Wes, currently part of the coaching staff team at FC Remy, grabbed a ball and volleyed it between his knees. Wes took emerging talent and got them ready to eventually fill holes in the starting lineup. "I was tired that day. Our striker—the great Austin Cade—kept missing and relying on the defense."

Wes was a few years older than me, and after that World Cup, he played one last season in the Premier League before joining the coaching staff here, the French football club, starting in the B teams and making his way up.

In the world of football—soccer—American players who played in the European leagues had a little social circle. We checked in on each other.

He chuckled. "Anything different about being back here?"

"Fewer cameras."

"Nice, right?" Wes gave a wide, knowing smile. He walked over, tossing another ball between his hands.

"Yeah . . ." I sighed, looking out to the empty stands.

"Our owner told me you were thinking about moving into coaching."

"I am." I shifted my weight between my legs. I wasn't chasing that rush anymore—adrenaline that poured into your veins when thousands of people cheered in unison, and then it all went quiet in your head, and you started to play. It was fun but it was short-lived. I wanted the feeling that came directly after. The incredible high that came along with being proud of what you'd accomplished. That was what I wanted again. "Seems like the perfect time."

"I was actually a little surprised." He dropped the ball between his feet and began to shuffle it slowly. "I always figured you'd stay Stateside after you went to play for the Lightning."

The reminder of why I was here whistled in my ear. I'd spent the last few years trying to figure out some direction. All I'd managed to do Stateside was get injured and let the Mistry Foundation fall into a precarious position.

He kicked the ball over to me and I volleyed it between my feet. "And let the international soccer world believe *you* were our legacy? Besides, there's nothing happening Stateside that compares to . . ." I looked around the stadium. The empty stands. The soaring walls that appeared to touch the sky. "This."

A part of me, a very small part, missed the idiot eighteen-year-old kid that I'd been. He'd made a lot of mistakes, prioritized the wrong things, but one thing he'd done right was walk through the world with a "how hard could it be" mentality— made easier by a best friend pushing him forward and literally nothing to lose at that time. I had been so sure everything would work out.

But I couldn't shake the urge to find that mentality again. I was hoping it was here.

"I think I might be chasing a feeling that's gone," I admitted. But at the same time, I wanted to escape that feeling of failing. I failed the foundation, Theo. I got injured. This was a way to turn things in a direction I knew I could do.

I shuffled the ball, a tightness in my knee reminding me I wasn't going to be playing for much longer.

"You think you'll find it here?" he asked. "Coaching?"

I shrugged. "I'd be good at it."

"You would. I'd love to have you here." Wes dropped the ball and shuffled it between his feet. "But there are other things you can do. Remember when Rivera started that winery?"

I chuckled. An old Premier League teammate from Spain had retired and gone home to buy a vineyard and run it. "I think I'd miss the game too much."

"There's *still* a lot more than coaching for a former footballer."

"Soon-to-be-former footballer," I corrected him and tried not to laugh at all those other options. "And I think I'd need *a lot* more media training before sportscasting, so staff on a team makes a lot more sense."

There were a few routes I could go but coaching got me back to what made sense.

"I guess, but you were the eighteen-year-old upstart thrown into a mess of a relegated team. Led them to victory and promotion the next season. The championship the season after that." He spoke like he was narrating a sports documentary. "If there's something else you want to do, I'm sure as shit betting you'll do it."

I smiled, remembering how I used to live in that feeling. When nothing felt impossible.

He kicked the ball over to me, challenging me to join him.

"I can't really play right now." I stopped the ball and rolled it back and forth under my foot a few times. "I'm on a schedule."

"Where do you possibly need to be in Paris right now?" Wes scoffed, shifting his weight, moving around me in an attempt to steal.

I turned, popped the ball up with my heel, and kept it in my possession. "I'm a wedding guest, actually. At the Amari wedding."

"No way." He chuckled, taking a step back. "How'd you manage that? Aww . . . are the happy couple fans?"

"It's sort of a long story," I grumbled.

He ran, then tracked it back, and suddenly became uninterested in the ball. "Wait. Are you here with someone?"

"Sort of." I crinkled my brow.

"Well, why didn't you bring her here? I could have met her and warned her," he quipped sarcastically.

"She's busy."

It wasn't anything like what Wes imagined. Last night made that very clear.

She said all she wanted was to be over it and leave with her dignity intact. But the way all the blood drained out of her face when she saw him—that wasn't someone who was over it.

It was a look that made me sure whatever I felt last night was one-sided. Besides, complications weren't what I needed right now. I finally had a clear vision for the future after years of blurriness. I had to hold on to that.

I threw more power behind a kick than I originally planned, and the ball spun perfectly around Wes and whipped against the net a second later.

Like the last time, a few inches off from where it was *supposed* to go.

Chapter 16
ISABELLE

I made my way into the welcome party that was beginning to fill the ballroom overlooking the Ritz's expansive garden. After having spent the afternoon with Selena, I managed not to think about Blake until I made it to the event.

Turning the corner to the gilded entrance of the ballroom to meet Austin, I checked my phone to see if any emails had come in. The Winthrop Fellowship Selection Committee would start sending out the first-round interview requests anytime after the application close date.

And that was two days ago.

It was silly to expect that I'd have word back by now, but a part of me was hoping for it today. A little reminder that I had a deeply important job and an important life to get back to.

A way to level the seesaw in my mind.

Taking a few more steps across the marble floor, my eyes landed on two people in front of the domed ballroom. Every worry about the Winthrop fellowship vanished. My body filled with a heavy dread.

Standing in front of the double doors were Blake and Francesca. In the middle of a conversation, they didn't seem to notice me until my heels made an audible click when I stopped short, the black satin from my floor-length gown swooshing against the back of my legs.

Their conversation stopped.

Looking as perfect as ever in a romantic magenta dress that swept against her knees at the front but bowed and hit the floor along the back, Francesca's gunmetal eyes rolled to Blake. Her mouth closed tight with her lips in a hard line.

My heart thudded into my stomach.

"Ummm . . ." I stammered for a second before pulling it together. I couldn't freeze again. "Hello."

Humiliation hit me like a wave. Fuck, why hadn't I planned to walk in with Austin? Why was I screwing this up? All I wanted was for this knot that pushed the stomach acid into my throat to loosen.

"Isa." Blake's voice was low and grated, exactly like it used to sound in the morning.

The urge to escape—pretend this wasn't happening, snooze this interaction as long as I could—climbed up my body, tempting my brain to find an exit, but pride kept my shoes cemented to the floor.

"I'm Isabelle." I stuck my arm out to Francesca, trying my best to not look at Blake, my heart slamming against my sternum. "The maid of honor."

Francesca's eyes moved down my body slowly in recognition. Her tense frame only became more jagged.

"Francesca." Her shoulders slumped down an inch, her lips tipped up at the ends. "And this is my fiancé, Blake Thompson."

"We've met," Blake mumbled, nearly under his breath, looking at Francesca almost pleadingly. They were *clearly* in the midst of a conversation that may have been about me.

Blake looked up at me apologetically. "Hi, Isa."

I opened my mouth to say something, anything.

Confident. Strong. A reminder that I was perfectly fine.

But like trying to run in waist-deep water, nothing moved me. I needed something, anything to pull me out.

Blake's eyes went from me to directly over my shoulder, going wide for a moment before they narrowed and his brow scrunched.

Just before I could look over my shoulder, Austin's voice filled the air.

"There she is." Austin's deep greeting loosened the constriction along my ribs.

I could breathe. The nerves, unease, all of it dissolved away. For a second, his reluctantly warm eyes felt like an anchor as one arm slid along my waist.

Blake's cheeks sank and his mouth parted slightly. At least I wasn't the only one to freeze.

"You're . . ." Blake stammered. *Finally*, I had him on the ropes.

"Austin, honey, this is Francesca and her fiancé, Blake," I delivered calmly, feeling some degree of balance.

"Nice to meet you," Austin said with what felt like a practiced politeness. Something he definitely didn't use in his day-to-day or even when it was something important—like interviews. But he put his hand out, careful to leave the other wrapped around me. "Austin Cade."

Blake's eyes flicked between Austin and me, the slow realization dawning on him as Austin leaned in and pressed a kiss on my head.

Playing along, I leaned in further, and he pulled me closer.

He shook Blake's hand like it was nothing out of the ordinary.

Blake, however, was stationary in disbelief. His mouth opened and stayed that way, loose, like he'd forgotten all his manners. He looked at us like we were the Sunday crossword and he'd *definitely* filled in an incorrect word somewhere. I tried to memorize the look, but my attention on him lost its sharpness.

Dulled by a new, mildly warm, almost sensual feeling on my back.

Austin's thumb grazed up and down against the thin satin, but I could feel it so keenly it was like there was no fabric there at all. Each swipe was like a wave that crested over my muscles with a sea of tingles.

"The American Footballer, of course," Francesca announced with a forced cheeriness after a couple awkward seconds. "The Amaris seem to know everyone."

"Oh. I'm not a guest of the Amaris," Austin explained. His eyes moved over mine slowly. I would have liked to chalk it up to acting, but something about his gaze kept mine glued to it. "I'm Isa's date. We actually met a few months ago, at work."

In my periphery, I could see Blake's shoulders hike up his body.

"Work?" Blake spat it out like he was trying to make a point, but whatever it was seemed to be lost in the argument he was having in his head.

"And then, when I was injured, being around Isa even *more* was my silver lining," Austin told him, but kept his eyes on me for an extended pause before looking at Blake and driving it home. Austin's hand moved to gently push a curl behind my ear. "Talk about a lucky break."

My stomach tumbled. *Why* was he so good at this? I was in on it and even I fell for it—for half a second.

"Mm-hmm." I ran a hand along his chest, hoping to get the high I was chasing from this, but it still hadn't hit. Austin's arm pulled tighter against my waist. "It worked out."

"It did," Austin agreed, a boyish grin snaking its way up his cheek, tipping up into an intrigued smirk on the side they couldn't see.

My heart raced, forgetting for a second what exactly we were doing. Lost in the magnetic draw from those crystalline eyes, I felt another round of tingles sweep up my back and along my skin.

"You're . . ." Blake murmured, breaking the short but heavy spell. "Together?"

I leaned my head on Austin's shoulder. "We are."

Blake looked at his fiancée. Her eyebrows drew together, and before he could stumble through the rest of the thought, she intervened.

"Oh." Francesca gently patted Blake's arm. She leaned in and her smile looked manufactured, like she was trying to find a way out of the conversation. "I think that's Misha. I wanted to talk to her."

With a polite goodbye, something stammered out of Blake's mouth, but he was pulled away before he had a chance to finish the thought.

"Someone get this woman an Oscar." Austin teased in my ear, ducking his head; mischief painted the steep cut of his jaw when he looked down at me.

I tried to get a handle on my speeding pulse and thoughts with a playful smack against his shoulder, taking a second to realize he still hadn't pulled his arm out from around me. "Told you. Quick study."

"I guess all you needed was the right inspiration." He cleared his throat and took a step back. "And that looked as close to skin melting as you can get. Feel better?"

Austin handed me a glass from a circulating waiter as we walked inside.

I did. For a second. The second Blake's face fell when he registered that I was just as moved-on as he was. I expected that high to last a little longer than it did, and now I just felt . . . empty and a little sick.

That feeling that sets in an hour after eating an entire bag of gummy bears. Nausea and regret. But as much as I interrogated my mind, I couldn't pin that regret on anything. Was it losing Blake? Was it not trying harder to keep him? Was it really just the letdown of petty revenge?

"Yeah." I let his hand fall back to his side. "That was exactly what I wanted."

Or at least, that's what I thought I wanted.

* * *

An hour or so after dinner, the guests floated through the garden and the ballroom.

Austin was pretty good company. And when we weren't attempting to fool anyone into believing we were dating, we got wrapped up in conversation about the research I did at the Lightning training facility. In fact, I hadn't realized that I was talking about it for almost an hour. But he kept asking follow-up questions, and what was I going to do? *Not* talk about pioneering minimally invasive robotic-assisted surgery?

I talked so much that I ran through my drink, and Austin went to get more, and I waited for him on the terrace that opened up to the gardens. The warm summer air competed with the cool air-conditioning as I stood between the two party spaces.

I glanced around the tall hedges. Just above them the city's lights glowed, but here inside the hedge perimeter was a lush garden that could have just as easily been in the middle of nowhere.

"Isa." His voice hit my ear like the melody of a song you'd memorized. The kind where you only need the first note to recognize and recite the whole thing.

My gaze moved to him. "Hey, Blake."

The dim light from the outdoor sconces cast shadows along

his cheekbones and down his hard-set jaw. His eyes met mine before they flickered all over, searching.

I hadn't seen him in over a year and this was the first time I let myself actually *look* at him. His hair had grown a little, slicked back neatly, but my memory showed it to me as I always remembered it. In my apartment, messy from a lazy day on the couch or a few hours in bed.

The tux fit a little more securely on top of a more toned physique.

"Can we talk?" He scanned the ballroom, and I did the same, catching a glimpse of Austin, who'd been roped into conversation with the mother-of-the-groom again. "Alone?"

"Sure." I sighed and followed him a few steps further out onto the terrace. It was a bit private here.

"What's up?" I asked. I hadn't actually planned how I was going to deal with him. I knew how I wanted him to react, but past that I hadn't figured out what I wanted, and that shadow had been following me around all night.

So, I let him take the lead and decided I'd figure it out at some point while he talked.

"All Francesca told me was that this was a family friend's wedding," he explained, running his hand through his hair with a huff. "I didn't know . . . I mean. If I *did* know you'd be here . . ."

I guess we were starting with why he was even here. It was something that had been bothering me, the blatant disregard for how I might feel. Or that he'd simply forgotten I existed.

An ache moved through me.

"I didn't know you'd be here. I didn't realize Selena was . . .

Selena," he went on. "By the time I did, we were already on our way."

My face scrunched. "You didn't bother to read the invitation until you were leaving for the wedding?"

That kicked a memory forward. The two of us getting ready—after a long morning in bed—for his business school graduation, and he hadn't even known where it was. He'd assumed I knew. I had, but that wasn't the point.

The irritation from that day set a match alight around my nerves.

"No," he scoffed, looking around aimlessly, frustrated. "Come on. You know how I feel about this stuff. I figured it was some society girl's wedding."

Society girl. The words rang in my ears. He could act like he was somehow above all of *this*, but he was *engaged* to a society girl.

Blake came from one of those long-standing American families that were nestled somewhere between DC and Boston. Not rich-rich like the Amaris, but well-to-do. They had legacies at certain schools. They weren't a part of the Manhattan high-society scene, but I'd met enough of his family in the past to know they wanted to be.

Was that why they were together? I hated myself for wondering.

"Maybe next time, read the invitation," I said, sharper than I intended, nearly flinching at my own reaction.

I was supposed to be acting unbothered.

"I wouldn't have come if—"

"Congratulations on the engagement, by the way." I pulled

my shoulders back, folded my hands in front of myself. "I hope you two are happy together."

I tried to make it sound genuine even though I had to force it through my lips.

"I was going to tell you," he added in a mumble.

"It's not like I gave you a play-by-play about Austin," I excused.

I didn't want to react. I didn't want him to see it. I didn't want to feel it. I was sick of feeling it.

That awful blurriness that made me question if I kept choosing the wrong path. That maybe I should have considered residency in California and forgone the best program in the country.

I hated that he made me wonder. My ambition was so bright that it led me forward. I chose to follow it, and I was always so sure about that choice until now. I hated him for making me question it.

He paused. "Yeah, you and . . ."

"Austin," I repeated, hoping that a tiny burst of dopamine from seeing him struggle with this would make all of the anguish go away. I wanted to see him caught off guard like I was.

"You're seeing him?" He blinked and scrunched his face like I was speaking a different language. "Like, an actual relationship?"

"No, we just play a couple on TV," I drawled sarcastically, rolling my eyes. "Yes, we're in an actual relationship."

His eyebrows drew in. "You don't have time for those."

"I made time," I lied, diplomatic but sharp. It helped mask the deep pain that clogged the back of my throat. I never made

time because I couldn't. I was busy. My first few years of residency had been nonstop work. When that schedule loosened
and I could've visited him, I found research obligations. I
couldn't make time for us, but neither could he.

"You made time?" His jaw was set on edge. Maybe I finally
hit a nerve. He mumbled something inaudible under his breath.

"Obviously." I motioned around, not sure what he was questioning, my dedication to the relationship or if it was a real one.
Either way, I was doubling down. "I brought him to Selena's
wedding. It's not some fling."

He let out a humorless laugh. "I didn't realize that making
time for a relationship was *possible* for you."

I swallowed hard to avoid that poisonous feeling distilled
down to a dull tremor in my muscles. Despite wanting to snap
at him, I took a deep breath. If I wanted to be the winner here,
I had to *seem* like I was perfectly fine, completely unaffected
no matter how twisted up I felt.

Before Blake could say anything, a pair of deep-blue eyes
caught mine.

"Isa." Austin walked through the open doorway, two drinks
in hand.

He set both on the balustrade a foot away, then took a few
steps to me. Austin didn't bother to acknowledge Blake as he
stepped between us and his palms spread over my waist at each
side. A warmth seeped into me. "Is everything alright?"

Gentle and strong, Austin's voice wrapped around me.

I nodded, trying to get my expression under control. Blake
was only a few steps away, but now that Austin stood between
us, his body would at least keep Blake from seeing it.

"Are you sure?"

I nodded again.

"Do you want him back?" Austin turned me around so he was facing the party; his gaze went from me to over his shoulder, then back to me.

Everything was foggy, but one thing was clear. That feeling from the lobby came back, cutting me so deep I could feel it in my bones. Seeing Blake and Francesca together was a different kind of pain than I was expecting.

It wasn't heartbreak—at least, not for him.

I just really thought Blake got it. That he saw what I was building toward, who I was becoming. I let myself believe he could wait. That we'd come back together when the timing was right, and everything I'd worked for would finally fit with love, too. That I could have both: the kind of career my mom sacrificed *and* the relationship I wanted, the kind I saw my best friend having, the kind that made me sure I couldn't settle for anything less.

Maybe I wanted to believe it so badly that I had ignored all the signs. Seeing Blake walk away was proof that the intrusive voice in my head—the one that always chirped up when I missed something important in sacrifice to my career—was right. It wasn't just losing him—it was the way it made me question everything. Was I pushing myself too hard? Was I choosing something that would leave me empty and alone?

Maybe I *was* angry at Blake for not being strong enough to wait. But mostly I was angry at myself—for letting someone else's timeline make me question my own. For thinking, for even one second, that I should shrink my ambition to fit into someone else's comfort zone.

Blake had confirmed what I should have always known to be true. I couldn't have my career and everything else, too. I had to pick. And I did.

"I . . ." I stammered, choking back the emotions until they were deep enough that I could assure myself they weren't going to come back up. With my back turned to the party, and my reaction hidden, I could relax a bit. "Why does that matter?"

"It informs my next decision," he answered steadily, a hand on my waist holding me tight. The other stayed fanned over the column of my neck. "Do you want him back?"

Austin's reassuring grip felt like a lighthouse. The storm brewed, but I could make out a few things. His cut-glass profile in the moonlight. The heavy stillness of his palm against my back. A chance to at least placate my pride.

Instead of acknowledging the pain, I wanted something to mollify it. And maybe I wanted to make Blake feel it for a while.

"What do you want, Isa?" Austin took a step closer. His thumb firmly swiped back and forth along my cheek.

His eyes flicked to look inside, then right back to me.

"I just want . . ." I took another deep breath, trying and failing to keep the emotion out of my voice. "I want him to *know* I don't want him back. And I want it to hurt."

His eyes immediately softened at the corners, and he drew closer.

His fingers laced up the back of my neck and through my hair. His thumb ran along my jaw, tilting my chin up.

"That's what you want?" His breath sent goose bumps along my skin. My heart raced for a new reason.

"Yes," I murmured. A spark popped between us.

Without another word, his fingers pressed firmly against me, and before I knew it, his lips were on mine. At first hard, a little menacing, but a second later, softer.

A tiny moan fell out of my lips. Responding, he pulled my body flush against his. I opened my mouth, and he deepened the kiss in an instant.

Like throwing gasoline on an open flame, my body ignited in an uncontrollable flash. He felt good—tasted even better. Every nerve lit up, a mind-altering high pulsing through me. Electricity roared in my ears, broken only by the low, ragged groan that rumbled from his throat.

An ache blossomed between my legs, and my knees began to give way. Not that it mattered; by that point he held me so tightly, he was holding me up.

It was all-consuming—deep, relentless, and passionate. He gave me no chance to breathe, no moment to pull away.

His fingers burned into my skin. His hand along my jaw kept me close as he controlled the pace and intensity. Seconds later, his other hand fanned along my cheek.

Every chance I got to take a breath was coupled with an uncontrollable whimper for more. The pent-up anger, angst, and heat that I had felt all night combusted into that kiss.

My shallow breaths were making me lightheaded. Finally, I pulled away—slowly, keeping my hand splayed across his muscular chest. His body rose and fell beneath my palm with deep, tortured gulps of air.

Alarms blared in my head for a whole new reason. Just moments ago, I was seething with anger at Blake, yet now my body had softened into Austin's with an ease I didn't recognize. For a brief second, I'd let myself get lost in that kiss. I'd felt calm. Safe.

But reality knocked me back into the present. Like a good fake boyfriend, Austin had played his part. Blake was watching.

"Did he see it?" I said between heavy breaths.

"Hmm?" His eyes, like spilled blue ink, struggled to focus as he blinked a few times.

"Did he see it?" I repeated, more firmly this time.

He flicked his eyes over my shoulder, then back to me.

"Yeah. He did," he answered gruffly, his hand loosening its grip on my waist, but he didn't let go. "Come on. We're going to leave, and he's going to go a little crazy wondering where we snuck off to."

Chapter 17
AUSTIN

My grip along Isa's waist loosened and my palm slid to the small of her back when we made a turn and were out of sight from the terrace. The music from inside was a whisper muffled by the summer breeze and my blood rushing through my ears.

Isa might not have seen Blake's reaction, but I had. Mostly, he looked surprised to see Isa and me together. But beneath that, he looked like he'd just spotted something he'd lost only to realize someone else had found it, too.

Isa may have been too blinded by her own pride or her petty vendetta to see it, but I wasn't. Even if it was fleeting, Blake was jealous, or at the very least bothered. She'd gotten what she wanted. And it made my stomach turn, wondering why she wanted it so badly.

My hand pressed against the small of her back. Walking on the two-by-two square stone grid path that led like a maze between the tall green hedges, she was silent.

Passing a few more feet until we hit a dead end with a gray stone bench sitting at it, I stopped.

"Sit," I told her gently. We could hide out for a little while in this secluded corner of the garden.

"Thanks for that, I guess." Isa ran a finger along her lower lip, wiping her ruined lipstick.

I watched her movement in what felt like slow motion. I replayed that kiss in my head as I watched her touch the aftermath smeared across her lips. A lightning bolt hurtled down my spine.

I cleared my throat. I needed to snap out of whatever it was I'd felt in that moment. I was just here to help the foundation. In return, Isa needed one thing: for me to play along. I'd taken things too far back there, I knew that.

But kissing her felt like amnesia.

"It worked," I reported awkwardly.

"Good." Her lips curved up one side of her face as she looked forward. Then some silent realization swept over her, the smile falling slowly with her shoulders.

We sat there like that for a few minutes, occasionally hearing a stray conversation here or there from party guests who wandered in and out of the garden.

The silence became its own noise, getting louder and more noticeable with each second.

"How was the meeting with that football club?" she ventured.

Meeting with FC Remy at the Stade went better than I'd expected. I would still be starting from the bottom, working with the B teams; but it was a newly promoted team with a lot of potential. I should have been thrilled, and the practically exuberant call from Jesse right after confirmed that. But in truth, the excitement never hit. I'd spent the entire time with the team thinking about getting back to Isa.

"Good, I think," I said with less enthusiasm than I meant.

I needed to accept that this was the logical next step. I had a meeting with my old team tomorrow afternoon. I planned to grab a high-speed train to London in two days.

"You don't sound too enthusiastic." Isa turned her gaze to me, confusion digging a frown between her eyebrows. "Isn't coaching what you want?"

Despite the ocean of differences between us, she managed to fish out a similarity. She envisioned her path into the future like rungs on a ladder. I used to do that, too.

I'd started as a rookie in the Champions League, helping lead the team to promotion. Then a starting position on the Premier League team at FC Farnham. A championship with them followed by getting closer than any other American soccer team to a World Cup final. And now coaching the next generation.

But instead of running toward a second act, all of it was starting to feel like I was running away.

This was supposed to be fulfilling, but all I felt was hollow. Like a rotted-out tree trunk that toppled over, one step on it and you'd fall right through—confirmation that nothing lasted forever.

"It is," I admitted. Coaching was the logical next move, and soon enough my heart would catch up with my brain. "I get to be around the game and have a legacy."

"Cheers to that." She stared straight ahead and tipped an imaginary glass in the air in the direction of the city just beyond the towering, finely trimmed hedges.

"So . . ." I began. "Blake?"

She let out a long sigh. "What about him?"

What happened between them? Why was she so surprised that he was engaged? Despite what she said, it felt like she was still holding on to something. And it was hard to deny that if there was someone who fit perfectly with Isa, it would be someone like Blake.

I'd spent enough time around high-profile people to know the type. One I never felt all that comfortable around. Ivy League educated. Successful. Someone who'd be invited to this type of party. He could probably hold his own in an intellectual debate with Isa and come out unscathed.

"What happened between you guys?" I asked.

Isa was too smart to let jealousy derail her like this. And he was engaged now, so they weren't getting back together. *Right?*

She couldn't possibly still want him back.

Maybe knowing would help me draw a more permanent line in my head and not let my imagination cross it.

"I told you, it's not an interesting story," she stated simply, staring at the ground. "We broke up. He moved on first."

"You asked me to come to Paris, put on this performance, all to save your pride?" I asked disbelievingly, a little frustrated. This was a lot more than that. She wanted to wound him. And if that was the case, then he must have done something to hurt her so deeply that she felt the need to return the feeling. "It was more than that."

After a few silent beats, she finally said, "We were together in college and long-distance in grad school. After that, we knew our careers had to take precedent, so we sort of came and went in each other's lives. I don't know, I always assumed we'd figure things out. We always stayed present for the big things; I assumed my finishing residency would be one of them. In the meantime, he had the whole whirlwind romance and didn't bother to let me know."

"Why'd you let him go if . . ." The question petered off because I wasn't sure how to ask it.

Isa didn't seem like the person that things simply *happened* to. If something was going on, *she* set it in motion.

"I didn't have time to nurture a long-distance relationship; neither did he," she defended pensively. "But I also didn't want to be one of those couples who were together since college and never matured on our own."

"Maybe that's what happened. You grew apart?"

She was twenty-nine, so she was past that part of life where every one of your friends stays close. It was a time in my own life when I saw that reality play out. Friends fell away because it was the nature of things. No matter how busy or carefree life was, weathering decades was a contact sport and not everyone made it.

Isa nodded. "I guess so."

It was the first time there was any inkling of vulnerability that she shared willingly. In the lobby the other night, she had faltered but recovered quickly, like she was trying to convince both of us she hadn't stumbled in the first place.

Tonight, it was different. Maybe she was tired of holding up

the mask: an uninterrupted stream of confidence and infal-
libility.

I paused for a beat, wondering if I should ask. Finally the
urge to know pushed it out. "Do you still love him?"

It felt a little beneath her, Isa waiting on some guy.

Her eyes flickered around the gravel path. Another long
pause.

"I know what I'm worth," she said, not answering the original
question. She took a deep breath and blinked away the emotion
from her eyes. "And it's a lot more than wanting some guy who's
engaged. I just . . . I thought I knew how my life was going to
go, and I'd pinned all of my—" She stopped abruptly, blinking
a few times. "I still have a bruised ego. And now, bruised lips."

I heaved a laugh, mostly from relief. Seeing the brunt her
lips took from that kiss gave me a similar high to the one after
a win on the field.

"You didn't call offsides, so I kept going," I confessed, leaning in.

When she'd kissed me back, I was sure it was more than
just trying to put on an act. It was a spark; she could feel it as
much as I could.

"Thank you . . ." She rocked to the side, gently nudging my
shoulder. "For making all of that a little less humiliating."

"Don't worry about it. I love meeting a fan."

She grinned. "See? If only you could be that nice on camera."

"You think I should try making out with the reporters?"

Her shoulders rose as a laugh bubbled out of her. "Well, we
do need to distract Malcolm."

"Come on." I stood. It had been a while. Whatever we were

pretending to do out here was probably done by now. I looked down at Isa. "You know what you do when you fall down during a match?"

She glanced up.

"Roll around and scream like you've just been shot?" She delivered it so matter-of-factly that you wouldn't have known she'd just had a few vulnerable moments.

The laugh that barreled out of me shook my entire chest.

Isa was like scoring directly from corner kick. So rare that—if you didn't see it with your own eyes—you'd question if it was even possible. And here she was, right in front of me.

Beautiful, smart, independent, funny, and compassionate, while sort of mean at the same time.

"And when you're done doing that," I answered, "you get back up and keep playing."

She'd eventually find some ambitious, well-read, scholarly, take-over-the-world type. Someone in her league who could keep up. Her bruised ego would heal. And in the meantime, if she wanted to see Blake squirm, I'd make sure he did.

Isa took my hand and stood.

"It's only been thirty minutes." Isa took my wrist and turned it to check the time on my watch. "I would have thought a pro athlete had more stamina."

Chapter 18
ISABELLE

The skin *definitely* melted off his face," Selena whispered to me the next morning over the sound of stand mixers spinning in unison. She threw a look over my shoulder, then back to me. "Not that it's a contest, but you win the breakup."

With two days between the welcome party and the first ceremonial event—the Mehndi—Selena and Henry's wedding planning team had arranged for guests to have any number of experiences during the downtime.

Today, any of the two hundred guests in attendance could take a macaron-making class with chef Gaston Phillip—the celebrity chef and owner of the three-Michelin-starred restaurant Sucre.

About fifty people filed into the giant, professional-grade demonstration kitchen for the activity. Blake and Francesca sat in the back.

Selena took a giant, crunchy bite out of a baguette she had taken from the enormous breadbasket that greeted us when we entered the kitchen. On the other side of her, at her workstation, Henry carefully read through the instructions.

Austin stood next to me, his brow lifted for a second before he looked back down at the bowl, stirring the batter while Selena discussed the events of the night before. We were busy gossiping while the men did the heavy lifting of actually baking the macarons.

"It *did* work," I noted.

After the kiss, everything sort of settled down for the night. Austin and I fell back into our usual banter like it had never happened and spent the rest of the night having a pretty decent time. Being around him was nice; there was no pressure. In a life that was filled with expectations, Austin was a person who wasn't expecting anything from me except to help with making connections for the foundation.

It was easy to fall into a rhythm with him.

"How was the kiss?" Selena whispered, even quieter this time since Austin was literally two feet away. "I bet it was good. Professional athlete of his age . . . probably a lot of experience under his belt. I know that sounds sort of red-flaggy but . . ." she yammered in a stream of consciousness. "Reformed playboy is . . ." Her expression glazed over a bit. One side of her mouth pulled up. "Well, being the recipient of all that experience . . . trust me, it's *not* a bad thing."

I cleared my throat, and my eyes went wide in warning. I tried to sort through what exactly I felt after that kiss. It gave me a high that, at first, I thought was knowing I got under Blake's skin. But, when I thought about it, it was something else.

"It was fine," I lied, mostly to get Selena to snap out of whatever daze she'd fallen into. But I could admit, to myself, that something about that kiss made my brain short-circuit, because I didn't want it to end.

I glanced around the test kitchen; nobody had heard her in that massive space. It took up the entire second floor of the Haussmann-style building. With five long countertops that spanned the room—each with four sets of burners and ovens—the fifty guests interested in coming along fit comfortably inside. Austin and I paired up with Malcolm to keep his attention, and any intrusive questions he may have had, away from Selena.

"Yeah . . . well." Selena blinked rapidly a few times. "Blake keeps looking over here like he's confused as to what's happening." Selena crossed a leg over the other while she sat on her stool, swiveling it in either direction. Her eyes went over my shoulder to the back corner where Francesca and Blake were with a few other guests. "He never was the brightest crayon in the box . . ."

I snorted a laugh. Blake was smart, graduated cum laude, but he had a tiny inferiority complex in his family since his brothers were higher achievers than him. It was a jab Selena knew she could make but usually was too classy to. "Selena, you don't have to be mean on my account."

"Either way, whatever that look is, you *definitely* got under his skin."

She took another bite from the baguette.

"Yeah?"

I should have been happy with doing what I came here to do—maintain some semblance of pride and make Blake feel a little small. I'd won.

But now that I'd done that, it felt hollow.

I felt a little hollow.

I reflexively checked my phone, hoping an invitation to interview for the Winthrop fellowship would give me the dopamine hit I was missing from seeing Blake get jealous.

No luck.

"How are you doing?" I asked, hoping to push past that empty feeling.

"Perfect," Selena admitted with a deep, shaky breath. At any given moment, it was like she was bursting with joy and wanted everyone around her to feel it. Her eyes became a little glassy. "It keeps being . . ."

"Selena . . ." I leaned in. Selena was *sentimental* but not usually teary when she was happy.

"I'm a little emotionally overwhelmed in a good way." She took another deep breath and blinked away the tears quickly. She turned her attention back to me. "I didn't think I could be this happy."

I heaved a relieved sigh. I didn't expect Selena to have second thoughts, but you never know. "You're sure that you're okay?"

Selena tended to stay pretty grounded when it came to keeping her feelings well contained. Lately, she was bursting with them.

She chewed her lower lip and grinned nervously.

"I'm pregnant," she whispered.

"What?" My voice bounced around the demonstration kitchen. Probably the wrong spot to be told a secret.

Henry's attention snapped back to Selena so fast it looked like reflex. All she had to do was give him a reassuring smile and his shoulders eased back down, the sharp lines that concern drew at the corners of his eyes softened.

"Sorry," I whispered, giving what was probably a ridiculous smile to everyone who had turned to look at us.

For some reason the rule that we always repeated back to each other in college played in my head.

Have fun. Be safe. Don't get pregnant.

In that order. Every time either of us had left the apartment we shared off campus. All of it crashed over me; how different everything was. How distant the tide pushed us away from each other. How I was slowly fading into the background. It was a good thing, a growing pain, but still pain.

She was getting married, starting a family, and I was on a completely different track. The inevitable conclusion was that those tracks wouldn't run parallel for much longer.

Right?

"We haven't told anyone and it's very early," Selena explained in a hushed tone, watching my face for a reaction.

"And you have a reporter lurking around," I added lightly, trying to shake off whatever I was feeling.

I glanced over my shoulder to see Malcolm and Austin entrenched in conversation—at least that was one thing I could still do for my best friend. Or, in this case, Austin could do.

"Yeah." She grinned nervously. "Thank you for keeping him busy. *Voulez* does seem to be holding off the paparazzi and it has been a huge relief to have peace. Especially now that I'm exhausted all the time."

My heart kicked at how adorably serious Austin took his charge to distract the reporter. Austin was even taking Malcolm along to London with him to meet with his old football club. Austin said it was his manager's idea, but still, it was important to Selena, so it was important to me. And he was helping.

"And you're feeling alright?" I asked, my mind switching into what felt like autopilot. The thing I was self-aware enough to know I did, happened. When faced with emotions I couldn't or wouldn't understand, Dr. Isa took the wheel. "You're resting? You need to drink at least two liters of water a day. Pregnant women are at higher risk for kidney stones. You need to eat folate-rich—"

"I'm fine. You're starting to sound like Henry," she interrupted. "Mostly, I'm just tired. I've been asleep for most of the time we've been in Paris. I'm sorry we haven't had a chance to gallivant the way we always planned to when we talked about coming here in college."

"It's okay," I blurted out in a whisper. We'd always talked about coming here and spending our days drinking wine along the Seine and our nights partying. But we were older, and things were different . . . she had a whole family now, a full life. "I'm happy for you."

She was my best friend. My sister. I was happy for her. How had I not said that yet?

"I know." She cocked her head; her brow scrunched, then released slowly. Her smile drew soft curves into her cheeks. "I think Henry needs my help with the macarons."

Selena hopped off her stool and walked over to Henry, who'd been doing the lion's share of the work. She gave me a look to do the same with Austin, all playing into the act. So I took a few steps back to my workstation and moved some pots and pans around to make it look like I was helping.

"You're suspiciously helpful when most of the work is done," Austin pointed out.

"Perfect timing." I swiped a finger along the bowl with one of the two fillings that we were making—well, Austin was making. "Besides, I prefer cooking to baking."

I licked the strawberry filling off my finger. Awareness prickled along my skin when I noticed Austin's attention fixed on me.

His throat shifted; he looked at the floor, then back at me.

"You mean the paella you never made?" Austin teased, casually.

"I'll get to it eventually." A buzz ran along my nerves at his smile. "So, how can I help?"

"Well . . ." He took an empty bowl and placed it in front of me, then moved around me, an arm bracketing either side of my body.

His breath skated down the nape of my neck. "You can help with the last filling."

With a hitched inhale, I tensed. "What are you—"

"Blake's looking," Austin noted offhandedly, his eyes still fixed on the instructions.

"Oh." I swallowed against a dry throat. I did a quick scan around the room like I was looking for Selena. "Good eye."

Austin didn't move, still unreasonably close, his warm body looming behind me as he continued to read the recipe.

"Part of the job," he answered flatly, putting the recipe card back on the counter. "Slowly add the confectioners' sugar into the mixer." His hand pressed against the small of my back, like it was nudging me to try. My breath caught. "Slowly."

Gliding gradually, his hand moved along my back until his fingers gently tapped around my waist. With the other hand, he took the bowl of confectioners' sugar and put a small measuring cup in it.

"I . . ." I stammered. I tried to focus, but his palm sent a slow ember moving up my spine, only intensified by the fact that his body still loomed around mine. "I . . . cut people open for a living. I can handle a pastry."

He took a step back. Trying to regain control after *that*, I dumped a cup of confectioners' sugar into the mixer.

"Slowly," he repeated, his voice rising slightly.

But it was too late—with a quick flip of a switch, the mixer went on at full speed and the confectioners' sugar became airborne.

I closed my eyes for a second when all the sugar slapped against us in a cloud of white. He pressed forward as he reached over me to turn off the mixer, his body crowding mine in the most unexpectedly delightful way.

I opened my eyes and glanced up at him from over my shoulder.

"Doesn't take instruction well," Austin noted calmly, his face covered in sugar. It sat along his eyebrows and lashes like freshly fallen snow. "Interesting."

"I'm sorry," I sputtered, then pressed my lips together as I tried not to laugh. Without thinking, I ran a finger along his cheek. I licked the pad of it. The powdery sugar dissolved on my tongue.

His jaw flexed, and then he took a quick step to the side and grabbed a couple towels off the handle on the oven.

"You know," he whispered next to me, wiping his face with the towel and attempting to tidy up our workspace. "You're going to need to decide what you want from him."

"What do mean?"

"Making him jealous is one thing, but if you want him back—"

"I *don't*." I stood up straighter, a little indignant that he kept doubting my intentions.

Maybe I still wanted some sort of an apology or admission of guilt or *something*, so I didn't feel so dumb. Because my head got tossed and turned for the last few weeks like a seashell tumbling in a wave toward the shore. And he just got to be *happy*? Making him miserable didn't have the same high I'd thought it would, but that didn't mean he *didn't* deserve it a little. "Honestly, I think his reaction during the party was enough. I don't want anything more from him now."

Austin's cheek twitched. "Understood."

"But we're not coming clean," I added quickly. Being an adult and realizing that vengeance was hollow was one thing. Telling Blake I'd made a deal with Austin to come here and piss him off, that was *never* going to happen. "We're in too deep."

Austin chuckled; his voice lowered. "I'll take the truth of this fake relationship to my grave."

"Good." My shoulders relaxed, and I did what I always did when things started going in the direction I needed them to. I went through my mental checklist of what to do next. And thanking Austin for being an effective distraction for Malcolm was one of them since that was never really part of the deal.

"So, all that's left now is to make some money for the foundation and continue to be a shiny object to distract Malcolm," I whispered. "Thanks for wrangling him, by the way."

"It's not so bad." Austin looked over to Malcolm, who was fidgeting with an empty mixer a few feet from us. Austin shrugged with a half smile. "He's actually a fan."

My ego was basically in pieces, and he was spending this week just short of signing autographs. I tried to think of something bantery to quip back, when I stopped and realized he'd completed the entire recipe. Start to finish. And was preparing to put it all together. All I'd managed to do so far was eat an entire demi baguette and half of a round of creamy Camembert. "Are you *good* at this?"

"Try to sound less surprised." He spun the pastry bag until it sat taut. "Zoya, my goddaughter's mom, is a chef. She has a demonstration kitchen and sort of forces it on everyone."

He put the bag on the counter and maneuvered around me, laying a gentle hand along the small of my back again. Austin grabbed an offset spatula from the other side and now I was fully sandwiched between his arms as he worked.

"Lucky . . ." I tried to think of something other than how distracting it was to be surrounded by him. His chest brushed against my back as he spun another pastry bag closed. The piney, musky scent from his cologne cut through the sugary smell in the room. My stomach dipped. "I have takeout most nights. I order from this Thai place Selena loves." Heat flooded my face despite my brain reminding me that he was simply putting on a good show, and my idiot body was falling for it. "It's . . . it's ummm . . ." I stammered, trying to think of anything other than how delightful his body felt pressed against me when he was wholly interested in the task at hand. "It's probably some of the best food I've had in the city. But still, a best friend chef is unbelievably lucky."

Four years of medical school, several more years of post-graduate training, and yet I sounded like an imbecile who just announced a stream of unintelligible consciousness.

Austin either didn't notice or pretended not to. "Except when she suggests I auction myself off."

I looked around and blew out a sigh. We were both getting what we needed. "I'd say it worked out."

"*And*, as it turns out, Malcolm is pretty interested in the foundation, too."

"Yeah?" I smiled, feeling lighter. "Look at you," I teased, and smacked his shoulder with the back of my hand playfully. "Marketing yourself."

"It's for the children," he answered dryly through a wide smile that played tug-of-war along his cheeks. He took a step back and pointed to a baked macaron half, silently instructing me to help by removing them from the sheet so he could assemble.

"That's really great," I thought out loud. I started picking up macaron halves. I wasn't as easily swooned at the mention of children as other people, but from Austin . . .

Maybe it was sort of cute.

"Right now, it's just a place where kids can go to keep them out of trouble and play a sport. But it's more than I had growing up."

"What do you mean?" I asked.

"I was a foster kid and sort of got lost in the system. Till I met Theo and the Mistrys sort of took me in as their own." The cords along his throat shifted. "Not everyone gets so lucky."

I nodded, not sure what to say but sort of hoping he'd keep going. He was brighter when he talked about the foundation.

"When we started it, that was the original purpose," he continued, gathering a few pastry bags. "To give kids a place to go and maybe find something they love. But we wanted to do more, outside of the charitable arm. Eventually we wanted to find talent and help place them in teams."

"Like scouts?"

"Sort of—more of a training camp like they have all over the world for kids that show some promise in soccer. It would be nice if every talented player didn't have to go abroad for a career. If there was a way to get talent to the American league easily, it might . . ."

He paused.

"Might . . ." I coaxed.

"Well, the dream is a long way off, but it would be nice to not go across the world to chase a dream."

Best friends were the family you got to choose. I imagined it had to have been lonely to have an entire career an ocean away from his version of that.

"That must've been hard."

"Yeah . . ." His voice lowered.

He swirled another macaron bottom with filling—and I watched.

"How far off is that version of the future?"

"A long way since up until a few weeks ago, we could barely

afford to keep the lights on in the center." He handed me a completed macaron. I assumed it was to eat, so I took a bite. The sweet strawberry filled my senses. "The auction helped. Good thing you've got that little crush on me."

My ego wanted to correct him, but the flutter between my ribs was distracting.

"I think you mean, good thing Selena has a limitless Black Card," I corrected.

For a moment, I remembered when Selena's way of talking about Henry had shifted to something that was laced with giddiness. It was after some story about walking in the rain together. She'd forgotten an umbrella, and he always carried one for her. The simple act of knowing that she might need it and coming prepared had practically wooed Selena off her feet.

I sat there, eating a delicious macaron I didn't help make—in fact I probably hindered the process. The strawberry filling was sweet, made sweeter because I could simply sit and be. I always wanted to make that paella, never had time, so it never happened. Here, I wanted to make macarons, got caught up with Selena, but they were made just the same.

The giddiness I could hear in Selena's voice that day was the same one I could feel moving through every muscle fiber in my body.

I think my version of walking in the rain was a man who could bake.

I picked up another macaron, readying myself for the rest of this week. This time, instead of feeling alone, I was sort of excited.

Chapter 19
AUSTIN

I was supposed to be thankful that I had any interest in my career from someone in the press. I kept telling myself that as Malcolm followed me like a shadow.

But I was helping Isa by keeping him occupied and that did make this whole thing a little easier. I liked being able to pull some of the weight from her shoulders.

The cloudy London sky hung over the redbrick facades and weathered stone buildings along the store-lined street in the West End as we left the Farnham FC training facility. All of it looked the same as I'd left it a few years ago.

The iron railing along the steps to some of the shops just down the road stood proud but some small imperfections in the ironwork showed their wear from the last few years. The concrete sidewalk on either side of the cobblestone streets had some new, noticeable cracks.

"Have you been back to London since leaving Farnham FC?" Malcolm chattered on from a couple steps behind me, walking and jotting things down.

We had gotten to the Farnham FC training facility early that morning and he'd been practically glued to my side since. He asked questions ranging from where I grew up to my early career, and even made a couple attempts at questions about my personal life, all of which I steered like I was supposed to.

The only time he left was when I talked to the manager and current coaching staff privately. Since it was early July, preseason training was underway, so a lot of the staff was busy preparing for the Premier League matches to start in five weeks.

"Nope," I answered as I turned down the same street I used to walk down every day.

The one where Jo learned how to walk, unsteady but brave along the cobblestone. It had been the first time they'd all traveled abroad as a family—three of them. Theo was doing great then. We'd all assumed he'd recover.

I glanced down at the messages that came in on my phone.

> JESSE: Great idea taking Malcolm with you to Farnham

> JESSE: Steer the conversation to coaching

I sighed. Jesse, while his heart was in the right place, had a one-track mind. I told Isa it was Jesse's idea to bring Malcolm because, honestly, it sounded like something Jesse would do. But I figured bringing him along would help her out and I sort of liked doing that.

ME: I was going to talk about the foundation

JESSE: Do both

Meeting with my old team had gone better than expected, not that I was expecting it to go poorly, but I wasn't sure how they'd receive me since I didn't provide much explanation, outside of wanting to go home, for why I didn't extend my contract.

"But, if I coach here, then I'll be back," I answered as Malcolm and I walked down the street.

After the meetings, I had kicked the ball around with a few of the newer players, and if I hadn't been sure my knee wasn't the same before, I was now. Playing against Premier League talent, even a few friendly drills, was as clear a sign as any that it would be years of nonstop training to maybe get back in the condition I had been in when I played here.

Despite sounding negative, it was actually a warming realization. I didn't want to play until I *couldn't*; I wanted to play until I was ready to stop. And knowing I couldn't play at the level I used to—it was starting to feel like it *was* the right time to stop.

Malcolm nodded, scribbled a few more things in his thin notepad, and clicked his pen. He caught up the couple steps he was behind. "How about a café?"

"I need to get something first," I answered, walking toward the same bookstore I used to go to before I'd leave for my visits to New York.

I needed a couple books for Jo, a tradition since the day

she was born. I bought her books because I knew there wasn't much I'd be qualified to teach that kid, but reading was one thing I knew I could.

"Lead the way," he said cheerily.

The gloomy, Victorian-style bay window displayed stacks of new books. I walked past to the colorful section in the corner with children's books.

This trip had actually been a decent distraction, but an entire morning at my old club and a reporter asking a thousand questions a minute was wearing on me.

"You think you'll enjoy coaching?" Malcolm ventured, the bell on the shop door ringing as we walked in. "B team, I mean."

Malcolm stated it like it was a well-known fact that I'd never get anything more than that. I knew.

"Gotta start somewhere." I flipped through a couple books absentmindedly.

If ever I had trouble remaining humble, I had all of sports media to correct that. The American Footballer had lost a lot of his sheen over the last few years.

"Why the abrupt move two years ago?"

"It wasn't abrupt," I defended, even though it was. My contract was up but nobody predicted I'd ever leave it, especially not for the American league.

Malcolm scribbled more down. "The American that joined the relegated Champions League team, instrumental in getting them back to the Premier League. Then becoming the champions of the Premier League a few years after that. Then, suddenly, you fell off the map."

It was the same question everyone asked. I just didn't want

to answer and, even now, it felt like a part of my life when I was going through the motions.

"Yeah . . ." I trailed off, looking through another table of age-appropriate books for Jo when something next to the cashier counter caught my eye. I put the three books I had so far under my arm and walked to the cobalt-blue book.

"It didn't make any sense," Malcolm nudged, trying to get me to explain something I didn't feel like getting into. "Especially not when you shocked everyone by staying in the States."

American soccer was still relatively new and nobody's first choice, especially not a champion's. Any American with talent got scouted to play in other parts of the world. I was that kid, and my luck was meeting my best friend who stopped at nothing to make sure I got a shot at something bigger.

"Everyone seems to think I dug my career's grave that day. Why not let them?" I added.

After Theo got sick, for a couple years it had seemed like he was going to be fine. Then he'd gone from being perfectly normal to frail in a matter of months. It wasn't long after that that he was gone.

I had wanted to go home; I owed it to him to take care of what was left behind after all that he'd done for me. But walking away from everything—that excuse would only invite more questions, so I didn't give anyone an answer. I wasn't ready to, and frankly, it wasn't anyone's business.

"Was it for your girlfriend?" He kept his eyes down, only looking up occasionally when he wasn't scribbling something down. "Did she convince you to stay Stateside?"

"No, we hadn't met yet. And let's keep Isa out of this," I

added reflexively, not entirely sure what was going on between us. There was something there, at least for me. She didn't want Blake anymore, but I didn't really know what she wanted past that. Isa was hard to read, and I wasn't sure it was worth trying, since coaching would bring me back here. She had her entire future mapped out on the other side of the ocean and this act would end in a few days. I picked up the blue book with silver font. I smiled, thought of Isa, and added it to the stack. "She's a very private person."

All I knew for sure about Isa were two things: she made her plans carefully and I wasn't in them. She fabricated this charade out of what was probably a little bit of desperation and a lot of pride. The last thing she needed was to have herself wrapped up in my work after we'd dropped the act.

"And I wanted to go home. That's why I left." I answered his original question and walked to the register. I needed the same thing I had needed from the second I got here—attention on the foundation. Once that was all zipped up and ready to go, and I hadn't left Theo's legacy in shambles, I could move on. "It's that simple. And the Mistry Foundation needed overseeing."

"Started with your friend, right?"

"Yeah. It's a great opportunity for young kids who enjoy the sport," I explained. "If all of the great players go abroad, then how can we build America's football league?"

"There isn't exactly infrastructure in an American league to keep talent," Malcolm countered, stating the glaringly obvious.

"Not yet . . ." I said to myself, remembering my conversation with Wes.

Nothing was ever going to change unless someone changed

it. Theo was sure that, one day, the Austin Cades of the world wouldn't have to go overseas. Maybe because he missed his best friend when I left. But maybe because he had a solid vision.

"And that's probably why everyone thinks I ended my career by going back," I said louder to Malcolm, ending the explanation exactly where I started it.

For now, I just needed to keep Theo's legacy alive and maybe, if the foundation ever found another person to lead it like Theo could have, it would grow.

I glanced at the time and realized that we should probably head back to the train station.

Malcolm's brow furrowed and he scribbled more down. "How very honorable."

I glanced up at the clock, then back at my case logs.

I couldn't focus.

Austin had left early this morning; I hadn't even noticed since the pillow wall sort of insulated me from the noise. Selena had been tired and took the day to relax and nap before the first event tomorrow—the Mehndi.

So, I planned to log some cases, but as the afternoon sun streamed past the white curtains and along the pearly white tabletop where I was *trying* to log those cases into my spreadsheet, I was restless.

I stood. Maybe I needed a change of scenery. Picking up my laptop and my purse, I thought maybe I'd try the garden.

Just as I began to turn the knob to the hotel room, the door swung open. I took a startled breath and a couple steps back, and Austin stood in the doorway. The deep-yellow afternoon sunshine flooded out to the hallway from behind me.

Casual in a pair of dark-gray joggers and a white Henley

T-shirt that made ripples along his muscular chest and arms, he made my heart jump. "Oh. Hi."

"Hey." He brushed past me, but I caught the lines around his eyes, the heaviness beneath them. He was tired. "Did you get some work done?"

My feet felt the need to move, so I turned my toes against the floor. "Yeah, it was super productive."

I lied. I didn't know why, but I felt like I had to make sure he knew I was busy and not wondering if he was having a nice time in London. Or when he'd be back. Because I wasn't his actual girlfriend, and he said he'd be back before tomorrow's party and that's all I really *needed* to know.

He nodded, walking back out into the living area. He looked over my shoulder to the table I was just working at. "Well, I'll leave you to it. I was going to grab something to eat."

Something told me not to let him walk away, propelling me to stop him. "Wait."

The tiny—truthful—part of me that sort of missed him while he was gone. I felt like, after that cooking class, we'd have had fun together today exploring Paris. With Selena so exhausted between events, she'd been napping a lot, and I wanted to make sure she got her rest.

"What about that place you mentioned a few days ago?" I added after a drawn out pause.

"The brewery?"

"Yeah." A nervous shiver ran along my muscles. Maybe he wanted to be alone; he seemed a little glum. But not even the unfathomable chance that I'd hear a polite declination stopped me. "Want to go? I've worked enough for the day. Selena's wedding team is outrageously well-equipped to do their jobs."

And Austin was basically doing the only other job assigned to me—dealing with Malcolm.

The corners of his mouth screwed dimples into the sculpted slope of his jaw. His face brightened. "Yeah, sure."

"Great." I put my laptop down on the console table and spun around on my toes to walk back into the bedroom. "I'll get changed."

"You look great like that," he called into the room as I shut the door. "I mean . . ." His voice lowered from the other side of the door. "It's casual. You don't need to dress up."

"Two minutes," I answered from my side of the door.

* * *

At the northeast tip of the city, in the nineteenth arrondissement, at the head of the large public pool that felt like a lake, were myriad outdoor activities. Tourists and locals alike sunbathed along either side of the pool, ziplines crossed the span, and tons of activities bubbled with life along its banks—a beach in the middle of the city.

On the wooden patio that hung over the top of the grand swimming area at its entry point, our seats gave us a view of the entire sun-soaked summer evening.

Austin's chuckle pulled me from my thoughts as I watched—with trepidation—as a few people dove into the water.

Across the square wooden table, Austin took a sip of his beer. "Imagining the injury?"

"It's hard not to after a few rotations on trauma. It can make one a little risk averse." I'd seen enough injuries that involved the cervical spine to know I was never going to dive into water unless it was unreasonably deep. "But traumas are pretty rewarding when they go well, seeing how quickly you can take someone from the brink and bring them back to something pretty close to normal."

I glanced back at him, and my eyes got caught on his. The flecks of darker and lighter shades of blue shifting in the sun like a calm tide. They were alive in the evening light. There was a playfulness about him that made it hard to look away.

"Is that why you went into surgery?" he asked. The wind wisped through the locks of his deep brown hair that fell forward before he brushed them back.

I smiled. It was what I liked to call an application question.

My answer was usually some poetic version of the truth. Surgery was demanding, one of the most difficult things you could set your plans on.

"It's tough," I answered. "But when you're in it—when you're operating—you're solving a constantly changing puzzle. You have a map and a lifetime of knowledge ready to go for all the intricacies, but that first cut . . ." I glanced over to the water, then back at Austin. "It's like a shot of pure adrenaline followed by hours of a challenge."

A half smile made a valley along his jaw.

He probably knew that exact feeling, I imagined that's what it felt like to play a hard game. Win or lose, it was a challenge.

"Sounds like a good reason."

"Well . . . it's not the only reason." I teetered between giving him the application answer—which was true—and the whole truth. "I would have never found it if it weren't for my parents. They're both surgeons, too. Who knows what I would have chased if they weren't."

His eyebrows lifted and fell slowly. "Big shoes to fill?"

"I guess," I began. "I know I'm talented, but sometimes it feels like I'll always be in my dad's shadow. I'm always fighting against the assumption that I've gotten the opportunities I have just because of who my dad is. I want to make a legacy of my own one day, one nobody can argue with. And I also want male surgeons to get used to the idea of me, and women in surgery in general."

Women in surgery got a particularly insidious line of assumptions made about them. That eventually surgery would be too tough, and we'd bow out for something friendlier to having a family. The assumption that we wouldn't keep up at this grueling clip in residency pushed me to put myself on countless papers, get prestigious awards, and now I was at the precipice of the most difficult fellowship offered in my subspecialty.

"Beating the boys out of spite?" He put his glass down and leaned in, crossing his arms on the table, an intrigued spark lit in his eye.

"No," I insisted. But maybe I was, a little. The days I was too exhausted to study or review cases, I would remind myself of that annoying trope. The one that assumed a woman's career aspirations just evaporated after she fell in love and had a family. Like suddenly she'd be lobotomized and *want* to ride off into the sunset with some guy, leaving everything she'd built behind. That thought pissed me off enough to keep going. "I'm just not letting anyone stand in the way."

Austin nodded. "Your parents must be proud, following in their footsteps."

"My dad didn't seem to even register it. It was the expectation. But my mom . . ."

"She was upset?" he asked disbelievingly.

"No." I laughed humorlessly to myself. My voice dropped in hollow disappointment. "She looked so proud. Like she was getting another chance, vicariously through me."

Confusion lined his brow when my dejected tone didn't match the words.

"My dad is a world-renowned orthopedic surgeon," I explained. Sometimes, I felt like I had to achieve the career my mom didn't have because of me. Raising me meant her life was on hold all those years and it wasn't like you could just pick up opportunities after you declined them originally. The world didn't wait. "He operated on former President Alders after he had that fall. When someone says Dr. Mercado, it's him they picture."

It had been all over the news and my dad was in a few press conferences outside the hospital. I remembered watching as a little girl and thinking about how that would be me one day.

"And your mom?"

"Top of her class. She outshined my dad in every measure," I said, running my finger up my glass, drawing lines in the condensation. I felt like I needed to highlight my mom's achievements because they were there, but nobody saw them. "But she's just a general surgeon now."

"And that's a *bad* thing?" His voice went up an octave, perplexed.

"No, of course not," I conceded, taking a sip from my beer. "It's just different. But sometimes she looks at me and tells me I have so much potential, and I feel like . . ."

My mom never really verbalized any regret about not pursuing a fellowship because she had me. But I could hear it in the way she pushed me to this fellowship. Whether she consciously knew that she was doing it or not didn't matter. For as long as I could remember, I had always had this feeling that stopping short of the top was a trap I couldn't fall into. So, I didn't.

"You don't want to let her down?" Austin finished for me. "I know that feeling."

In that moment, another interesting similarity gleamed between us. Big dreams and a cheering section that maybe we felt like we owed something to.

"I know she wants me to be happy," I insisted. "But anything short of the best is . . . I dunno, I just don't want to feel like I wasted my potential."

Austin didn't say anything, rather he nodded in a quiet understanding.

After days of blurriness, focus finally came together in my mind.

I think that was why seeing Blake spun me out the way it did. He made me question my drive, if putting my career first was really the right move. The temporary heartache had cracked my resolve and made me wonder how I could have avoided it—what I could have changed to make a relationship with him work.

But, despite being painful, all the Blake stuff was ultimately just proof that we were never going to work—that no relationship could. I'd been right to put a relationship on the back burner because there was no alternative.

I *had* to be successful.

I couldn't let myself just be Dr. Felix Mercado's daughter forever. I had the talent to be even better, and I wanted to prove it.

I didn't want to dwell on this anymore, so I decided to move the topic of conversation along. "What about you? Who do you feel like you owe? Your agent?"

He chuckled. "No, but Jesse is known to use a good guilt trip strategically." He turned his glass for a second before going on. "Theo, my best friend. He was pretty much the person who made everything good that's happened in my life happen. When I was a kid, after a string of really shitty foster homes, I almost got moved pretty far from where I grew up in Queens, so Theo's family fostered me until I was eighteen. Theo practiced with me every day till I got scouted to play in London. I sort of owe him . . . *everything*."

"Wow." My mouth hung open a bit. I didn't know that about him and it made my heart ache. I was almost thirty and didn't really feel grown sometimes. I couldn't imagine being a kid without a stable home. Or eighteen, on my own and my best friend an ocean away. "Premier League superstar: Austin Cade. I'm sure he was proud."

"I guess." He chuckled offhandedly, almost self-deprecatingly, as if his notable career was something to scoff at. "Although, there were a lot of lucky breaks involved."

It irked me and I couldn't figure out why. At first, it sounded

like he was being humble, and now it felt like he was reminding himself.

"The professional athlete who's trying to build an entire
sports infrastructure where it doesn't exist," I stated almost
harshly. "That requires a lot more than *luck*. You'll figure that
part out, too," I went on, not waiting for a response. "If you
weren't going to, you would have given up," I explained. He was
here doing this favor—which was all sorts of unconventional—
for me in exchange for my help with the foundation. That was
determination. "Your heart's in it, so you'll do it."

His cheeks lifted, but not in a smile. It was like recognition
of something. A silent realization. Maybe my manner of tough
motivation worked.

"Are you . . ." The smile finally crested again into a wide
grin, a bright one that made my body warm. "Being nice?"

"No." I crossed my arms with an almost offended dip in my
brow. "I believe in you and I'm right about most things. So,
don't make me wrong, Cade."

He watched me for a few extended seconds, like he was
taking notes in his head or wordlessly trying to solve a puzzle.

"You make a lot of sense now," he admitted, looking com-
posed but sounding a little flustered.

I couldn't help but grin, my heart beating a little faster.
"What's that mean?"

He looked up at the city's skyline in front of the early sunset.
"I don't know, I was just curious how Isa became . . . Isa."

I swallowed against the butterfly-inducing reality that he
was *thinking* about me. And I sort of liked that.

"What do you mean?"

"Based on how you start, I always figured life either hardens you or softens you," he continued.

In a knee-jerk reaction to something that made me a little nervous—feelings I wasn't expecting—my lips sealed together with the joke I wanted to make. They tried their best not to open with a laugh, but the corners tipped up and gave me away.

He rolled his eyes. "Don't make a dirty joke."

Just like that, the conversation that was leaning toward intimate, swung all the way back to playful. I leaned forward and across the table to smack his shoulder with the back of my hand. "Come on. You set me up."

Despite the confidence I carried most of time, suddenly I felt a little nervous. I kept this part of myself guarded. I always told myself it was because I didn't need to bother opening up—that I didn't have time to make new relationships. But in truth, it just wasn't easy for me. It always felt like an editorial review, where all the messy, complicated parts of you were laid bare for scrutiny, and maybe you'd get feedback you didn't want, if not outright rejection.

"I can't believe they let you operate on people." He squeezed his eyes for a second.

"It could have been on you," I added. His eyebrows arched. "If I had asked to scrub in on the case."

He dropped his hand around his drink, taking a pause like he was deciding which direction this conversation might go. "Is that what you want?"

"To be your doctor?" I teased. "I feel like we've been through this."

"No." Despite my light banter, his tone stayed immovably serious. "The job. What Dr. Reinhold does."

"It's not . . ." I stammered, having been dragged away from playfulness again. I took a long sip of beer—it was a sour one from Alsace and I was finishing it faster than I had expected because he was pushing me to share things, and despite the knee-jerk reluctance, I sort of wanted to.

"The Winthrop fellowship was always the goal." I failed to answer his actual question.

Winthrop meant I'd spend a lot of time operating and a lot of time researching. I'd burn the candle at both ends, but I'd live a future where the work I did was used by orthopedic surgeons around the world. In comparison to that, completing a sports medicine fellowship and going on to simply *enjoying* operating felt like an insult to my potential.

"But Dr. Reinhold's work is fine, I guess. I could take it or leave it," I finally spat out.

Regret dug a hole in my lungs; a long sigh that I didn't mean to make slipped out. I wasn't sure who I was trying to convince.

"Okay." Austin's eyes ran along the horizon. A few seconds passed as he took a sip of his beer. "That little crush you have on me probably influenced your experience anyway."

A reflexive laugh popped out of my mouth.

"I liked being there because I liked the work. Did that ever occur to you?" I rolled my eyes. "You egomaniac."

"Yeah. It's *my* ego that's the problem," he said glibly, sitting forward. "And it *did* occur to me that you liked the work, judging by all those yellow highlighted cases. Those are sports injuries, right?" He leaned both arms on the table with a taunting

little flourish. He didn't wait for me to confirm that he was correct. The optional cases I requested to be in were largely sports
injuries, highlighted in yellow in that case log. "And since you
spent the little free time you have working on research for it.
So yeah, it did occur to me that you enjoyed the work. I happen
to be a part of that work, but that's neither here nor there."

My stomach flipped again. I *did* like the work.

The joy any regular person feels when they see someone
they helped, to some degree, do well was a universal feeling.

"Yeah," I reiterated with an unamused scowl that fought
a smile. "The *work* I've dedicated my life to is something I
enjoy."

"You're absolutely sure, nothing else had you so *engaged*?" He
leaned in and tucked a few stray strands behind my ear. "Because I thought you said sports medicine was just 'fine' and you
'could take it or leave it.' Which one is it, Doc?"

"I . . ." I was caught in a game. The more I told him, the less
I felt like I knew. "Just because I like something doesn't mean I
have to pursue it. I like blowing out birthday candles—doesn't
make me a firefighter."

He pulled away completely to lean back in his seat, leaving
behind a haze that took a few seconds to clear. One side of his
mouth climbed up his cheek. "Got it."

As much as I hated that he cornered me into the logical
conclusion that I was ignoring the fellowship I might actually
want, I couldn't help but smile back.

The clever bastard.

Chapter 21

ISABELLE

*T*he next day, I sat next to Selena on one of the many tufted, silk-upholstered, multicolored ottomans that had been arranged in a circle. I tried to ignore the unstoppable need to move.

Below the gilded ceilings and in romantic light from the torchères, Opéra Garnier's grand staircase was the setting for Henry and Selena's Mehndi. Decorated with calla lilies, jasmine, and marigolds, the space was steeped in the traditions of both Henry's and Selena's families. Garlands wrapped around the grand marble stairwell, where servers carried trays of what was probably Michelin-star-quality food.

Not that I'd know.

My stomach groaned, interrupting the whispered sound from the violins being played at the landing.

"Hungry?" Austin chuckled across from me, taking note of my attention on the circulating servers.

The spiced scent of masala and chili wafted past, and I sat perfectly still.

I was starving, and the mehndi had been on my hand for over an hour, with hours to go before it was dry.

I looked directly ahead. From my vantage point at the top of the long landing between the central staircase and where it bifurcated, I could see all the servers below at the main level, each carrying a tray of something tantalizingly delicious—caviar toast points, bite-size samosas, masala vada. My patience wore thin as I got dangerously close to hangry.

"Yes . . ." I said as I shifted on my seat.

The ottomans were set up in a small circle for the bridal party to relax and have their mehndi done. At the bottom of the central steps, anyone in attendance was welcome to have an artist complete theirs as well. Some guests had taken the opportunity.

"I can help with that." Austin shrugged. "But you're going to have to ask *nicely*."

A baiting playfulness glimmered in the flecks of blue and gray in his eyes, lit under the golden glow of the ornately painted domed ceilings. That flirtatiousness became more than the occasional occurrence while pretending. Now it was pushing the line we never really agreed *not* to cross.

"You have to *feed* her, dear." Beatrice Amari—the mother of the groom—gently tapped Austin's shoulder as she walked past. Her seat was actually next to mine, but she hadn't sat down yet, busy greeting guests. "It's how the men make themselves useful at this event."

I scrunched my nose, leaning forward an inch, propelled by an electric excitement that made me want to move. It had to have been because I was sitting so long. I was restless. "Make yourself useful, *dear*."

Restless or not, I was on pins waiting for his response, watching his eyes as closely as he watched mine.

He didn't say anything else. A grin played tug-of-war between his cheeks, but he got up and made his way down the steps, seemingly taking the hint. Moments later, he climbed back up the steps with a small plate in his hand, having followed orders.

But the mocking smile on his face made me sure his obedience ended there.

"Say please," he teased, sitting across from me. I pushed my lips together in a tight line. His grin grew wider. "Come on . . . ask for help."

"I don't like asking for help," I admitted curtly.

When you were a woman of color in surgery, you had to be twice as good to get half the recognition by patients or colleagues. I never gave anyone reason to pin my success on anything but my own skill. I also had the privilege of being Dr. Felix Mercado's daughter. Trying to grow out of that shadow meant never asking for help. Because he never did.

"Someone tell Malcolm we have breaking news," he drawled sarcastically. "Why not?"

I paused.

A truth pushed up the back of my throat, so I swallowed hard and shoved it back down. I didn't ask for help because then I'd be in a position to hear that call go unanswered. I simply didn't want to get used to having someone I could count on. I got used to the idea of Blake eventually being that person. That blew up in my face.

"I don't *need* help," I clarified.

Like I was trying to prove it, I used the tips of my fingers on each hand, the tiny bits of surface area that weren't painted, as chopsticks and carefully picked up a perfectly rounded pastry dipped in syrup.

"*Clearly.*" He watched, holding the plate steady beneath the path my fingers took, like he was expecting what happened next.

It dropped back down to his plate and, thanks to Austin, not my dress.

"It's not that hard," he goaded.

"Easy to say when you can use your hands."

"I meant asking for help." He leaned in, holding up a tiny rolled pastry. Finally, I gave up and opened my mouth and took a small bite. His eyes watched me with every ounce of attention he had. That moment was suspended, slow. I scraped a crumb that fell on my lower lip. The lines along his throat shifted. His voice lowered and became a little gravelly. "And I based an entire career off of not using my hands. I can do *a lot* without them."

That taunting smile paired with the intense focus from the stare—that didn't leave me once—fanned heat down my body.

All of it felt like foreplay.

A drop of the syrup pulled at the corner of my lip. I lifted my hand reflexively to wipe it but stopped when his fingers gripped my chin.

"No hands, Isa." His reminder was low in the inches between us. His thumb dragged slowly across the corner of my lip, picking up the syrup on its way.

A buzz filled my stomach, like I'd swallowed two handfuls of popping candy, and they were going off like fireworks in there. It moved through my nerves, making everything tingle.

He looked at his thumb for a moment like he was deciding. I opened my mouth, and the pad of his thumb pushed just past the entrance. I ran my tongue over it.

A growl was just barely audible under his flexed jaw.

My mind filled with how he tasted. How good it felt when his body was firmly pressed against me. When he kissed me like it was the last kiss I'd ever have; like he didn't want it to end.

The memory prickled my skin with goose bumps. A heat welled in my core.

My heart roared in my ears, but I realized it was all I could hear. The grand staircase, a place where conversation was meant to echo, quieted.

And it yanked me back to the present.

Feeling eyes on me, I swallowed hard against a dry throat and looked around to see that I was right. Everyone seated at the top of the landing and many of those mingling below had stopped and looked because we were doing such a good job at selling this that maybe we were attracting attention.

A little proud and a little mortified at how obvious the heat between us was, in a relatively public setting—a high-society event—I cleared my throat.

Next to me, Selena's wide eyes met mine, then darted right back down to the intricate design painted on her hands and arms.

"So, where's Henry's name? It should be here somewhere, right?" someone from the wedding party asked Selena. She looked down at Selena's mehndi and drew everyone's attention back to the bride.

"What an excellent question," Selena announced a second later, and everyone became unconvincingly interested in the design.

Austin's cheek twitched as he pulled away.

As if pressing play, the rest of the room went back to normal. I was thankful we didn't occupy too much more of the room's collective attention and it went back to where it belonged—the bride.

We were supposed to look like a couple, not put on a show. I tried to think of something else to talk about that wouldn't immediately route us back to flirting.

But that was basically nothing.

So, I asked the first thing that popped into my head.

"The Stade is where the World Cup was, right?" I looked down at my own mehndi, needing to fill the space with words to get my face to cool down from all the heat that flooded it. "The one before you came back to the States?"

I remembered it distinctly because Blake had been watching from my place, wearing a Cade jersey, of all things.

Something switched in his eyes. "You *have* been googling me."

"Relax. It was a quick search. I was curious why you came back to the States."

"I came back for a few reasons," he admitted, his eyes moving along the golden moldings.

"And those are . . ."

He took a long sigh and sat up a little straighter.

"I'm more of a plan follower, not maker. My best friend always had a plan, and I went along with it. When he died, I sort of dropped the ball, so to speak. I went back to the States to take care of everything that was left behind."

Three puzzle pieces set themselves up perfectly, but left just enough room between for me to speculate, telling me so much about what brought him to the same training facility I was doing research in without telling me much at all.

"Like the foundation?"

He nodded. "It's the least I can do. He was like a momager, best friend, and tutor all rolled into one."

"If I had functionality of my hands, I'd lift a glass to toast." I tipped my chin up. "To excessively involved best friends."

I could relate to that. So much so that I could feel the pull along my heart, knowing a familiar dynamic was changing for me, and it was scary. I glanced over to Selena, deeply immersed in her mehndi with her soon-to-be in-laws.

The melancholy must have been visible.

"Not much changes," Austin offered, drawing my attention back. "Don't worry. She's not leaving you behind."

"I know that."

"Well, if you didn't," he noted in a playfully taunting tone, like he knew better than to cross my pride.

"Okay . . . if I didn't?" I conceded. "For argument's sake . . . was it hard? Not being around when your best friend got married and moved to a different place in life than you?"

"No, not all. His wife, Zoya, was like a part of the duo we never knew we needed."

"Oh." My shoulders slumped.

He chuckled. "But when they told me they were pregnant, I was thrown. It didn't hit me till I visited during the offseason. Everything in their lives had changed and a part of me was a little annoyed. I was happy for them, of course. But I was a little resentful they didn't just stay frozen while I was gone. That they moved ahead and built a life I didn't feel like I had a place in."

A lump in the back of my throat made it hard for me to ask what I needed, but I managed to croak it out. "What did you do?"

"I became their kid's favorite person as revenge," he said quickly and flatly. A slow smile grew along his jaw seconds later.

I grinned. I couldn't help it.

"I didn't do anything," he answered more seriously. "Love isn't finite; it makes room. And you can't slow things down but eventually—in one way or another—you catch up to each other. One day you will have whatever your version of that looks like. Everything settles out."

I wondered what Austin's *version* of a family looked like. Probably a kid or two. He was patient and caring. It was probably the type of thing he'd eventually have.

Everything I'd probably never get to. I didn't want to think about that. I was finally having some fun. I didn't want to weigh it down with truths that didn't even matter since we weren't really a couple, he was moving somewhere here soon, and I had a legacy to get to.

I wanted to revel in the fun.

I smacked his shoulder with the back of my hand since it

didn't have any mehndi. "This is what they mean when they say listen to your elders."

He waited a beat, studying me for a drawn-out pause.

"Careful." His voice lifted, becoming lighter—like he was teasing. My shoulder relaxed. *This* I could handle. "I can still use *my* hands."

"Is that a threat?"

A curl fell forward into my face and he brushed it back, his fingers leaving goose bumps in their wake.

He was pulling me back into the haze. This time I let him.

"No." His fingers pulled my face toward him, sliding past my cheek to curl gently around the base of my head. I leaned in. Under the sparkling lights, the blue in his irises was riddled with little facets of gray.

His lips brushed against mine.

It was hardly a kiss. It was warm and intimate.

It gently pressed and passed along my lips, drawing me in slowly.

"Offsides?" he mumbled.

"No," I breathed, my eyes closed.

I let my mind go blank and not harp on what the hell we were doing. Because if I did, I would have noted that this wasn't like the kiss before. It was slow and tempting. Tiny brushes that were so teasing that my body warmed like it was so much more. Desire curled deep in my belly.

Maybe because I hadn't had sex in something like two hundred and four days, but who was counting?

Austin pulled away. Both of us barely opened our eyes to watch each other.

"Was he looking?" The words pushed out of my mouth like a reflex, some flimsy attempt to remind myself of the boundary between us.

His jaw flexed, but his gaze stayed glued to mine. "Do you care?"

I started, realizing what he was really asking, and what that meant. Even if we were pretending on all other fronts, this spark between us was real. That realization lit a fire in my chest that danced between my legs.

"No . . ." I admitted, watching him carefully now. My mind flashed to all the ways we could make use of our gorgeous hotel room and insanely comfortable bed. A bed I wouldn't mind being pinned to after a nearly yearlong dry spell.

A smirk tugged at his cheek. "Then why ask, Isa?"

"I . . ." Maybe I wanted to see his reaction. That glint of heat in his eyes that told me he wanted every wicked scenario playing out in my head just as badly. "I'm giving you the chance to back out, you know. A fling might offend those Regency-era sensibilities."

Both of his eyebrows lifted. The dim lighting carved streaks where his jaw flexed. "I've been waiting for the okay to go."

"Oh." My lungs burned, every breath laced with something hallucinogenic when I was that close to him. "You have it. You can take control."

"Good, because I plan to." Eyes unmoving from mine, he watched me. For those extended seconds, all I could think about was how much I wanted to touch, feel, *taste* him. Then he moved a few inches back from me and his eyes flickered around my face. "How long till you can wash that off?"

"A few hours."

He let out a slow, controlled breath. "How about I help?"

My heart raced.

The space between our bodies crackled with electricity. It sent a buzz down my spine. I nodded. "I could probably use a hand."

"Or two."

Chapter 22
ISABELLE

*L*ike a flame moving down a wick, the rest of the night was a slow burn that kept getting hotter. Flirtatious whispers. A few well-placed comments about using his hands. Small touches—all perfectly appropriate—like a hand at the crook of my neck, or fingers occasionally sweeping back and forth along my collarbone. The gestures rasped against my skin with an undercurrent that was carnal and just a bit possessive.

They scattered tingles in my stomach all night, lacing the entire evening with anticipation that thickened to a haze as we made our way back to our suite.

My heels clicked against the marble floor. A few steps behind me, the metallic clack of the lock sliding into place filled the silent room.

In the dark living area, the city lights streamed in through the sheer curtain. Austin didn't say anything, but I could practically feel his footsteps thud at the bottom of my belly as he placed my things down on the entryway table.

"Isa." The baritone in his voice plucked a string deep in my belly.

"Yeah."

In the dim glow from the lamp in the corner, my eyes became transfixed on the quick flick it took to loosen and remove his cufflinks. Whether it was the dexterity or the way they *clinked* against the wood, cutting through the heavy tension—I couldn't tell. But my heart raced.

"What do you want?" He looked up. Sky-blue eyes drowned out the entire world. All I could see, hear, think was everything I wanted to happen.

Caught in a heavy current, my thoughts tumbled out. "I need to put my hair up." I swallowed against a dry throat. "So I can wash this off."

He nodded and picked up a hair tie from the table. Ambient streetlights that spilled through the windows passed like bars over his body as he closed the space between us.

"We'll get to that." His words prickled against my skin. "What do you want?"

Desire curled between my thighs.

My teeth scraped over my lower lip. "*Help* me wash this off?"

He leaned down and hummed close to my lips, taking a second to wait there. Pulling the tension so taut it stretched and thinned, getting closer to snapping. An inch away from the kiss we'd been waiting to have, he didn't move.

He watched with carnal amusement, and a smirk dug into his cheek. "I knew you could ask for help."

He pulled back a few inches. I was pinned by his controlled stare. Those nimble fingers undid the clasp that held up the billowing skirt of my lehenga. It pooled on the floor. Seconds later the bodice came loose, and his index finger ran a slow line along my collar.

He watched me like a lion watched prey, and I let him. I stayed absolutely still.

He nudged one strap off, then the other. It skated down my body on its way to the floor. Completely naked aside from my lace panties, trembles and goose bumps laid claim to every inch his gaze touched.

His jaw flexed under a groan that rumbled in his chest.

The electricity cracked and popped between us. Finally, his mouth dipped to mine and, a hair's distance from my lips, he said: "Get in the shower, Isa."

My pussy clenched.

His hands splayed along my hips and turned me around, an arm looped around my naked waist, and he dropped a few stray kisses on the nape of my neck as we walked into the bathroom.

One blink and the shower was running; the next and he was unbuttoning his shirt and discarding his clothes. My eyes took their time wandering down his sculpted body. The deep-cut V in his abs arrowing straight down to his dick.

I licked my lips.

Before I could gawk, he moved behind me.

His fingers gently weaved through my hair, pulling it up.

Static yoked up my spine. The momentary surprise evaporated in the steam that billowed around us. "What are you . . ."

In the partially cloudy mirror, I could see our blurry reflection as he gently pulled my hair into a neat bun.

"You said you needed to pull your hair back." His breath fanned down my neck. I leaned against his body, feeling every inch of his erection against my back. "And the sooner we wash the mehndi off, the sooner we can get to *that*."

His palm slid over my stomach. A finger looped around my panties and yanked them down.

Anticipation arrowed between my thighs.

The ache begged for attention, and, my hair surprisingly well-secured, I made the only move I could make.

I stepped into the shower with Austin right behind me.

The water only intensified the feeling that jumped along every nerve ending. In seconds the dried powder on my hands melted off, and the brilliant orange disappeared from my palms, leaving behind a slightly paler design. I turned around, and his muddled blue eyes met mine.

Rivulets of water dripped down his face. Finally, I could touch him, and the first place my hands went was that slab of marble that was his chest. His hands on either of my hips, his thumbs ran tight circles on each side. Slow and controlled, his lips lowered to mine.

He kissed me with a gentle peck at first, barely pressing against my lips.

I exhaled a pleading sigh, and finally, his patience snapped.

With the speed and intensity of a firecracker going off, the kiss exploded, filling the air around us with sparks. A groan climbed up his chest, and he deepened the kiss. His fingers gripped my hips, bruising with how firm his hold was.

His hand smoothed down my stomach and his fingers

stopped at my naval. A jittery fog filled my mind as the steam filled the shower.

"Isa." Ragged and gravelly, his voice pulled with desire between heavy breaths.

The water gently lapping down my body mixed with the static building in my core. I was so aroused, I felt slickness between my thighs despite the water falling over me.

"More." My fingers weaved into his hair and yanked.

"Like this?" He paused, let his thumb wander down, and ran it lightly over my clit.

My hips jerked forward.

"Yes."

He sank a finger into me.

"*Fuck,*" he gritted out. "You're tight."

My head tilted back slowly against the shower tile and I grinded against him. Every nerve ending was aware and waiting, the tension pulled tighter and tighter, making the air thin.

Using the heel of his palm against my clit, he sank another finger into me, and everything went topsy-turvy.

"Remember when you questioned my stamina, Isa?" he asked through a tight jaw.

Lost in every sensation, all I could do was let the moan and whimpers for more fall loose from my mouth. I wanted more in any way he'd give it to me.

Molten pleasure moved up my spine. I ran my hand over his shoulder to his back as I tried to hold on.

"Austin," I murmured just before it all came together. The

electricity, the heat, the cliff every one of my nerves was about to fall off.

The world around us muffled under the filthy chorus of my breathy moans, the water dripping down intermingled with the slick sounds of his fingers stroking and curling until he found *that* spot.

I gasped. My leg swung around his waist, shamelessly grinding against him for more. A static began to move through my legs, concentrating at my core. My eyes closed and I let the feeling pull me under, so close I could almost . . .

"For the rest of the night." He pressed firmer against my clit. "We're going to set the record straight."

The tension tightened, getting me so close with every progressive push against my sensitive skin.

Then, it all stopped. His hand and body moved away from mine. My eyes blinked, I tried to regain some focus, and the shower door swung open.

A whoosh of air and the suffocating steam dissipated.

My eyes fluttered open as a towel wrapped around me.

"What are you . . ." My brain was scrambled, my body frustrated, and more than anything begging to be touched.

He held the towel closed with both hands and leaned down to my ear. "Taking control, like you asked."

A towel around his waist, he stepped out and dried off. I stood there, stunned for a moment. I reveled in that feeling.

It was nice to have someone else take control, to simply ride along for a bit.

I stepped out of the shower and stood directly in front of him.

"If you keep teasing me . . ." I warned, but it got lost in the look he gave me. A stare like a boxer waiting in their corner.

"You're going to what?" His broad chest at my eyeline, his hand snaked into my towel, and his thumb barely touched my aching clit, my body jolting at the tiny, provocative contact. "Come on, Doc. Threaten me."

The words sent sparks down my naval.

"If you do that again," I clarified. My skin, dried but dewy, filled with a renewed heat.

"If I don't let you come?" He dragged his thumb over my clit again, slower this time. Static filled my legs.

My breath hitched. "Yes."

"How about this. I'll let you come. I'll even let you pick." He tossed my towel to the side. Pushing the bathroom door open a bit further, he took my hand and led me out. His eyes moved from the doorway to the small writing desk to the armoire and then to the bed. "Bent over the desk or the bed?"

My teeth sank into my lower lip. *God*, if every one of his requests came alongside this feeling, I'd be a lot more accommodating.

"Desk," I whispered. Anticipation slickened between my thighs.

Without another word, he led me the few steps to the desk in front of the bed and fanned his fingers out on the small of my back, bending me over.

His other hand roamed. Touching, squeezing, teasing all over my body. Finally, it nudged my legs apart. I flicked a glance over my shoulder.

"You sure you're okay in control?" I taunted, aching to feel just how serious he was.

His hand was heavy on my back, pushing against me in warning, bringing me down to my elbows. "Don't test me, Isa."

He moved away for a second, and the sound of foil ripping open filled the electric quiet.

Then he neared, his hand moving up my spine, gently gripping the base of my neck. His fingers stroked my collarbone.

His dick slid across my entrance a few times before he pushed into me tentatively, the tip moving into me just enough to torment me. To show me how good he'd feel when he was inside me.

My mouth fell open and a shaky moan came loose.

"You want it all?"

Chills erupted down the back of my neck.

"Yes," I breathed. It was meant to be coy or provocative, but it came out pleading, because he felt *so* good.

I looked over my shoulder. Our eyes connected, the lines along his throat grew taut, and he pushed himself in with one swift motion.

My breath hitched from the light sting from his roughness. But it lit a spark that fanned down my muscles. Overcome, I lay flush against the desk. He waited a moment before his strokes started slow and deep.

"Fuck." He groaned. "*Baby*, you're so fucking tight."

My skin pebbled. I rolled my forehead against the cool polished wood, letting the words and that tone wash over me.

"Austin," I called, wanting more. More contact, more friction, more of him.

I wanted him so intensely that filling and stretching me wasn't enough. He was stroking me slowly, sensuously. But I wanted him deeper and rougher. I wanted to feel everything I'd been imagining.

"*Fuck*, you look good." His breathing went ragged. I looked back again and this time it nearly pushed me over the edge. He watched where our bodies met intensely for a moment before looking up to me. "Taking every inch like I knew you would."

His movements became rougher, his fingers pressed firmer against my skin. With each heavy thrust, he got deeper inside. The hair tie holding my bun came loose and my curls cascaded down my back.

Pants and moans mingled together in an incomprehensible web of sounds and noises that fell out of my mouth. "Harder," I begged.

With a fist full of my hair, he gave it to me. The sound, the tiny pricks of pain, the overwhelming pleasure all converged and pushed me over the edge.

It rocked me, knocked me over like a giant wave at the beach. I was pulled under in a flash. Overcome from the pleasure bursting from the inside out, my legs gave way, and my entire body slumped against the desk as my breath began to slow.

Moments later, Austin helped me to my feet, turned me around, and instead of the dominating version of him that I wasn't used to but *was* enjoying, I got the Austin I was expecting. He pulled me into a gentle kiss. Slow and passionate; laced with something addictive because I didn't want it to end.

His one arm stayed tight against me while the other moved up and down my back, a finger tracing my spine, as I caught my breath against his muscular chest.

"Are you okay?" he asked.

I nodded against him, and even though I could keenly feel everything we just did when I moved, I rolled my hips against him. He was still hard. My heart raced.

"I'm not letting that stamina crack go." His voice lifted from a whisper, and he grasped my chin. "Ready for more?"

I looked up, my teeth sank into my lower lip.

"It was a simple observation," I said between breaths.

Challenge flared in his eyes. "On the bed. On your back."

I walked gingerly to the bed, knowing I was going to be sore in the morning. My shaking legs barely held me up as I knelt on the perfectly made bed waiting for him.

"Isa . . ." he warned, closing the distance between us. "I said on your back."

I smiled, defiantly. If he wanted me like that, he'd have to do it himself.

He stood at the edge of the bed and pulled me into a searing kiss. This one was anything but sweet; it was hungry and domineering. Teeth, hands, lips, every part of me buzzed with a need to touch every part of him.

I traced a finger down every rigid dip and rise of his washboard torso. A tortured groan rumbled up his throat when I got to his navel.

He pulled away, a hair's distance from my lips, his hands squeezed below the swell of my ass, his expression turned wicked. Before I knew it, he dropped his hands lower to my legs, then pulled them forward and in one quick motion, and my back hit the mattress.

It dipped as Austin hovered over me, pushing my legs further apart.

"Doesn't take instruction well." He ran the head of his dick along my wet pussy, pushing it in only to pull it back out.

"Oh . . ." I moaned softly. Sparks popped along my hips.

"It's a shame . . ." He *tsk*ed, his hand moving down my body to between my thighs. His thumb found my aching clit and ran progressively firmer strokes around it, torturing me slowly. "If you'd just do what you were told, I could get to the part you want."

"Austin . . ." I panted. My fingers carded through his hair, forming a fist when he teased me.

He pushed a finger into me. My head tipped back, and my body bowed into him. A short whimper leaped out of me.

"Isa . . ." He moved the other hand down my thigh and encouraged my leg over his shoulder. "Who's in charge here?"

My nails dug into his scalp, and I rolled my hips, aching to create some friction against his fingers. His breathing faltered.

"Isa," he warned through a tight jaw.

At that point I'd have done anything to feel him stretching me again. I was lightheaded; the air was impossibly thick. "You."

Without another word, he pulled his fingers from me, positioned himself at my entrance, and slid in to the hilt, slow and purposeful, making sure I felt every single inch.

Electricity moved up my legs. He started slow, leaning down and pressing a few reassuring kisses along my neck before pulling away. The movements picked up in tempo.

"Don't ask for a break tonight." His voice was tight and restrained like it was the only thing keeping him from going completely undone.

"I don't need one," I taunted between powerful thrusts. My head arched into the pillow. "But good for you. It's important to stay active as you get ol—"

He slammed into me, harder this time, with a satisfied groan. He chuckled—low and controlled—which nearly got lost under the sound of the increasingly rough strokes.

He panted my name as I barreled to the edge again, so close this time, the room started to blur. The pleasure built, quick and intense. I couldn't hold it in any longer. My nerves tingled with waves of consuming heat. Then a second later, a cold sweat broke over me.

Everything went hazy until his guttural groan filled my ears, pulling me back to the present. He got out of bed momentarily before rejoining me with a deep kiss.

My hand ran along his neck until my fingertips combed back a lock of tawny brown hair. He pulled up to look at me, and I pushed away some that had fallen over his forehead.

"Are you okay?" he whispered. He was so close that his blue eyes were almost gray at the edges.

I hummed in sated reassurance, relishing how good he felt.

How good all of this felt.

Our legs intertwined, we lay there, and the thin film of sweat began to evaporate. I nestled in his arms; I outstretched my own and looked at the now burgundy-color pattern on my palm. "Look at that, no smears."

"Good for us." Austin's chest rumbled with a chuckle. "Keeping our hands to ourselves for an *entire* evening," he drawled sarcastically and pressed a kiss on my head.

It was intimate.

A different kind of intimate than what we'd just done.

The gesture rang clarity between my ears.

My heavy eyelids became lighter, and I fully realized we'd crossed a line we hadn't *actually* talked about crossing. If this wedding had taught me anything, it was that knowing where you stood was important. Because maybe if I'd known that with Blake, I wouldn't have spun out the way I did when I heard about his engagement. I never wanted to feel that safety yanked away from me again.

My body caught up with my mind. "We should probably talk about that, right?" I whispered against his chest.

I didn't want this to stop because *that* was great. More than great. But I had a bare-bones kind of life right now. I couldn't do a real relationship with everything else going on, and in the future the fellowship would only make it harder.

Most men I'd encountered were intimidated by me. No matter how feminist they proclaimed to be, they'd hear the things I wanted—an independent life, maybe without children—and scoff, assuming I'd "come around." I didn't neatly fit in the box they'd ascribed. Surgery instead of a "family friendly" specialty like pediatrics or internal medicine. Fellowships and research instead of "settling down." A life lived in service to my own goals rather than in service of a family.

But if I made the boundaries clear early on, maybe I could avoid all that. I was having fun right now, a kind of fun I hadn't had in a long time. I didn't want this to stop. I wanted to enjoy myself while it lasted. As long as we were clear with each other, we could avoid those pitfalls. Right?

"Talking is the last thing I was thinking about." His voice, gravelly and deep, scrambled everything. He dipped his head down, brushing his lips in a few sweeps against my lips and cheek.

A delightful static spindled around my spine, moving lower with each purposefully teasing brush.

"Oh?" I ran my teeth over my lower lip. "Is it because of the little crush you have on me?"

A smile touched his lips, and he shook his head. Then, not taking a second for me to process it, he rolled me onto my back. "It's a big one."

My stomach did cartwheels, probably from the sudden change in position and the feeling of his muscular body pressed against mine. But still, the words—direct and forthright—were a surprise. The willingness to put his intentions out there, vulnerable to attack, was *a choice.*

"We're having fun, so we might as well enjoy ourselves until the wedding is over." I pushed my fingers through his hair. "Right?"

I was having trouble being as direct as he was. Because I liked him, but at the same time, I wasn't in any position to be putting my feelings first. I had a life and plans to get home to, and so did he.

He paused for a moment, brushing a loose curl out of my face. "Really committing to the bit, huh?"

"It could be fun," I teased, running a finger up that unreasonably solid chest. "And we clearly play well together."

He chuckled, low and rich. It warmed me.

"Sounds good to me, Doc." He pressed a kiss against my lips.

Maybe this was exactly what I needed.

Chapter 23
AUSTIN

*T*he pressure of satin-covered hips rolling against mine jostled me awake. Still foggy and half asleep, I didn't think and simply threw my arm around her and pulled her close. The sound of her soft moan coupled with another slow hip roll woke me up completely. That and the blood suddenly rushing to my groin.

Heat ran up my spine and I pulled in closer to her until we were on the same pillow—hers. The silk-covered one she slept on was just as soft as it looked. And she felt better than I had imagined.

Every memory from last night flashed in my head.

I didn't want to be the guy who did one-night stands anymore. I was past that stage in my life. But there wasn't any point in denying this thing between us. She didn't want anything serious, and honestly, I wasn't in any position to ask for that sort of thing with my most likely impending move. So, what was the harm in enjoying it?

Originally, this had felt a little too complicated with all the ways Isa was wrapped around Blake, but that seemed to loosen over the last week. Maybe this was good for both of us, because I finally had some direction in my life.

I wasn't going to question any of it right now, not when all of it felt so good.

"Mmmm," she hummed and rolled her hips again. This time I knew she felt how hard I was.

"Isa . . ." I dropped a kiss on her neck.

My hand slipped under her camisole and spanned across her stomach. Her satin skin pricked with goose bumps. She felt good. And we had a few days left here; we might as well enjoy them.

My heart's erratic rhythm got faster.

A little more awake, she moaned softly this time and ran a hand up behind her through my hair.

Fuck.

Suddenly, a loud rumble against the nightstand made her tense.

"Don't pick it up," I whispered.

She nodded, her mouth slightly open, and my hand moved up against her chest—running gently over the curve of her ribs before reaching the tempting swell of her breasts.

Another loud rumble against the nightstand interrupted us.

"It's a reminder," she told me. Her voice was low and a little scratchy with a mix of sleepiness and lust.

Blood rushed through my ears, hot and loud. I held her tighter against me.

That sound.

Her voice wasn't the normal steady and confident one—it was wobbly, almost vulnerable. And, fuck, I wanted to protect it. Keep it. All for myself.

I groaned into her ear. "Ignore it."

She paused for a second, I closed my eyes and ran my lips along the curve of her neck. And she eased back into me. My hand spanned over her breast, running a finger slowly over her puckered nipple.

One last rumble against the nightstand convinced her to pull away.

With a disgruntled growl, she went from slowly raking her hands through my hair to reaching across the bed for her phone.

"Oh." She sat up, her eyes scanning the screen. The room came back into focus. "You have your playdate today."

The electricity in the room stretched and disappeared altogether.

I was meeting Xander Sutton, the banker, at the Stade today. He was a founder of an enormous capital investment firm and a guest at the wedding. The meeting was informal since it would be over a friendly game, but he was an important person to talk to and, if anything, it was a business opportunity. But right now, all I could think about was staying in bed.

"Please stop calling it that." I was still trying to get my heart rate back down to something normal. Isa pushed the sheets off her and got out of bed. She stood in front of her nightstand with her eyes on the screen, and my eyes lingered on the curve of her ass barely peeking out from the bottoms of her shorts. "Can you come along?"

She was great at making small talk since she seemed to know a little bit about *everything*.

"I figured he might like to play at the Stade," I added. I'd cleared it with Wes right before I left, riding the high that I could do what I needed for the foundation. But now I wondered what exactly that was. Set it up and get it in a place where it could sustain itself or maybe more. "You could see it, too."

"Look at you," Isa teased gently. "Who needs a pushy manager now?"

"So . . ." I got out of bed and rounded it till I was right behind her. Putting both arms around her waist, I dropped my head to the crook of her neck. "Wanna come along?"

"Ummm . . ." Isa looked down at her phone. She refreshed her email, but nothing updated. Her shoulders dropped.

"Why don't you stay here and work." I could see that was where her mind was at.

"I believe in you," she said cheekily, turning in my arms. Just the slightest feel of her breath sweeping against them sent all that electricity back down my spine. "You'll do great."

I knew she was being cute or flirtatious, but the words felt different when they came out of her mouth. "I'm not as quick a study as you, but I think I can hold my own."

She smiled but didn't say anything. She only looked up at me, and her eyes held mine for a moment. "I know I was supposed to help—"

I pressed a kiss against her lips. She was adorable when she was a little nervous. "Find a way to make it up to me later?"

"I can think of something."

"And I'll meet you here before tonight's thing?" I asked before moving a few steps away to the bathroom. My mind flashed to the memories in the shower last night.

She nodded and walked over to the armoire at the other end of the room where her laptop sat. Just as I stepped into the bathroom, her voice stopped me.

"What's this?" Isa picked up a book from where she'd put her laptop last night.

Taking the large book in her hand, she walked back to the bed. She crossed her legs beneath her.

"Oh . . ." I realized it was the blue one with silver lettering I'd bought in London. "Just in case you get bored with plan A and plan B," I told her casually, a bizarre sense of dread, or maybe nerves, wrapping around me. Suddenly I was very aware that I'd done something forward and not in a physical way.

While I was picking out books for Jo, I'd found that book. It was more like an encyclopedia, but it had every question and answer over the last thirty years of *Jeopardy!* It seemed too perfect not to buy. And then I got back and I second-guessed why I'd even got it. It seemed dumb to give to someone like Isa. I didn't know what I'd been thinking, but I liked having something that was between the two of us.

Isa paged through it. "I'll keep that in mind."

She closed it, held it tightly with both arms, and smiled; it brightened the room like all the morning sun shooting through it at that exact second.

That.

That was why I'd bought it—what I was hoping for.

"But I already know a lot of these answers," she teased lightly.

My heart dipped and a chuckle rolled through me. I was both expecting and not expecting that answer.

"Of course you do." I pushed the door to the bathroom open. "Get to work, Doc."

"Go make a friend," she called as I stepped into the shower.

* * *

I got out of the elevator and made the turn that gave me a direct sight line to the gardens. Among the clusters of white hydrangeas and magnolias, Malcolm was sitting at the end of a semi-private alcove nestled among the hedges where he was able to both catch the wedding planners when they were leaving and still have some seclusion—he had picked a pretty good spot.

A part of me really liked the feeling of doing something to make Isa's life a little easier. Today, maybe that meant I could distract the reporter a bit. He was a fan. Maybe he'd like a friendly game, too.

I made my way to the small wrought iron table with the circular marble top where Malcolm was enjoying an espresso and scribbling in his notepad.

He didn't look up at me, sighing deeply as he continued with his notes. "Where are we going now?"

"I thought you might like to see the field at the Stade."

"And why is that?"

"Site of the last World Cup and probably more fun than discussing centerpieces, right?"

"My job is to discuss centerpieces," he grumbled.

"You seem like a creative guy." I sidestepped the fact that Malcolm clearly understood the bride and groom were as excited to have him here as he was to be here. "I'm sure going to the event tonight is more than enough."

He finally stopped his writing.

"You know, most fans would love to play a quick match on the field at the Stade." I shrugged. If keeping him out of the way did something to make Isa's day a little better, I was going to do it. And if not, I'd have time to fill his little notepad with more information about the foundation. "But do what you want."

He tucked his notepad into his pocket. There was no way he was going to give something like that up for table decorations.

"Great, it's settled." I grinned.

Chapter 24
AUSTIN

I was expecting Xander Sutton—the billionaire and cofounder of the venture capital group—to be a little less approachable. But he was unbelievably friendly. He'd pulled together a group of guys who were basically a captive audience at this wedding and gotten them together for a game. And this was the perfect venue to talk to him about investment in the foundation.

I walked onto the field and my eyes landed on Blake.

It made sense that he was here. He was around the same age as Isa and probably just as good at making new friends. He likely was invited to join when Xander gathered the rest of his buddies.

I tried to ignore Blake, because it took five minutes of chatting with Xander to understand why Isa had sent him my way. A former Division 1 soccer player, he ran a venture capital firm now and carried a love for the sport. And happened to own stakes in numerous football clubs around the world. There wasn't a person more perfect to share my vision for the foundation and eventual training academy.

He'd understood it and happened to have a lot of capital.

"So, you asked a few people to join a quick pickup game and all these people show up?" I walked over to the bench he was sitting on as he put on a pair of cleats.

Inside the Stade again twice in the same week was a bizarre feeling of déjà vu. I stared out to the empty stands, then looked down at the friendly billionaire.

"People tend to like me." Xander shrugged with an upside-down smile, then ran a hand through his tawny blond hair. "And the Ritz Paris is filled to the brim with rich people who have nothing to do between events."

He stood and shifted his weight between his legs, like it had been a while since he'd played.

"I'm guessing the groom put you up to this?" he asked.

"Huh?"

He chuckled lightly. "Playing hot potato with the reporter sounds like a Henry-type request."

"It's a mission for the maid of honor," I told him, looking down the field as the group of around fifteen or sixteen filed onto it. Blake was one of them. "Thought maybe I'd make her day a little easier."

The competitive fire in my gut flared, but I reminded myself there wasn't any glory in beating a beginner. I needed to take it easy, and it would be tactless to humiliate Blake up and down the pitch today.

"So, are we playing, or is this a mean-spirited game of target practice?" Xander looked at Malcolm with suspicion. "I'm up for either."

"How about a friendly game?" I suggested, raising my hand

over my eyes to block the sun. Malcolm was a scraggy chain-
smoker; there was no chance he'd survive anything more than
an easygoing match.

"Fine, but your team gets a few less players." He jogged onto
the field and turned to run backward with a charming smile.
"You know, professional and all."

"I'm basically retired," I retorted mostly to myself.

"Still counts," he called, turned back around, and ran to the
group.

* * *

Trying to be a good sport when playing against civilians was
frustrating. And we had to stop when Malcolm became a con-
cerning shade of gray.

"You okay?" I walked over to the bench where Malcolm was
nearly doubled over.

He nodded, taking a bottle of water from me but still so
winded that he couldn't drink it. "Sorry we had to end early."

"Don't worry about it." I wasn't supposed to be playing, not
that the last thirty minutes were anything close to actual play.
"You did . . . *great*."

I tried to sound genuine over the lie.

The first ten minutes, he'd seemed fine. He took a break
after fifteen, and then around a half hour in, he just sat down.
But given that it would be an hour back to the Ritz and another
one to Versailles, we'd successfully distracted him and he was
still alive. So, all in all, a good day.

"Well, that was . . ." Xander walked over to the bench and

grabbed a bottle of water. He looked over to Malcolm with a pitying smile. He grimaced. "Movement?"

I chuckled a little under my breath.

"Too bad Isa couldn't come. She's always a lot of fun," Xander told me.

Right when I opened my mouth to tell him why Isa was busy today, someone else answered for me.

"Isa doesn't like soccer." Blake's voice cut into our conversation, cold and annoyed. He took a seat a few feet away from Malcolm. "Never has."

He was *clearly* bothered. Isa got exactly what she'd wanted; he was going a little nuts. That specific bit of information would probably make her happy to know, and that made a pit form in my stomach. She didn't want anything from him but still cared enough about Blake to want to see him hurt.

"She finds it tedious," Blake continued, looked up with a half smile, smug. Like he wanted to make sure I knew how well *he* knew her. "She watched it for years with me and never learned a single rule."

"I taught her a few things," I replied offhandedly. Blake's jaw lined with tension. "People change."

"Not some people . . ." he grumbled, standing up and making sure to knock my shoulder as he pushed past.

He walked over to one of the tunnels that led out of the stadium, along with everyone else. Malcolm took a few deep breaths and followed behind Blake.

"Isa's ex?" Xander stated once Blake was out of earshot.

"Yeah."

"An ex showing up, unexpectedly; been there." He slapped

a hand on my shoulder before he started walking in the same direction. He didn't explain any further, only kept toward the exit. "So, I was talking to the owner—are you considering coaching here?"

"You know Hugo Sellier?"

Apparently, I was talking to exactly the right person. I tried to shake off the brief frustration from talking to Blake because I needed to make sure I thanked Isa.

"Mm-hmm," he answered casually.

I puffed out a breath of air. "B team coaching," I clarified. "But yeah, maybe."

"Nothing wrong with B team." Xander nodded at a few of the other guys as they all began to file out. "I never made it past collegiate level, so . . ."

"I was also thinking . . ." I pushed myself because, even though this felt a little weird, knowing Isa sort of set this up gave me a nudge I didn't realize I needed. "I started the Mistry Foundation. It's based out of Queens, and funding sort of depends on me staying relevant. I was thinking of starting an academy-type facility, you know? Find talent and keep it in the States."

"Invest in the American league. Like the individual clubs do in the Premier League," he surmised, his eyebrows raised. "I like it."

Some days, when I saw just how much American kids liked the sport, it didn't feel so far off. And maybe our dream of expanding the foundation's reach, recruiting talent, creating a program for young talent—maybe it might happen at some point.

"It's a long way off," I added. "It's not exactly a safe investment, the training facility. Building a program that feeds into a fledgling league."

"Yeah," he said shortly, unfazed. "Returns won't be for decades, but that's what venture capital is for." Xander grinned. "And that usually means a pretty big upside. When we get back to New York, you should come by Dawn Capital."

"Yeah?" Anxiety and hope filled me at the same time.

"I like to think the world isn't nearly as complicated as we make it." He shrugged. "How hard could it be?"

The words echoed in my head.

He took a last look over his shoulder to the pitch as we made our way to the tunnel to leave. "So, you're done playing?"

"I think so," I admitted out loud for the first time.

I *was* done playing. I knew that; it was the whole reason I was here. But I'd always figured that realization would be some big moment in my mind.

But it wasn't. Instead, I had a new idea, a new thing I wanted to chase. All this time I'd put that energy into finding a way to keep in the sport through coaching. But maybe there was another way I could hold on to it. A way I was genuinely excited to try. Maybe Theo's vision wasn't meant to be passed along to someone to manage it. Maybe I could do it. I knew now that I wanted to.

Chapter 25
ISABELLE

$\mathcal{H}$ours after Austin got back from the Stade, guests entered private cars and left the Ritz for the last venue before we left for the mountains.

Versailles.

It was the last night in Paris; we'd leave for the castle in the morning. Tonight was a night of music and dancing—the Sangeet—that Henry and Selena had decided to make a masquerade.

The gold-and-brass gates opened as the line of black SUVs began to file in and drop the guests off. Even though there were staff to lead all the guests to the Hall of Mirrors—where the festivities would take place—Austin and I got a little caught up taking in the castle.

I linked my arm in Austin's, and we began to make our way to the path. "How was your big-important-not-at-all-silly mandate?"

A grin stretched across his face. I had been busy getting ready by the time he got back, so we hadn't had a chance to talk since the private cars had been filled with other guests on the drive over.

"Honestly . . ." he began. Austin's eyes ran along the sweeping angular roofs and ornate sculptures that seemed to adorn every corner of this place. "I think the Mistry Foundation has investment. Real investment."

I stopped. "Yeah?"

"Yeah." He nodded. He looked straight ahead, the sunset casting a shadow along his jaw.

I'd met Xander, a friend of Henry and Selena's, enough in the past to know he could make friends with anyone. He loved soccer and ran a venture capital firm. He was the perfect person for Austin to meet and schmooze.

We stopped in front of the entrance that led straight into the Hall of Mirrors.

"Seems like it worked out." Like I was filled with helium, I lifted to my tiptoes and smacked his chest proudly.

I was a little invested in his success. The chance that his next dream might become a reality filled me with an excitement I'd only felt in regard to myself before. Maybe it was selfishness back then or a greater empathy now, but seeing him gain traction in something he wanted felt like a victory.

His hand ran along my waist, and he turned to me.

"It did. And did you get time to do some work?" he asked.

"I made a solid dent in the cases."

He chuckled and shook his head like he was expecting that answer. "The ones that don't matter."

"Yup." My cheeks hit the bottoms of my eyelids, I was grinning so wide. I looked over his shoulder to see guests filing in.

I took the masks he had been holding in his hand. "I guess we should put these on."

I took his mask and got on my tiptoes. I reached my arms around him and tied it. He let me, running his hands down my sides and holding me steady as I did.

He could tie it on himself, but I didn't mind the way his breath felt when it faltered and sailed along my skin.

When I was done, he circled his finger in the air, motioning for me to turn around.

I did a quick turn, and he fastened it on, but right before I could turn back, his hands gripped my hips and pulled me to him. He whispered in my ear from behind. "There. Done."

Goose bumps rolled down my body.

* * *

The entire night ran like clockwork according to the planner. And Austin and I basically flirted with each other without any real attempt to rein it in. We both knew where this was going tonight. Same place it went last night.

I adjusted the mask that sat just above the swell of my cheek and turned the corner from the bar to go back to the Hall of Mirrors—where most guests were mingling and having drinks. My eyes traced along the painted ceilings. Lush blues that created a bright sky and muted yellow clouds that peppered it. Sliding my eyes along the fleurs-de-lys carved into the crown moldings, my head craned back a bit more with every step.

The warm summer air drifted through the patina windows.

It was beautiful here.

I took a few more steps moving in the same direction, and it wasn't until I clocked how quiet the hum from the orchestral music had gotten that I looked around and realized I was nowhere near the Hall of Mirrors.

I turned in place looking for a placard, peeking down the hallway.

"There needs to be a map in here," I mumbled to myself.

"Down the hall to the right." Blake's voice cut through the quiet. Behind a golden mask was the same set of eyes I'd put too much stock in.

I jumped in my skin. "Oh."

"Sorry, I was just . . ." He looked down the gilded hallway I'd walked through. He stood in front of a portrait of what I assumed was some old, dead royal. "It was quiet in here; I was walking around."

"I . . ." I pointed to the ceiling. "Got distracted."

He nodded and pushed his hands into his pockets. An awkward silence settled between us. Just as I was about to turn around, his voice stopped me.

"Look, Isa." He rubbed the back of his neck. "I know I should have explained—"

"It's fine, really." Honestly, I hadn't really thought about him all night. And I didn't want to think about him. "We don't have to do that."

"I should have told you about Francesca. She and I sort of just happened. It felt right. Things with her are simple . . ."

The timbre in his voice pinched my nerves. After asking to *not* hear the story, because I didn't want to, it felt cruel of him to tell it. "Well, I guess it's a good thing Austin can *handle* complicated."

His eyes went wide for a moment before his shoulders stiffened, telling me I hit my mark, because if there was one thing Blake and I had in common, it was proving that our respective family names didn't factor into our success. I was doing it in the male-dominated surgical subspeciality of orthopedics. Blake, a trust fund baby, had to do it in his family and he always struggled to succeed on that front.

"I think I handled complicated just fine for *years*." The venom in his words made me take a step back. "Maybe I got sick of it, Isa."

His jaw sat on a hard line.

My brow crinkled.

He couldn't seriously be upset with *me*. He had an entire fiancée he didn't tell me about, and I'm the one who screwed up our relationship? "You can't be pinning our relationship not working out on me."

I didn't even know it was over. He didn't have the decency to tell me. We had a plan; he deviated. Not me.

He yanked the golden mask off his face.

"You're unbelievable," he said through a frustrated huff. "What was I supposed to do, Isa? Wait for you to take over the world before you finally decided you wanted me? To finally *make time* for me?" He took a few steps toward me. Those two words stuck out like pins. "I asked you a thousand times, begged you, to consider a residency in California. But no, you never gave an inch. Now all of a sudden, the infallible Isabelle

Mercado is 'making time' to make it work with someone she hardly knows? But you're right, you're not culpable in anything."

Razor-sharp, each syllable pierced my gut. Because despite how badly I wanted to pin it all on him, he was right.

"It was the top program in the country," I reminded him. Every one of my internal shields went up. "And what about you? It's my fault you chose to leave for a start-up?"

"No, Isa, because *nothing* is ever your fault," he huffed, but he didn't move back. He was too close.

I opened my mouth, but nothing came out.

Part of me *wanted* to lay into him about everything that had happened. Because I had to find out about his move back to New York from Selena. I had to find out that he was engaged by seeing the ring on his fiancée's finger. But more than that, I wanted this conversation to be over.

That fact cleared some of the anger that fogged my mind.

Blake laughed bitterly to himself. "And in true Isa fashion, you won't even have this conversation with me."

"Because it doesn't matter anymore."

"And you wouldn't have this conversation when it *did* matter. So, I made it work for *us*. I waited till residency, hoping you'd choose to *make it work* with me," he continued. I tried to duck his gaze when it moved to follow mine. "But no, you asked me to wait. Till we both had what we wanted. And I was the idiot because I was hoping maybe you might—"

"What? I might *not* put myself first?" I snapped, losing grip on the momentary balance I felt in realizing that I didn't care to argue, because now *he* was the one who hit a nerve. "You expected what? I would take some lesser arrangement so that *you* wouldn't have to deal with a few tough years?"

"No, so *we* didn't," Blake bit back. "I was thinking about *us*, while you were choosing you."

Every single word ached. He kept doing that, making my world feel cloudy.

My ambition was so bright that sometimes I worried it blinded me. When things got tough, I followed it like a beacon. Reminded myself why I was working toward a sterling future, the kind my mom had to give up for me, the one so many male colleagues were sure I'd never have. The type of sterling future that was often inhospitable to women, and that wouldn't change until women like me changed it.

"Then why didn't *you* stay? Why was it so easy for *you* to chase your dream, but so hard to imagine me chasing mine?" The indignation in my voice rose, sharp and steady. "You needed to go after your ambition, I get that. But you just assumed mine would . . . what? Sort itself out?" I shook my head. "Why was it *your* future we had to prioritize?"

He was silent.

I gathered every fiber of strength left to deliver the next words so they wouldn't waver. "So, you see? *You* chose."

I didn't wait for him to respond. I turned sharply and walked in the direction I'd come from.

"Always right, aren't you, Isa?" Blake taunted under his breath.

I ignored it, following the sound of laughter and music until it got a bit louder, continuing down the marbled floor until I got to the part of the hallway I'd made a detour in earlier. My eyes landed on a few gilded chandeliers and, instead of walking into the party, I walked past it. Right to the terrace that overlooked Versailles's massive, perfectly manicured gardens.

I blinked away what felt like stars in my eyes. I took a few steps down to the main garden, then a few more past the fountain. Lost in my thoughts, I didn't register a presence at my side until he spoke.

"Isa." Austin's voice cut like a scalpel through the sound of blood rushing in my ears. His body was relaxed next to mine. "I saw Blake walking through the Hall of Mirrors looking like he'd been punched," Austin noted casually, keeping his eyes directly forward as he walked with me further into the garden. "Figured you had something to do with that." We walked a few more steps. "You okay?"

My shoulders relaxed. I took a deep breath.

I was.

The crack that Blake made in my resolve was patched, filled with the knowledge that if I had *chosen* him, I would have lost myself.

"Yeah . . ." I looked around at the tall hedges surrounding us, blanketed under a dark, diamond-studded sky, realizing just how far I'd walked off from the palace. "I think I know why he got under my skin the way he did."

Austin looped an arm around me. "Don't keep me in suspense . . ."

"His engagement made things blurry for me," I said plainly.

Having Blake made me think that vision of finding some happy middle ground between my mom and dad's life was possible. But it wasn't. The myth of having it all was just that: a myth.

I should have known that, because my mom had already tried. Blake getting engaged had been confirmation I wasn't ready to receive.

"It made me question what I wanted," I clarified. "What I gave up getting here. But the truth is, I've always wanted the same thing—to make my own legacy."

Not my father's or my mother's. Not a husband's. *Mine.*

Because I was tired of constantly proving that I deserved my accolades. My own legacy—procedures named after me, textbooks with *my* words in them—would prove to every mediocre man that this *woman* was not only an impeccable orthopedic surgeon, but I got what I had on my own merit, despite all the headwinds. I'd have what so many female doctors were locked out of for so long because of the nature of medical training. I couldn't fumble that.

"You'll have it." Austin's reply was strong and swift, like it was a fact of nature.

I smiled. After weeks of feeling lost, my vision was finally clear again.

Wanting Blake had been a detour, not the destination. A part of me saw what Selena and Henry had and simply slotted Blake in, thinking it was my version of their love. But I was okay on my own, chasing the life I'd always dreamed of, and I didn't need anyone beside me to make it real. And I'd rather be on my own than with someone who wanted me to be simpler, because I'd always be a little complicated.

"Thank you." I let out a long sigh and leaned into him as we walked. The gardens were quiet and cool. The breeze sent an occasional rustle between us. We took a few more steps along the tiny stones, further into what was sort of like a maze. It was an elaborate set of paths anchored between towering hedges and perfectly manicured trees. In that moment, all of the prickly emotion slid off me like I was Teflon.

His eyebrows raised. The tips of his mouth slanted up. "Thanks for what?"

With Austin, I could relax. He was a good guy, we had fun, and he didn't ask me for things I couldn't give. He gave me what I wanted: amazing sex, good company, and a willing partner to enact a little bit of petty vengeance. "For being a great fake date."

He hesitated, his gaze drifting past me to the maze ahead before settling back. For a moment, something hardened in his expression—then it softened. He gave a quick nod and a small, tentative smile. "Of course."

We'd have to get back inside soon, but for a moment, in the hypnotizing quiet, I felt better. Even-keeled. Steady again.

Chapter 26
ISABELLE

The next day moved so fast, it felt like it happened in flashes.

Waking up in our Paris hotel room, tangled in each other. Getting dressed and getting on the plane to the mountains. Spending the day being a very convincing couple as we settled into the castle. Now I had the night with Selena—her last night as a single woman.

"To the future Mrs. Amari." I held up my glass of sparkling cider, and Selena held up hers.

At the final venue for the wedding in the Vosges mountains, Selena grinned like she had all day on our way down from Paris to the castle where they'd be married tomorrow. She was acting almost nonsensical. Honestly, if I didn't know her, I would have thought she was high. I guessed she kind of was.

The cool mountain air rolled over the large balcony in Selena's bridal suite that overlooked the sweeping hills.

"Thank you." She took a sip and sat on one of the teak chairs that sat on the balcony.

Selena and I had a whole night planned. While the guests

for tomorrow's ceremonies made their way to the castle and got settled in their rooms, we had a night of movies, facials, and spa treatments, then going to bed early.

A text message notification lit up my phone screen.

AMI: Robert got an interview for Winthrop fellowship

AMI: I wanted you to know

My heart rate skyrocketed. Robert was my cochief resident. That meant the first-round invites went out.

I opened my email and refreshed it three times.

Nothing.

My stomach churned, pushing acid up my throat.

It meant I wasn't a first choice. But the next round of invitations would go out in a few weeks. I was *sure* I'd be in those.

I tried to suck in a breath and remind myself of that.

I'd become so comfortable with the idea this fellowship was mine for the taking that I didn't think I'd be anything other than the first choice.

Hearing shuffling behind me, I clicked the screen off.

"You okay?" Selena's voice cut through the beating I could hear in my ears.

"Yeah."

"If you need to check something, you can." She tried to reach over, but I kept the phone from her. The last thing I wanted to do was turn this into a night about me.

"It was just Ami telling me my research paper was accepted

to that conference in Oslo." I tucked my phone back into my pocket and tried to hide the lie and the physical reaction I was having.

"That's great!" Selena began. I could see her gearing up to ask me a million questions about it, because my best friend was so many things, chief among them supportive.

"Tonight isn't about that," I reminded her.

If I let her, Selena would spend the next hour talking about it, telling me she was proud and asking thoughtful questions.

There were times—so many of them—in our relationship when I felt undeserving of Selena's friendship. In the moments when the pressure to be flawless became too heavy and it concentrated into frustration or isolation. And Selena met my jaded and sometimes domineering moods with patience and understanding.

I tried to make up for those times by being there for her in every way I could, knowing it probably would never be the type of support she'd given me. I knew there weren't many people who would stick around while I continuously put myself in a pressure cooker.

But Selena would; she was permanent.

"Now back to you. Any cold feet or any other things I should be checking for?" I playfully lifted the blanket she sat under.

I leaned back against the teak loveseat I was sitting in. The balcony overlooked the valley. The castle was on a mountain, so just below us was a steep drop. In these seats—with the valley shrouded in darkness in front of us—it was like we were hanging above the clouds.

Selena shook her head. "No, just a little morning sickness some days. And then some cravings."

"I was wondering how Thai ended up on tonight's menu for the two of us." I looked at the massive table filled with all of Selena's favorites.

I chalked it up to Henry because I was pretty sure this was from a restaurant in Manhattan. Meaning the chef was probably somewhere in the castle at the behest of the groom.

"Cravings and being tired. I've been napping a lot," Selena noted, throwing some spicy chicken satay into her mouth. "Thanks for keeping Malcolm busy. I would have done it if I was feeling more energized."

The article that Malcolm was writing was set to be published in *Voulez* a few weeks after we all got back from the wedding. Henry and Selena would still be on their honeymoon at the time, but she'd get an advanced read before it went to print. That meant Malcolm had to be writing as he was here attending events, so Austin's intervention came in pretty clutch because it meant Selena wouldn't be bothered with a reporter buzzing around her while she was tired, newly pregnant, and trying to relax before her wedding. She had plenty of press attention already in everyday life as the soon-to-be Mrs. Amari.

"Stop thanking me," I insisted. It was the only way I felt useful and I was happy to do it. Not to mention, I wasn't doing much. "It's been easy. He acts pretentious but basically melted when Austin took him along to his old team at Farnham . . ."

A tiny smile crept up the sides of Selena's mouth. "I know you're trying to keep this all about me, but I gotta know . . ."

"Know . . ."

"Isa." She leaned forward and took a sip of her sparkling apple cider. "*Come on.*"

"What?" I laughed, feeling my face heat.

"The tension." She threw her head back with a loud giggle. "It's palpable. You're sleeping together, right? You have to be. That chemistry can't be fake."

"Okay, fine." After getting almost no sleep last night, Austin and I had spent the morning locked in our hotel room. Getting out of bed and having to be presentable for the short flight from Paris to the Vosges mountains felt like slow torture. "It's not serious. But it's been . . . fun."

We were keeping it casual, but oddly, I felt a strange sense of gratitude that we were still pretending to be a serious couple for the other guests. It had given me a reason to touch him on the plane—as part of the act, of course—but that didn't stop me from privately appreciating the cords of muscles in his bicep beneath my fingers. I couldn't exactly explain the way I'd snuggled into his shoulder as we'd wandered the castle's dark corridors earlier, when no one was looking. Or the way he'd pinned me against the cold stone and kissed me breathless. I'd spent the entire day with him before I came here.

A wolfish grin painted Selena's face. She stood from her chair across from me and squeezed in next to me on the loveseat.

"This castle has stone walls. You can be as loud as you want." She leaned her head on my shoulder. She shifted, tucking her legs beneath her. "Trust me."

"Noted."

"And . . ." she added in a singsong fashion. "He seems to be making friends. And he's doing a huge favor to your best friend by keeping Malcolm busy."

"Because it helps him, too," I reminded her, knowing what she was getting at.

"Mm-hmm," Selena hummed disbelievingly.

For all the time I'd known her, Selena had always been completely single or in a committed relationship—never anything in between. She didn't do casual or situationships. She liked the security in knowing where she stood with someone and having those lines clearly drawn.

I wasn't like that. To me, neatly drawn lines were a way to box me in. I needed flexibility and a backup plan.

"Don't read into it," I told her resolutely. This was quid pro quo. A hot one. "We're together while we're here. Then we each get what we need and can go our separate ways."

Maybe one day I'd find what Selena had with Henry without losing myself, but for now, the sex was more than enough. We both needed to focus on our respective futures. The Winthrop fellowship was still on the horizon, and I needed to keep my slate clear for it.

"Okay, got it. You have what you need." Selena looked out onto the horizon. "And there's nothing wrong with a palate cleanser. But what do you *want*?"

The idea that I wasn't going to see Austin much after this did rattle a bit in my chest. Maybe the occasional hello while I finished my work at the Lightning facility. I tried to ignore it. It was a path I'd been down before and gotten burned from, and I had no interest in putting myself through that again. Especially when the outcome was going to be the same. Someone was going to have to give something up and that wasn't fair to anyone.

"I already have what I want." I thought about the interview invitation I was still waiting on. "Well, I will. Just like we planned since college. Back when we probably drank too much and ran around New York City in sky-high heels and miniskirts in the middle of winter."

"Now, here we are on the night before my wedding." She lifted her sparkling apple cider. "And I'm knocked up, too."

I laughed, clinking her glass. "A big family, happily-ever-after, the whole package."

We sat like that, quietly smushed together on the loveseat.

"Isa." Selena's voice settled into something serious. "My kids are going to need their cool aunt to remind them how to be normal. Things won't be all that different."

I nodded.

In the last couple years, I realized I had become the loneliest I'd ever been. Not because I wasn't busy with my own life, but because everything was changing, and I couldn't help but feel I was left behind.

"We're a package deal. You know it's not going to change, right?" Selena repeated.

Selena had fallen in love, and Henry and his family had become a huge part of her life. That happened around the same time I was in the toughest, most demanding parts of residency. Now that things were easing up, it felt a little bittersweet. I was finally going to have some time and as I reached that milestone, my best friend reached a different one.

Austin's words from the Mehndi pushed a sentimentality to my eyes. It condensed to a glassiness that coated them. *Love isn't finite; it makes room.*

"Of course I do."

It wasn't really a loss but a change. The realization that those days of just the two of us traipsing through the city were over hit me in waves. Things were going to be different, but it didn't feel as dark as it had even a few weeks ago.

Selena leaned her head on my shoulder. "What would those crazy college girls think of us now?"

I laughed, blinking away the emotion. "I think they ended up where they planned to be."

Back then I had a map for where I wanted to be in life, and now I was there. I'd get the interview and I'd nail it when I got back. I'd get everything I wanted.

"Not where they planned," Selena corrected, sitting up and motioning her arms at the darkness ahead of us, lit only with the occasional lantern in the vineyards. "But I think we are where we're supposed to be."

"Your personal castle?"

She shook her head. "Together."

Chapter 27
ISABELLE

A sunset stained the cotton candy sky in deep pinks and oranges as the sun made its final dip under the horizon. The twilight it left behind blanketed the reception that was in full swing now.

Henry and Selena's wedding ceremonies took place in the castle's chapel and the north-facing lawn that overlooked miles of vineyards. The reception took place a little further down that same vast green, closer to the peak of another rolling hill that opened to a view of the stunning river valleys, each lined with rows of vines.

"Usually, reporters covering weddings get some insights into the couple from the wedding party." Malcolm stood next to me at the bar. "Or maybe the couple deign to give them a few words."

All day, I had tried to put the text from Ami out of my head and be present for one of the most important days in my best friend's life. Up until now, I had succeeded. But now with everything all settled, my mind kept returning to it.

I had thought a drink might help and I ended up at the bar with Malcolm.

I didn't get a first-round interview, but I would still get one eventually . . . I had to. I tried to swallow the sour taste in the back of my throat.

"Selena and Henry are very private people," I told him, even though he had to know that by now. The only reason he was here was because one magazine was the lesser of the press evils they might have been subjected to. "And what else do you need to know besides china patterns and floral arrangements?"

"I could write about the guests," he challenged, almost like it was meant to sound like a threat, but immediately after the surge of protectiveness wore down, it actually sounded like a good idea.

"Well, you have plenty of fodder," I agreed. "Assuming any of them let you."

Considering this party was filled with people who valued their privacy and tried to stay out of the public eye, he'd be up against a mountain of shit with his magazine and editor and probably their legal team if he published any names he wasn't allowed to.

"Like your date?"

I smiled. Pride shot through me. "Between being an *American* Premier League champion, the former US World Cup team captain, and a philanthropist, I'm sure you could do much worse."

His eyebrows rounded up, and he wrote something on his notepad with an upside-down grin and a shrug. "Are you his girlfriend or his publicist?"

He said it plainly, but his eyes were intense. The implication being that he saw through us. I probably should have practiced a bit more before fumbling our performance that first night. But I'd thought we'd done a pretty good job selling the act since then, and it was far too late to backtrack now.

I crossed my arms. "Is there a reason you're baiting me?"

He chuckled to himself and shook his head. "Not at all. I'm actually going to try to arrange a sit-down with your date later this summer."

"Oh yeah?" I took a sip of wine. A win for Austin felt like a win for me.

"Yeah." Austin's voice, deep and strong, was like a shot of espresso. My muscles jumped when his hands spanned along my hips, then his arms wrapped around my waist and yanked me back to him.

AUSTIN

*I*sa bragging about me delivered the same adrenaline rush as the sound of wind whipping around a net when a ball moving at ninety miles an hour swung against it.

A wave of pride followed by relief, followed by pride again.

She leaned into me, her skin warm and soft. I glanced up to Malcolm, who raised an eyebrow, opened his mouth, but then closed it immediately. "Will you excuse us, Malcolm?"

Without waiting for an answer, I took her hand and began leading her across the green along a stone path into the castle.

The wedding now over, our time together was fading as quickly as the sunset had, and I wanted to wring every last second dry.

"I heard that." I squeezed her hand.

"What?" She stopped and looked around with some curiosity as we stood between one of the stone entrances into the castle and the slowly dwindling reception. She turned and innocently smoothed her hands over my lapels. "You happen to have accomplished a lot and ambition is sexy."

I didn't know what it was about her, but her determination was contagious. She loved her life and her work, and that type of excitement was evident in everything she did. It made me want to find that feeling again.

A feeling I'd lost years ago.

Reawakened by that look in her eye. The one that made me think I was capable of more than I let myself believe. I didn't care what people thought of me as long as it benefited the foundation, but suddenly I cared what Isa thought.

"You didn't tell me you are getting an interview with *the* Malcolm Parks."

"Yeah, well, he has spent most of the trip as my shadow."

"What can I say? You're a good honey trap." Her eyebrows knitted together when I pulled her inside. "Where are we going?"

"I wanted to get you alone." I stopped in front of a curved mahogany door.

We didn't have much time left in this arrangement—twelve hours, but who was counting?

I was going to go from seeing her nonstop to maybe a few times at the training facility. And I wasn't going to be able to touch her the way I had the last few days. I knew what this was and what it wasn't, but for now I wanted to enjoy *this* while I had it.

The castle was enormous, and it would take twenty minutes of hallways, corridors, and steps to get her in our bed, too much time wasted when we had so little left. So, I improvised and happened to see this wine cellar earlier when all the guests were filing through to get to the reception outside. It was a little hidden behind a stairwell.

I glanced back and Isa rolled her lower lip under her teeth. "Well, if you insist."

The door opened to a room filled from wall to wall with massive oak barrels, each with a wooden placard with the year written on it. They were all lined up next to one another, the only space a small set of paths between a few rows that met in the center of the room at an old wooden table.

With a firm hold on her hips, I maneuvered her to the table.

She sat down. This place was secluded and private and we could walk back out to the reception quickly before anyone noticed we were gone.

"Go ahead . . ." She grabbed either side of my suit jacket and pulled me in until my lips were a hair's distance from hers. The woody scent of barrels and the musk from the cellar wisped around us. "Take the lead."

The entire wedding party was filing out of here tomorrow. The weekend would be over soon, and for now I wanted to sink into how good she felt.

My heart raced and I pulled her into a kiss. She eagerly deepened it, running her nails through my hair along the scalp. Electricity shot down my back.

My hands moved up her thighs. I nudged her back slowly, and she rolled her hips against mine as I did, stoking my erection as I laid her down.

Laying slow kisses down her body, stopping at her breasts, I nudged her dress aside to leave a few languid strokes around her nipples. Her breathing shallowed.

"Austin," she whispered, her face already a little flushed. The space between us got hazy and thick.

I moved down her body, kiss by kiss, making my way between her thighs. My index finger looped around her panties and dragged them down her legs.

Tossing them to the side and parting her legs, I took a second to look at her. On her back with her legs spread for me, waiting for me.

Fuck. It was the sexiest thing I'd ever seen. I wanted to savor it.

I wanted to savor *her*. Every part of her. The soft moans she let out into our kisses, the tiny hitches her breath took when I slowly grazed my teeth against her neck, the electricity her nails sent down my spine when she grasped on to my back as she neared her climax.

I wanted to feel it all, slowly, and make it last forever.

She whimpered as I leaned back between her spread legs, and I tried to maintain some restraint. Her thighs glistened with her arousal; she was already so wet that it took every patient fiber of my being not to bury myself between her legs.

"Isa." I released a tortured groan. I leaned in and gently ran my teeth across her clit. "Fuck, you're wet."

Her hand curled into my hair. A few hitched breaths rewarded my patience.

Lapping my tongue over her clit again, more firmly with each stroke, her hips began to move in time with my mouth, begging for more friction. I sucked on it with more voracity alternating between that and hard presses with my tongue before her thighs began to tremble.

I flicked a glance up, and her chin tilted forward on a desperate whimper.

"Austin," she begged just as her legs jerked around me. I pulled away and pushed a finger inside of her, then another.

So tight and wet I could feel every pulse inside keenly. I stroked faster, using the heel of my palm to push and stroke her clit.

She bucked against me. A few unintelligible pants and pleas slipped through her mouth as the climax broke over her.

"Kiss me," she begged between breaths. The final waves of her orgasm undulated through her body.

I took a step back from her, just long enough to get my pants undone and the condom on.

I leaned in and kissed her again, slowly pushing myself into her at the same time. Inch by inch, she moaned into the kiss until I was completely inside of her. I didn't move, taking the moment to enjoy just how perfectly we fit together, like the ocean to the coast.

Her tight pussy teased me, goaded me to move faster, but I held back, keeping the sensuous pace.

My muscles, my jaw, my teeth all held taut with every ounce of control I could assemble. I lingered, leaning closer, gliding in and out, and took my time relishing the slick pulses around my cock.

Her mouth hung open slightly; her breaths taking a few more tiny hitches.

"*Baby*." Her back arched up from the table, a tiny cry broke through. I sank in even deeper. *Fuck*. "Harder."

My patience finally slipped. I couldn't hold back anymore; I needed it all.

Pushing into her faster and with more force, her breathy moans became louder and more frequent.

My fingerprints became bruises on her hips, gripping them tight while mine snapped back and forth, plunging deeper, chasing the high only she could give me.

Her eyes closed, her body became rigid, and I leaned back down to kiss her through her climax.

Her walls clamped against my dick, setting my own free. In a blinding flash, I came deep inside of her.

The fog began to clear, and Isa's eyes opened to meet mine. Her hands spanned either side of my face and as I began to pull away, she kept me there. Something flickered under the soft glow of the lantern lights. She held me there for another extended beat, looking at me differently. Without the bravado and sass, slightly wide eyes with an unsure smile.

We stayed tangled up in each other for another few seconds before finally pulling apart to put ourselves back together, and we made our way out of the cellar.

Taking a few steps forward along the stone hallway, she leaned into me, and I threw my arm around her shoulders, still basking in the warm afterglow.

"Blake." Isa stopped and took half a step back, when my palm stopped her.

"I was heading back to my room." Blake's jaw went tight as he stopped a few steps short of us. He pushed his fingers through his hair, and his eyes darted around before finally landing on Isa.

"We were just . . ." Isa's startled eyes looked up at me, begging for help.

My heart soared only to fall back down, because all the steps forward we'd made would be washed away in hours.

"Touring the wine cellar," I finished for her, running my thumb below my lower lip, where some of her lipstick had smudged, to get the point across. Although the wrinkles in Isa's dress were doing a pretty good job for me.

Isa looked straight ahead, past Blake, but I looked him dead in the eye. Because I didn't want him to guess about what we were doing in there.

I wanted him to know.

I had kissed her. I'd touched her. I'd made her moan.

"We should get back." Isa looked at me and we quickly brushed past him.

"You don't want to rub it in?" I asked, pulling her a little closer as we walked back out of the stone corridor.

"No," she said curtly, like the thrill had been pulled out of it. "I'm more concerned with enjoying the last bit of this vacation before I get thrown back into a crazy work schedule." She pulled me back toward the lawn with a devilish grin. "Let's not waste time thinking about him."

I smiled. She was right. Our deal came to a neat end soon, and I was going to spend the next few hours putting my hands all over her.

Chapter 28
AUSTIN

My first full day back in New York, I didn't know what to do with myself. I got a call from Jesse early this morning with good news on the coaching front, but all it did was make me want to move around.

So, I did what I'd been doing a lot the last couple years— seeing if there was anything Zoya needed.

She had her hands full with her demonstration kitchen in Park Slope. The storefront in Brooklyn was lined on one side with windows, and on a bright day, the sun filled the entire room and bounced off the stainless-steel fridges that spanned the back wall. She worked with a couple culinary schools and did private classes and events. Zoya also used the space for her catering business, which had been picking up steam over the last year.

"Two teams are interested?" Zoya slapped a proud hand on my back. "They grow up so fast."

My meetings with Farnham and Remy had gone well, and it took the pressure off Jesse at my management company since I was making strides to secure my future.

"Gee, thanks," I drawled, tapping my fingers against the dark counters.

We sat on stools next to each other in front of the largest countertop at the front of the room, usually where she'd demo before letting the groups go off to attempt recipes on their own.

This was exactly what Jesse wanted, and honestly, I was ready to move on. Move in a different direction. But the more I pictured it, the more I was sure it didn't involve me leaving the States again. I wanted to work on something that meant more to me than a next step. And that had become crystal clear in Paris.

"Speaking of, I was actually hoping to get your help with something."

Before Zoya owned and operated a demonstration kitchen and burgeoning catering service, she had run Theo's company. It was how they'd met.

She was the MBA behind the man with an incredibly successful tech start-up. When Theo got sick, it was right around the time of the IPO; they had made a very comfortable nest egg with that sale. And Zoya had decided to slow down, spend time with Theo while she had it, and when he was gone, she'd started doing something else she loved.

"Sure, but try this first." She handed me what looked like a pastry from across the counter.

I took a bite of the flaky crust, expecting it to be sweet.

I coughed and heat spread all along my mouth, pushing a few tears from the corners of my eyes. I covered my mouth with my hand as I chewed and looked up at Zoya. "Why do you need to throw chiles in everything?"

I coughed and happily accepted the water she handed me. "Too spicy?"

I winced. "A little."

I coughed again; it was like eating fire.

"I'll have someone else try it." She scrunched her nose and ran a towel over the counter one last time before taking a seat. "What do you need help with?"

"The foundation has new funding. But also, we might have capital investment, real capital. I think we have an avenue to create a youth league. Training faculty. With enough funding, it can be self-sufficient, maybe expand like Theo and I always hoped."

Wide eyes paused on me for a second before blinking a few times. Her mouth hung slightly open before it closed and she sat up straighter. Her face filled with all the questions she probably wasn't going to ask, because I'd seen that face before— every time Joseen would reach a new milestone and Zoya didn't want to overreact.

"Okay . . ." she said slowly, the excitement rising in her shoulders.

I'd never really taken the lead, but over the last couple weeks I had stopped feeling so lost. I had a direction, and it was an uphill climb, but so was my entire career and that had worked out. I chalked it up to luck, but maybe I had it in me to be more than just the athlete.

Or at the very least, try.

Whatever questions she had, she ignored. With a beaming smile, she looked up in thought. "How much capital are we talking?"

"Probably more than we need," I told her. Taking Xander Sutton up on his offer meant proposals and plans and math. All things I was terrible with. "But I might need some help."

"Lucky for you, my job is pretty flexible." She grinned. She took the pastry I couldn't eat and finished it off like it was made of nothing. Not a single reaction to what had felt like the fires of hell in each bite.

"They really *do* grow up so fast." She beamed proudly. Then she looked at me with an inquisitory smile.

"What?"

"Nothing." Her smile only got more suspicious looking, crooked on one end, and she looked like she was inspecting every single one of my features, hunting for something.

"You're looking at me like you look at Jo when she sneaks a cupcake before dinner."

"You're just . . ." She leaned back against the high-top chair's metal backing. "Different."

I rubbed the back of my neck. "I know where you're—"

"How was Paris?" With a flourish, she pulled herself forward and folded one hand on top of the other on the countertop. "You know, the wedding."

"Good," I answered curtly.

Her shoulders fell dramatically.

"So, you had that hot doctor in a hotel room for a week and nothing happened?" She wiped a hand down her face. "How are you a professional athlete with *zero* game?"

"It's not any of your business. Besides, I don't kiss and tell."

I tried not to smile but all the ways things had happened with Isa flashed through my mind.

"Oh, *please.*" With a dismissive flick of her hand and an eye roll, Zoya crossed her arms. "I remember you and Theo practically giggling on the phone when you had that penchant for dating models years ago."

"We weren't giggling," I snapped. "It was serious and manly."

"Fine, don't kiss and tell. But . . . that grin"—she pointed around my face—"leads me to believe you had sex, so . . ."

I winced. "Please stop."

"I'm not asking about *details.*" She recoiled. "I mean . . . tell me what you're going to do now. Are you going out?" Zoya slapped her hands on the counter and looked around the space as if it were brand-new and her mind was filling with ideas. "You should bring her here. The demonstration kitchen is a hit for—"

"She's busy. It was just a fling for the wedding." I stopped Zoya before she started picking out china patterns.

"So, you're not going on a date with her?" Zoya pressed. "Ever?"

"Well . . ." I rubbed the heels of my palms against my eyes, tired. "Instead of trying to live vicariously through me, *you* could go on date."

"*Or.*" She swung forward menacingly, sitting up straight to make her point. "You could stop being a little bitch and make some actual plans with her. You're practically beaming. I cannot believe she has nothing to do with it."

I wanted to see Isa and hadn't stopped thinking about her since we'd gotten back. But that was only a day ago. And I didn't want to be a thing on her long list of tasks. And, quite frankly, Isa was intimidating as hell. And sexy.

Funny. Beautiful.

I *wanted* to see her again. And regularly.

I pulled out my phone to text her. Just as I started, Zoya slapped it away.

"Oh my God." Her whole face contorted. "You're a grown-up. Call her. Or even better, you know where she occasionally works." She gestured her hands open in front of me like it was obvious. "Be cute. Or thoughtful or charming." She put both hands on her face and shook her head. "Zero game."

I was sure something real with me wasn't in Isa's plans. But plans changed. Hell, over the last few weeks more had changed in my vision of the future than in the last decade.

Excitement filled me.

It didn't have to become anything, but it didn't mean I couldn't try. Blake let himself lose her, and I knew not to be so stupid as to let someone like her go.

Chapter 29
AUSTIN

Zoya was right.

And while I thought accosting Isa somewhere in some bid to be romantic was a terrible idea, I *did* know she came to the Lightning training facility every Thursday evening. So, that week, I decided to hang around awhile.

"We could have done this tomorrow." Trevor handed me my bottle of water, and we walked off the training mat to the exam equipment. He looked up at the clock; it was nearly seven in the evening. Usually, only staff were here this late in the off-season. "You didn't have to stay this late."

But then I'd miss Isa. I looked over his shoulder to the open door and empty hallway, hoping she'd be here. "I don't mind."

"Well, your mobility looks good." Trevor looked at some of the readings from the dynamometer, a device used to measure different forces along the muscles. "And I can run these results by Dr. Reinhold, but you're probably on track to play in a few weeks, once he clears you."

I smiled. Now that I had been back from France for a few days and I'd given my knees *some* rest, I was anxious to get back to training. If this was going to be my last season, I wanted to make it a good one.

One I was proud of.

"Great." I heard a few footsteps down the hall, my heart raced, and I was thankful I wasn't on any of the heart rate monitoring equipment.

A few more steps and the person I was waiting for walked in, her attention flickering around the hallways before finally looking inside.

Her eyes landed on me, and her lips pushed up against her cheeks in the most adorable grin. Her trademark mint-green scrubs, the New York Lightning zip-up on, and her hair in a neat bun. A jolt of excitement ran up my body.

"Dr. Mercado," I greeted her, and this time a slight shade of red ran across her face.

"Hi," Isa said nonchalantly, but her eyes lingered on mine for a moment. She walked in and went straight to one of the computers. She cleared her throat and started on her work like nothing had changed from the last time I saw her in here. "Don't mind me, I'm just going to draft some of the findings for the research report."

Her eyes locked on the screen; I could see her lips quake as they tried to remain straight and serious.

It had only been a few days, but I missed her.

"I thought your research report was mostly done," Trevor asked.

"It is . . . I wanted to . . ." Isa stammered, the cool casualness breaking for a second. "I was going to look into some of the data we had from the college team. You know, for good measure."

"No rest for the wicked?" Trevor flipped through a file and gave me the okay to get up. I was free to get going as he packed up a few of his things and prepared to leave himself.

"Apparently not," I added.

He looked between us speculatively.

"Well, I have to go, but there should be some staff around for the next couple hours if you need anything," he said to Isa.

I waited until he was out of earshot and out of view, far down the hallway and around the turn he'd need to make to leave, before I talked to Isa. "You came here for research . . ."

"Mm-hmm. As discussed, I enjoy the work." Isa's eyes stayed on the screen. "The team allows a few college programs to use the training facilities. Some of the college athletes agreed to use some of the de-identified recovery stats."

"Oh yeah?" I nodded and crossed the room to stand right next to where she sat.

"Yeah." She looked up at me for a second. Air filled her lungs like she was just *waiting* to tell someone about it.

There was a way her body stilled with focus, but her eyes came alive when she read something that excited her. Or when she explained it. She may have had her hopes pinned on that fancy research fellowship, but she practically glowed when she was here.

"In younger athletes, we're more likely to go in with a surgical repair first because they recover well, as opposed to . . ."

"Older ones?" I leaned down and looked at the screen like I understood anything she was reading on it.

She glanced over her shoulder to where I was crowding her, but she didn't seem to mind. She didn't move a muscle.

"The older ones require more . . . finesse. Operatively, I mean," she added with a hard swallow that shifted down her throat. "So . . . you're here late."

I braced each arm around her now, keeping her locked between them. That close, every memory with her flashed in my mind. I let out an exhausted breath. I wanted to take her home, but more than that I wanted to take her out. On a real date. I wanted this thing to be real. "I wanted to see you."

A blush ran along her cheeks. I was realizing pretty quickly if I wanted to startle her, all I had to do was be direct. "Is it because you have a little crush me?"

"Yes," I answered definitively. I wasn't giving her any cutesy ways out. "I want to take you on a date. A real one."

Her frame tightened for a moment. Her eyes flickered around. My pulse hiked up. But then she turned and her gaze met mine, and finally, her expression stilled, becoming serious.

"Okay . . ." she said with all the confidence of someone standing at the edge of an open plane door being coaxed into skydiving.

But while her voice needed some steadying, her eyes were balanced. And honestly, a part of me was expecting a much more scattered reaction. I smiled. "Great, how about this weekend?"

"Sure." The word was heavy as it sank down my body, pushing excitement up in its wake. She glanced up at the time and pushed her chair back. I gave her some room to stand. "We can hang out tonight, too. I have the de-identified data, so I can do this from anywhere now."

She pulled the portable drive out of the computer and tucked it in her bag, then closed the tiny space between us.

"Hang out?" I was a little disappointed that after I mentioned a date, her mind went right to a hookup.

"It's what us young people call—"

"I know what you mean." I yanked her close, running my palms over the rough fabric of her scrubs. I could see what she was doing, pushing this back to what it was at the wedding, a fling or friends with benefits or whatever she was thinking. But I didn't want to be her friend. And I had a feeling the only way to make Isa believe something was to show her it could happen. So, I would. "I want more."

She nodded; this time her eyes and voice were steady. "I have an early morning, that's all, so I can't go out on a real date *tonight*. But we can stay in . . ."

Suddenly on defense, a jitter ran up my spine. "Fine. But you still owe me that date this weekend."

"I already agreed. We have plans this weekend." She put her hands up innocently. "A *real* date." She smiled cheekily. "I know how to do that, promise. And you're not exactly being subtle."

"Maybe it's because you're a difficult woman to pin down, Isabelle."

A spark lit in her eyes. She leaned in and whispered against my lips. "Let's go back to your place and I promise I won't make it difficult for you to pin me down."

* * *

A drought of not seeing—or touching—her ended the second we got back to my place. With our dinner out on the kitchen counter and our clothes somewhere out in the living room and probably the hallway, we lay there, covered in a thin layer of sweat.

"So, you know about the Blake of it all." Isa lay with her back against my chest. She took my hand that gently stroked her hip and weaved her fingers into mine. "Who's your Blake?"

"Don't say his name when you're in bed with me," I warned in her ear.

She rolled her hips against me. "Don't dodge the question."

I didn't have a Blake and I really wanted to stop talking about him. Mostly because she said it with a casualness like I was a buddy that she happened to be sleeping with. Not the guy she was dating, and I wanted to be that guy.

"Well, at first, I did the thing most pro athletes do when they go pro." I answered her question without actually answering it.

"Whored around?" She lifted her head up to look at me with a mischievous grin.

I cleared my throat, not expecting her bluntness even though that's what I'd become so familiar with when it came to Isa. "Yeah."

"Respect." She looked back up at the ceiling. "Everyone needs a ho phase."

"Yeah well, after that, life became . . ." I went home and I felt like I had to put all the energy I used to put into serving my own interests into something else. "Different."

"What do you mean?"

"Theo got sick," I said curtly. I tried to be around more when he first got sick—it was when Joseen was only a year old.

Isa didn't say anything, but she looked at me with a soft curve along her lips, encouraging me to keep going.

"He was the reason I didn't fall through the cracks. With everything from home life to struggling in school," I admitted. I didn't talk about it much, not because I was ashamed of my past but more because I was a little ashamed of not being around more. When I left, I was kid—eighteen—and suddenly went from dirt poor to a million-dollar contract and attention from all angles. I spent too long entrenched in it. "But when nobody cared, Theo refused to let anyone forget about me. It didn't sink in that I wasn't spending enough time here until it was too late."

When he got sick, I came back every chance I got.

Isa was stoic, stone-faced. Probably good for a surgeon given they had to deliver the type of news I was sure she'd broken over the years. She swallowed hard, her jaw set tight, serious.

"And you feel guilty," she said softly, almost in a whisper. She turned around and snaked an arm around my neck. Pulling forward, she pressed a light kiss on my cheek.

It was sweet. Intimate.

And she was right. I did feel a little guilty—always did when I talked about him with anyone else. But with Isa, it was easy.

"A little." I cleared my throat.

She was still naked in my bed, and this conversation became *heavy*. A type of heavy Isa usually steered back to light, but she hadn't at all, and despite the knee-jerk desire to change the subject, I liked that she knew this part of me. I pulled my arm around her waist and kept her chest flush against mine.

"Is that why you act like you *aren't* a famous athlete?" she asked.

"I don't do that."

"You *definitely* do."

"A part of me hated that while he had always been there for me, I was an ocean away for so long," I confessed for the first time out loud. I didn't come back and spend much time in the States until I was well into my career. I thought back to all that time I'd lost with my best friend and what I traded it for. "And *formerly* famous is probably more accurate."

The idea for the soccer schools was Theo's. Equal parts best friend and investing genius, Theo knew an open market. Creating a way to keep talent in the States would have meant me staying here if it had happened years ago. Since it hadn't, he made a way so it *could*.

She looked up, opened her mouth like she was going to ask more, but she stopped. She turned around, grabbed a clean jersey folded on my nightstand, and pulled it over her head.

"Well, I'm glad someone understands what it feels like to be the friend that's a success but also kind of a mess."

"I never said I was a mess. Just a little lost for a while," I said, glancing over to the nightstand when my phone buzzed on it. "I always had one vision for the future."

"I get that." She nodded, running her fingers through my hair. Her nails sent tiny sparks along my scalp. "Have you considered being a professional wedding date? Because I had a great time."

With that, the heaviness was chased away. I liked her like this, relaxed and a little silly. It was a stark contrast to how she was out in the world. An intimate look I wanted to hoard all for myself.

"I'm choosing to take that as a compliment," I said lowly in her ear as a warning.

Chapter 30
ISABELLE

A few days after seeing Austin at the training facility, I woke up feeling like death.

My heart sank; we had plans today. The weekend date we had agreed on.

The one I'd been looking forward to despite being a little nervous about going from fling to actual dating. But with Austin, it felt like an easy transition.

I rocked forward on my living room couch, where I'd landed after getting up for exactly ten minutes before my muscles dragged me down like sandbags. I grabbed my phone and sent the text I didn't want to have to send to Austin.

> ME: I can't see you today

> ME: I'm definitely sick

I sighed and dropped my phone somewhere on the couch and tried to keep warm under the rolling shudders. Today was supposed to be a day-date at the farmers market and other cutesy things.

I dragged my weighted blanket onto the couch as another wave of icy shivers hit me. It wouldn't be long till it was on the floor. Because I'd spent most of last night and this morning in a cycle of blistering sweats followed by debilitating chills.

Wrapped up in warmth, I looked around at my sparse apartment and my eyes started to close again.

I was always pretty good at being alone because I could wait it out. As a teenager—when I had a private tutor teaching me all the material I'd learn in school the next year while my friends were at summer camp—I waited for the summer to end and, like clockwork, I was happy again when my friends reconvened at school in the fall.

As I got older and the waits became longer as my friend group thinned out because not much survived my schedule, I could always count on Selena to show up and fill the quiet.

Alone and sick was always the worst to wait through. But I refused to call Selena and get her sick; besides, she was still on her honeymoon.

My eyes closed and, in the warm sunlight, I fell asleep.

Hours later, a loud knock at the door woke me.

The afternoon light was overhead. I'd been asleep all morning. Did I end up ordering that soup for delivery? In my feverish delirium, I wasn't sure.

"Isa. It's Austin." His voice, heavy and low, rolled over me.

I sat up.

"Coming," I shouted against a sandpaper throat.

Knowing he was there was like a shot of epinephrine. My

sluggish body stood and took the heavy blanket, wrapped it around me, and walked to the door. Hoping the stimulants in the decongestants I'd taken did something to make me look less like a zombie, I ran my hand through my hair, then pulled the door open.

His eyes ran over me once.

"You're sick," he said out loud, like his assessment confirmed something for him.

I guessed the decongestants did nothing to cure sick-face. "What are you doing here?"

"You're sick," he repeated, brushing past me with whatever was in his canvas grocery bags. I closed the door behind him and followed as he began to make himself busy at my kitchen counter.

He pulled out two large containers with what looked like soup.

My heart's unsteady rhythm became more erratic. "You made me soup?"

"*Technically*, I'm injured and it's the offseason," he explained, pulling the lid off one container and then opening and closing a few cabinets until he found a bowl. "I had some time."

"You didn't have to do that."

I wasn't expecting anything from him because I knew I couldn't return much in the way of time spent. This wasn't like the trip abroad at a decadent wedding. Here, in reality, that attraction wouldn't survive my schedule. It never had before.

"Well, I knew you weren't going to *ask* for help," he drawled.

I tried to steady myself enough to take a seat on one of the barstools, telling myself that I'd lean against the back of it to keep from falling over. "I don't need help."

I was *planning* to order soup . . . until I passed out for four hours.

He looked around the sparse fridge, my apartment, and finally at me—a shivering mess wrapped in a weighted blanket.

"I know," he said. He stopped pouring the soup in a bowl.

Without another word, he put his arm around my waist and assisted me back to the couch, pulled the coffee table closer, and placed my legs on it. My shoulders relaxed and I leaned into the couch.

I gave him a silent smile, and he nodded.

He was giving me the dignity of not making it obvious that I could use someone here, and I tried not to revel in the feeling—knowing it wasn't going to be permanent, not for me.

I didn't need a partner to help me. But the warmth that fluttered in my chest reminded me it was nice to have someone who did anyway.

"I don't want to get you sick," I told him as he finished getting a bowl of soup for me and grabbing a spoon.

This was nice but this wasn't casual territory. This was best friend territory, or relationship territory. *Real* relationship territory.

He chuckled and walked back over to the couch. Dropping a fluffy, beat-up old throw pillow on my lap first, he then handed me the soup. "I'm not leaving. And it's not like I can even play until I get cleared to by my . . ." His voice swung up playfully and he look at me with eyebrows raised.

"*I'm* not your doctor."

The steam rising from the bowl wafted with the scent of herbs; it eased my congested nose as I breathed it in. And a long, languid sip ran over my inflamed throat, soothing it. The warmth sank into my bones, and so did the sentiment.

I let out a sigh and took a few more slow sips and slurps of soup. It was so good.

"So, it's settled," he whispered, and flicked on the TV but kept the volume so low I wondered if he could even hear it. It was set to operative videos of knee repairs. He was right—I loved sports medicine. It was interesting to see it, learn it, perfect repairs, and then see the results.

We sat there like that, quietly. He mostly winced and looked away from the screen.

My appetite was essentially gone, but I managed to finish most of the bowl. I guessed I was hungry and did, sort of, need help.

"Thank you," I whispered.

He nodded, running his arm around my shoulders. His eyes searched my face and concern softened lines around his mouth. "Can you take some time off if you're feeling this beat?"

I groaned. "That's not really how it works."

I just got back from two weeks off, and that almost never happened in residency. The only reason I was able to line up two weeks back to back was because I hadn't taken a single day off in almost a year.

While technically, per the national residency accreditation standards, I had a few days off left for the year, it wasn't like taking them was something you did unless you were deathly ill.

"When I was a junior, one of my seniors had a crazy high fever; he looked like death but still took call for seven hours." I repeated back the toxic cycle we were trying to break as a profession, but that didn't mean much when I was up against an institution riddled with subconscious discriminatory beliefs. "He still finished his call shift, signed out, then moseyed over to the ER to have his appendix removed before it burst."

I knew how that sounded, and I was pretty sure all I had was a case of RSV or something. But I was a woman in surgery—any extra time I happened to take would always be tinged with the idea that this was too much to handle. That I was weak. It didn't help when there were stories like that one repeated with reverence by your attendings.

"And that's a story about what you *should* do?" he asked, confused. "If you look like this tomorrow, I'm taking you to the ER."

I huffed a sigh, too tired and too weak to go through all the ways residency and fellowship weren't fair. It wasn't like other jobs, and every time I tried to explain it to someone who didn't go through it themselves or see someone they love do it all, they didn't understand.

That made Austin's kindness all the more painful. He was trying to be there for me, but he'd get sick of it soon enough.

"Can we talk about something else?" I leaned my head onto his shoulder, the warmth from the soup beginning to weigh heavy on my eyelids. "Did you hear from the teams?"

"Yeah, actually." He shifted a bit. "I may be in a position to choose."

My body felt heavier than before. That meant he was planning to go back abroad. Even though that was exactly what

I was expecting to hear from the question, it still felt like a surprise.

"That's great." The words propelled out of me. It *was* great, the next logical step. "So, which do you want: Paris or London?"

"I was actually thinking maybe something else."

I turned my head up to meet his eyes. "Yeah?"

My body eased into his.

"Now that there's more attention on the foundation . . ." He waffled over his words and looked ahead. "I was working to get some real capital behind the football academy idea. Well, I guess we'd call it a soccer academy. But yeah . . ."

I smiled. When we left France, it seemed like it was something he'd work on in the background, not that he'd throw himself into it. I wondered what prompted the change.

"Paris gave me a little perspective," he admitted.

My pulse fluttered. The muscle aches felt a little less intense. Maybe it was the tachycardia secondary to viral-illness-induced hypotension.

Or maybe it was because I liked the idea of having him around. I liked making plans with him and the way he helped me think about things other than work.

My heart beat a little faster. Because *maybe* I was getting a little attached to that feeling. I couldn't help the tiny cloud of fear that bubbled up at that realization, warning me the warmth blossoming in my chest would be painful to lose.

But I was tired, and I didn't feel like chasing the happiness away just yet.

"I guess your little crush led to something good," I answered, feeling a little delirious.

His chest rumbled with a laugh, and it chased away the momentary concern.

My eyes began to feel heavy again. The soft and hypnotic feel of his thumb moving up and down my arm slowly lulled me to sleep.

Chapter 31
ISABELLE

$\mathcal{A}$ few days after pushing through work while sick, I was recovering. I felt like myself again.

In the trauma bay, a nurse hung an IV bag filled with a vasopressor—a medication that would keep the patient's blood pressure stable and heart perfusing blood for the short term, and the victim of a side-collision car accident stabilized so we could get him to surgery.

"We can take him back now. Can you call the OR?" I asked the trauma nurse and felt a few vibrations from my personal phone in my back pocket.

The nurse nodded and I checked my phone.

An email came in.

Winthrop Reconstructive Surgery Fellowship Admission Committee: Interview Invitation

I scrolled down and read the invitation three times.

My guiding light was as bright as ever. The goal I was running toward was back in clear view. This invitation was the assurance I was on the right path.

Relief moved down my body.

Everything was perfect. I was seeing Austin later for dinner. We were going out and it was all I could think about. Maybe this was what it felt like to *have it all*.

I tucked my phone back in my pocket and went back to the workstation on wheels that was specifically designated for the trauma bay. I typed up a quick note as the nurses and transport began taking the patient to the OR.

The next three hours blended together as my brain went straight into autopilot. It was a kind of peace, in the cold OR under the hot lights, where I found balance.

When the case was complete, I walked out of the OR like waking up from a trance. The rest of the world bled back into full color for the first time in hours. I swiped my badge against the access pad and walked through the double doors toward the residents' room next to the OR.

I leaned against the doorframe and happened to catch Ami on the computer, meaning she'd already checked on all our patients and was writing notes.

"How's the list looking?" I asked.

"Fine." She shrugged. "Nothing new, a few scheduled admissions. That'll probably pick up soon when all the college kids filter their way back into the city."

Traumas always picked up around the time the universities in the city resumed classes.

"Great." Today was shaping up to be perfect. "I'm actually going to head out soon."

It was early in the evening. I wasn't on call, and the floor was handled.

"Are you going to the visiting-professor lecture tonight?" Ami asked, not looking away from the screen.

"Actually, no." I smiled. I knew I probably should schmooze, but tonight I didn't want to.

The longer the day dragged on, the more excited I was to see Austin. And the more I was sure I'd rather see him than endure a long dinner with octogenarian surgeons, even if it was "good for networking."

I was *going* on that date. Not a steamy hookup and not me on the precipice of death with a particularly nasty case of RSV.

A real date.

Anxiety and excitement filled me in equal measure, because Austin was making me want things I hadn't expected. Like forgoing a night of networking to go on a date. Now that my interview was securely in hand, I figured I could take a beat to be with the guy I *wanted* to see. It felt like I couldn't possibly be knocked offtrack.

"I have dinner plans."

Ami's eyebrows shot up and she looked at me. Her face lit up with a thousand questions, but I wasn't ready to grin and squeal about my date just yet. She was probably equally surprised I was missing the lecture since Charles Winthrop would be there, but I was tired. I had six years of nonstop work under my belt; I was allowed to skip this.

"Have fun," she said with a short, coy smile.

"I plan to." I grinned and turned on my heels toward the elevators.

Just as I pushed the down button, a few texts came in.

> **AUSTIN:** Hey, can't make tonight, something came up. It's a long story.

> **AUSTIN:** I know you probably won't get this till later, but come over instead?

An *actual* date cut down into something else. I didn't expect to feel as winded as I did.

Disappointment curled in my stomach. I tried not to let it because this was the sort of thing I did to dates. I had to reschedule. Or minimize them down to just a quick night together because I didn't have time.

So why did it bother me?

Maybe because I didn't want to reschedule with him. And he made me *want* to be available.

I tried to reclaim the high I'd been floating on earlier. I'd gotten the interview invitation I'd been waiting for.

I took a deep breath as the elevator doors opened.

Maybe this was just a sign that my focus was never wrong to stay where it always had, on building my career. Everything else . . . it was just something nice to have, but not worth compromising over.

Chapter 32
AUSTIN

I checked my phone as I opened the door to my midtown condo. I held it open, letting Joseen scurry in, then closing it behind us. I checked my phone so many times during the trip to the market, Joseen had asked about it, so I tried to hide it better.

Zoya, who seemed very committed to making me go out on a limb with Isa, was making it pretty hard to do it. She had a last-minute opportunity that I couldn't let her skip, so I had to make some changes to the date I'd planned for Isa.

Hopefully, she didn't mind a plus-one tonight. But Isa hadn't responded, so I was beginning to think she did.

"I love your house, Uncle Austin," Joseen yelled. She put the flowers she carried on the leather seat of one of the barstools that sat in front of the countertop and ran toward a kids' bike I kept for when I watched her.

I'd had this place since I got my first big signing bonus. I did the thing every financial advisor tells you not to do when you sign your first big contract—I made a large purchase. Luckily a lot more lucrative contracts came my way and buying real estate in Manhattan ten years ago ended up being a pretty solid financial decision.

"Please don't ride that in here," I said firmly, putting my bags on the counter of the industrial-style kitchen: stainless steel appliances, large exposed metal beams overhead. There were a few cabinets along the exposed brick wall but mostly floating shelves.

I looked up from under the tin lantern pendant lights and Joseen was gone. So was the bike.

"Jo," I called sternly through the house as I started pulling all the vegetables out of the bags.

"What?" she yelled from down the hallway. I heard the pedals as she turned and made her way back.

My house didn't have a lot of rules, outside of not getting injured. It was the only line I drew, and Jo didn't just cross it, she jumped rope with it.

Every time she was here, she found a new way to potentially maim herself.

"Jo." The mental exhaustion started to bleed into my words. "Come on. Help me make all of this."

She ran back into the kitchen, ditching the bike somewhere for me to trip on later. "What are we making again?"

Joseen climbed up the little tower I'd bought for her so she could reach the countertop.

"It's written right here." I pointed to the top of the recipe I had on my phone, zooming in on the word PAELLA in large letters.

Jo loved to help out in the kitchen, and when she stayed with me—usually when something came up for Zoya—I turned it into something we could do together that kept her safely in one piece.

And the paella . . .

"Pa . . ." Joseen ran her finger along the screen,. She smiled when I nodded and kept going. "Eee . . . la."

I leaned down. "You got it, keep going."

She squinted. "Pa-e-la?"

"It's a hard one. You did a good job." I congratulated her with a high five and handed her a giant bag of rice. I reveled in the fact that I might be able to teach her something. "Two scoops, into this bowl."

She nodded while I started unpacking the rest of the groceries.

"I'm not good at reading." Her shoulders slumped.

"Yes, you are," I promised her. Joseen was smart, like her parents. She'd started putting words together at three and could cobble together sentences now. "It'll get easier, I promise. Soon you'll be helping me."

It wasn't too long after, when everything was washed and ready to prep, when a knock came at the door. I'd become so focused on keeping Jo in one piece and getting things settled here, I hadn't obsessively checked my phone like a lovesick teenager.

I walked down the hall and opened the door, knowing it was probably her but still surprised with confirmation.

In a bright lilac sundress that skated around her knees with her hair down in tight curls that bounced along her back, she stole the breath I was about to take just as easily as she did in those mint-green scrubs.

"Isa." I didn't realize I whispered it until her shoulders lifted with what seemed like excitement.

"Sorry, I texted but . . ."

"Hi!" Joseen appeared from out of nowhere, suddenly at my side and staring up at Isa. The quiet delight that wrapped around us at the threshold was replaced by loud curiosity. "I'm Joseen. You're tall."

Wide-eyed and bewildered, Isa looked at me, then at Joseen.

It was actually kind of cute. Isa's eyes searched for something and her mouth hung open with words she couldn't find. Was she nervous?

"I'm Isa, and you're a little short." Isa's features immediately went from soft to tight with panic. "I mean . . ." Isa stammered. She looked at me apologetically. "I didn't mean—"

Joseen only grinned wider.

"I'm actually the tallest in my class . . ." Joseen spun on her heels and skipped down the hallway. "C'mon. We're cooking!"

I glanced back at Isa, who walked in and followed a few steps behind Jo. She smiled.

A whirlwind kicked up in my chest.

$\mathcal{T}$he scent of garlic and saffron filled my lungs as I walked into Austin's entryway.

Austin closed the door behind us. Joseen, with dark black hair pulled up in a ponytail and large dark eyes, stared up at me with a toothy smile.

"I was going to call," Austin explained, trailing a few steps behind us. "But I figured you were in a surgery or working."

"Oh," I answered him, trying to keep up with whatever Joseen was saying at a mile a minute.

"Her mom got a really big opportunity this weekend, so she's out of town," he went on. "With the catering thing."

I turned to him once we got to the kitchen and his weight shifted between his legs.

"I get it."

"We were just making dinner." Austin put his hands on my waist as he moved between me and Joseen to grab a few bags out of the way. "Right, Jo?"

"Mm-hmm." She nodded exuberantly. "We're making pa . . ."

She looked up at him for help.

"Paella," he finished for her, looking at me with a boyish smile.

My heart took such a giant leap that it left my lungs empty.

Spending time with his goddaughter, having dinner with her, *making* a dinner that he knew I wanted to eventually get to. I swallowed against a tightness in my throat. This was so sweet, and I wanted to keep my guard up, but it was impossible when he was so good at pulling it down.

"Creative," I teased. Walking along the line of the kitchen island, I looked out the large windows to the view of the Lower Manhattan skyline. Strewn along the countertop were neatly placed bowls, then one with rice that had a bunch spilled over it. "How'd you think of it?"

"I had most of the ingredients and—"

"We went to the store!" Joseen interrupted and grabbed my hand. "I'll show you."

I looked over my shoulder, and Austin rubbed the back of his neck. "Yeah, that, too."

Joseen stopped at a barstool and handed me a bouquet of flowers. I looked up to Austin, who was becoming the cutest shade of red. "These, too?"

"Mm-hmm," Joseen confirmed in a high-pitched affirmation.

I busied myself with getting a vase and water to put the roses in. He'd bought me flowers and it wasn't a far cry to think he would, considering he'd made me soup last week. And now I was starting to get used to that. Him being the kind of guy who was easy to lean on.

There was this fleeting moment when my nerves kicked up, but his smile laid them neatly back down.

"You're the doctor," Joseen stated plainly like she was putting me in her head under a specific category.

"She's a surgeon, actually," Austin answered.

Joseen's eyes went wide. "Wow."

I laughed to myself at the fact that I was standing next to a professional athlete, and she was taken with me—deservedly so—but still, most regular jobs didn't hold up in a child's imagination like a famous athlete.

I loved *that*. A little girl's eyes lighting up knowing that she could be one, too. I was one of a few female surgeons because not enough little girls got to see women in that position living happy and fulfilling lives.

There was a lot that got lost in a life so heavily tied to a career like surgery, but none of it ever cracked my resolve to keep going. Blake may have gotten close, but I stayed undeterred, because I couldn't break or falter, not when seeing Joseen's eyes light up was more rewarding than all the institutional validation I had hanging on the walls in my apartment.

"Wanna learn how to stitch up a wound?" I glanced around the counter and took one of the tomatoes and a peach from the fruit bowl.

I loved that Austin's place always had groceries and a fridge filled with food that hadn't expired. It was a level of having your "non-work-related shit" together that I hoped I'd have one day. Once my life slowed down enough to pay attention to other things.

A million-watt smile stretched across Joseen's face. Her eyebrows shot up and she nodded vivaciously. "Yes!"

I rounded the counter to my purse, then pulled out the emergency suture kit I carried around and never actually used. All the sterile supplies had probably expired by now, so why not use it as a demonstration kit?

Joseen climbed down the kitchen tower that allowed her to stand at countertop height and sat next to me on a barstool at the kitchen island.

"So, nobody is helping me?" Austin looked at us with his hands out expectantly.

We both looked up at him and answered, "No."

* * *

Everything about the last three hours felt comfortable even though I was exhausted from a full day of work and then hanging around a five-year-old—it was . . . fun.

Domestic.

A type of domestic I never really let myself think about, mostly because I didn't know how it could possibly fit with my life, so I kicked the idea down the road.

Future Isa could deal with that. Present-day Isa had enough on her plate.

After dinner, Joseen was pretty entertained with practicing stitches until we ran out of tomatoes and peaches. Then she jumped around here like an acrobat until about an hour ago, when she fell asleep.

"I got that interview, the Winthrop one," I told Austin as I collapsed onto the couch next to him.

His body tightened for a second. Silence stretched over us before he said, "I'm not surprised." His hand was stretched along the back of the couch. I leaned into his chest and took a deep sigh. "Congratulations, Isa."

He didn't make a display like Selena would have. Jumping up and down, squealing, the whole thing. But the deep and soft way his words bounced around between my ribs gave me the same feeling.

I craned my head to look back at him. "Thank you."

Austin nodded, reached forward to the coffee table, and handed me a glass of wine he'd poured after Joseen went to sleep.

The flirtatious banter, the kind that kept me mentally and emotionally on my toes, was fun. It was what drew me to him. But it was the quiet moments we had together that I liked the most. I could sit with him and just *be*.

Another silence dropped over us. When I looked up at him, he seemed a little lost in thought. I let it be. "So . . . paella?"

"Someone gave me the idea in Paris. Figured I had the time," he answered casually.

"Oh, is that all?"

His arm moved from the back of the couch to snake around my waist. He leaned his mouth to my ear and whispered, "You know it's not."

My thigh involuntarily clenched at the heat of his breath as it sent electricity down my body.

My mind pushed past the ways I was planning to end tonight

since there was a child in the vicinity. I shifted a bit against his chest again, enjoying how big his body was. It could wrap around me on command.

"You have this full life outside of what everyone knows you for," I stated, mostly to myself, a couple minutes later.

"Yeah, I do." He looked down at me curiously.

I was a little envious. If anyone were to come by my apartment on any given day, the only sign it was currently being occupied might be an occasional dish in the sink.

I was more than my work. I knew that, but it was hard to see sometimes. It became glaringly evident I didn't have much of a life outside of work when I saw other people's.

"It wasn't built overnight, you know," he told me, his head bobbing down to meet my eyes. His tone softened from speculative to encouraging. "Dreams don't just come true. Sacrifices are always going to be made; it's the way of things."

I hated that he was probably right. Sacrifices had to be made, but I was trying my best to avoid that. And with dating him, I hadn't thought about it since things were so new.

His eyes on mine felt heavy, too heavy. I looked away.

"Was it worth it?"

"I remember being where you are. Giving up a lot for the thing I wanted most, wondering if it was worth it. But I try not to think that way anymore." He ran his fingers up and down my shoulder. "I got to play a game I love. Make something of myself. And now . . ." He looked out the windows at the city below, then back to me. "Something new, I guess."

"What changed your mind?" I asked, shifting a bit so my

legs were curled beneath me and I was facing him. "About the foundation? In Paris it seemed like you were just trying to get it stable enough to continue on its own."

He gave me a look like I knew the answer. When I didn't say anything, he took my glass of wine and placed it on the coffee table with his.

Instead of answering my question, he leaned forward, spread both hands along either side of my waist, and his lips met mine in a sweet, unhurried kiss. Instead of overthinking what that meant, I rocked into him and enjoyed how good it all felt. He had a way of doing that, keeping me in the present instead of running down my mental list of implications.

His fingers laced around the base of my neck and into my hair as I opened my mouth and he deepened the kiss.

Moving slowly, he leaned in, and I began to fall back against the couch, only breaking the kiss for a short second. Before I knew it, he was on top of me.

His lips recaptured mine, this time hungrier. A groan rumbled up his throat as he slowly pushed my legs apart and kept his body flush against mine between them.

"Offsides," I whispered, spreading my hand wide on his shirt. I pointed in the direction of the guest bedroom. Lines arched on his forehead questioningly. "There is a small child in the next room."

Down one hallway was the primary suite, which was the only part of his place I knew. The hallway on the other side of the living room had been a mystery to me. And now I knew why. It seemed like Joseen had rein over all of that.

"After how she ran around here for the last three hours, she's definitely asleep." He leaned back in, but I pushed him a little firmer this time.

"I'm not taking that risk."

He groaned playfully. "Do you think every set of parents stops kissing in their own house because kids are around?"

Something about that statement sucked all the heat out from the room.

"I don't know, and I don't plan to find out," I blurted, pushing him back until he was far enough away that I could sit up on the couch.

With Blake, maybe I would have been happy, but I would have probably had to make some concessions in my career—like my mom. I'd managed to avoid that.

"Oh." His brow wrinkled. "Okay."

"I mean. I'm not sure. I still have the fellowship and . . ." I added, realizing how sharp that sounded. My mind raced with more anxiety-inducing questions. He probably wanted kids. He was practically oozing dad energy with Joseen earlier. I was only nearing thirty, but he was thirty-seven and he probably wanted a family of his own soon. That fact, the one I sort of avoided these last couple weeks, glared right through me. "It's going to take up all my time. There are conferences, medical missions, international surgical collaborative workshops."

I didn't know if I wanted kids; it always felt like something I'd decide later. I tried to remain apathetic to it. And now I was beginning to realize that apathy was protection—for the day I didn't get something I admitted I wanted.

So, I *couldn't* want all of those things, because I may not get them. And that felt worse.

"Isa—"

"And even in the downtime, I'll be working and operating a ton. If I plan to pioneer techniques, I have to master them first."

"Isa." He put his hands on my shoulders, cutting off the spiraling thoughts. "I really didn't mean anything by it."

Maybe not, but the truth still hung over me. A family was a perfectly normal thing to want.

I nodded, but like a big wave at the beach, the realization knocked me off-balance. He was staying in New York and he seemed happy about it. But was that for me? It couldn't be. We hardly knew each other, and I *couldn't* reciprocate that kind of sacrifice.

"I don't want to disrupt *your* plans," I choked out.

I cared about him, and now an ache pulled at my heart because I knew what it felt like to be asked to give up something for a relationship. I couldn't ask him to do that. And how the hell could *I* live up to him giving up kids and coaching in an international league? I was barely around as it was.

This perfect night went upside down.

"Isa." Austin waved his hand in front of my face. "You're not disrupting anything. I'm sorry I brought it up."

"Yeah." I blinked a few times and tried not to think about it. "Sorry, I didn't mean to . . ."

"I'll keep my hands to myself tonight," he whispered, putting them up in the air innocently, trying to pull the conversation back from the cliff it was headed down. "Promise."

I smiled and forced a small laugh. I didn't want this to end, so for now I was going to ignore a truth I wasn't ready to face.

I leaned forward, picked up my glass, and took a giant gulp of wine.

"Can we go to bed a little early?" Every part of my body screamed to run, but I didn't want to hide from him. I didn't want to freak out, even if I *was* freaking out a little. Because for the first time, *having it all* felt like it was still within reach. I had the interview, I had a great guy, and getting this close to perfect was scary. If I could shut off the little voice in my head telling me I had to choose, maybe it would all work out. "I'm exhausted. I think I just need some sleep."

He pressed a kiss on my forehead, sweet and understanding, then nodded.

Chapter 34

AUSTIN

$\mathcal{I}$ said bye to Jo and Zoya as they left through the front door quietly the next morning. I shut the door behind them, walked over to the kitchen to grab two mugs of coffee, and headed back to my bedroom.

At the end of the hallway, I peeked in the door to my room and saw Isa still asleep. The curtains were still drawn and tiny streaks of light flooded in at the sides, dimly lighting the room. I put the coffee on the nightstand.

A surge of possessiveness filled me, seeing the sun streak across Isa's back. She was wearing one of my jerseys; she slept in it when she stayed over. I loved her like this, sleepy and without the armor she put on for the day—when she was completely unguarded.

With a deep inhale, she turned in bed, her eyes met mine as they slowly opened, and she yawned. "Hi."

My chest warmed.

In the stillness, I took a second to just look at her. The morning light reflected the flecks of honey that sparkled in her deep brown eyes. Her hair was bouncy and a little askew from the silk pillowcase I had here for her. "Morning."

Isa sat up in the middle of the bed and reached forward to take a mug from the nightstand, taking a deep breath while she stared down at it. "I'm sorry I freaked out last night."

I threw off my shirt and got back into bed with her. Leaning against the headboard, I watched as she fidgeted with the cup. "Honestly, I was sort of waiting for it."

It was why I hadn't woken her up when Zoya came to pick up Joseen. Isa seemed to spook pretty easily last night. I didn't want to send her running in the opposite direction because Zoya could not be cool if her life depended on it. I didn't want to throw more at Isa than she was ready to take on.

And I could see her eyes filling with panic, as though any step we took forward was a step back in her professional life.

She took a long sip of coffee. "You're not . . ." She turned the mug in her hand. "I'm not part of the reason you're staying, right?"

My brow crinkled. "What do you mean?"

"If you're choosing to decline coaching offers because you want to be here for me . . ." She shifted in the sheets, leaning forward over my legs to put her coffee down on the nightstand. "I can't let you do that."

"Look, Isa." I stopped her before she moved back to her spot, instead pulling her onto me. Her legs straddled over my waist. The jersey she had on ended along her thighs. "I need you to understand something."

"Okay." Her fingers played with the sheets at her sides.

"I know what it's like to leave everything behind and chase

a dream. I also know what it's like to walk away from it for a while. And then figure out something new. This direction is what's best for me."

"Oh." Her eyes flicked around the bed. "Good, I'm glad."

"But I won't lie to you. When I think about the future, I like the idea of having you in it." I lifted her chin. "I should have said this last night, but I'm not going to ask for anything that you're not ready for. I'm not going to wreck your plans. I promise."

A cautious smile moved up her cheeks.

"Is that okay?" I asked, splaying my hands to sweep up and down the silky smooth skin of her thighs.

The lines along her throat shifted. Her eyes wide but soft at the corners, she looked at me in a different way than she ever had before.

Hopeful. And I was coming to realize the most vulnerable she'd ever be was when she hoped for something she couldn't control.

"Yeah," Isa whispered, drawing close. Her fingers ran through my hair, the short nails scraping against my scalp. Static strolled down my back.

I pulled her into a kiss. Her fingers curled around the back of my neck. Slow and sensuously, she melted against me.

My hands slid up her back. She had a jersey at her place, too, and I sort of loved knowing it was there. The mental image of her wearing it when she was alone burrowed down my spine to my hips.

I dropped a couple kisses on her neck; she tipped her head back with a quiet moan. I pushed her panties down a fraction of an inch as she sat there. She got up momentarily to fling them off before straddling me and rocking against my groin the way that always drove me crazy. The slickness between her thighs made my mind go completely blank. Focused only on her.

My phone went off on the nightstand and I ignored it.

"Do you need to—"

"No," I groaned. I had her in my bed all night and for the first time since we crossed the line in Paris, all we did was sleep. Laced with concern about *this* conversation, I didn't get much. But now everything was falling into place and all I wanted to do was touch her everywhere.

She rolled her hips in my lap and my restraint wore down.

My fingers dugs into her perfectly round ass. *Fuck.*

I flipped her onto her back and kissed her intently. Her pillowy-soft lips were like a drug and I was finding myself needing a fix more and more.

I took off my boxers and got back into bed. Running my hands up her sides, I started to pin her before she pulled away.

"Wait," she said breathless, bucking her hips and rolling me onto my back with a wild look in her eye.

She kept her gaze locked on mine as she slowly peeled the jersey up and off her body, gently grinding her hips in a slow swivel against my rigid dick. I watched in what felt like slow motion. Her naked body on full display, aching to be touched, licked, fucked.

"Baby," I practically begged. My grip on her hips tightened when she stopped moving, pushing her back and forth against my erection. "Don't tease me."

I ran one hand to the swell of her breasts, taking a puckered nipple and rubbing it with my thumb. Her head tipped back slowly. Shaky sighs told me my window to roll her onto her back was open.

But just as I started, she leaned forward and her hands pinned my wrists to the mattress above my head. And I let her. Her tits were just close enough to my face that I ran my tongue along the nipple I'd just played with.

All of it was unbelievably hot. Her, naked, grinding against me. Pinning my hands down and giving me a view of her tits while she did it.

"No hands, Austin." She ran her teeth over her lower lip, muffling her tiny moans from a flick of my tongue against her nipple. Her pussy was so wet I could feel it dripping onto me. "If you move them, I'll stop."

I nodded, waiting for her. She got a condom from the nightstand, and I watched as she took her time rolling it down my shaft, torturing me with how slowly she moved. She stroked me a couple times, making it known who was in charge.

"Isa . . ." I grunted out alongside a labored exhale.

She finally sank onto me. Static ran up my legs, inch by inch, as her tight pussy slowly lowered onto me.

Wet and tight—fuck—my muscles ached to flip her back over. "Let me touch you."

"No." She leaned forward, and her arms braced on my shoulders. She swiveled at first, then bobbed up and down.

With Isa, every sense felt heightened. I could *see* the way her muscles tensed when she got *so* close to an orgasm, *hear* the nearly inaudible rise in her pitch, *taste* the sweat that misted off her body. Feel her so keenly that the only explanation was we fit together perfectly. The shoreline at the beach. Every single piece fit exactly like it was made to.

"Austin," she called out with a dip in her voice—it begged to me to touch her.

Pleasure rippled down my dick. I couldn't wait anymore.

My hands snapped to her waist, and seconds later I had her on her back. My thumb ran along her sensitive clit and I pushed into her in one quick motion.

She yipped a tiny gasp, a pleading look in her eyes before she closed them and her head arched back against the mattress.

"My turn." My hips snapped into her, ruthless. Every drop of restraint evaporated when she called my name.

Too far gone and mesmerized by the sound of her breathless moans and deep, pleasure-filled whimpers, I plunged into her deeply.

Faster and harder until her pussy tightened around me. Her legs snapped around my waist.

Her walls clamped against my dick; nails dug into my back as she rode through her climax. The sound, feel, and sight of it set my own free in a roaring flash.

We stilled.

Still deep inside her, I leaned my head against hers.

Isa's eyes stayed closed as her fingers weaved through my hair with a sated smile. "I think I like it when you take over."

"Good." I kissed her soundly on her lips. "Because next time, you're not using *your* hands."

Her airy laugh filled the room.

Chapter 35
ISABELLE

After a morning in bed, we ventured out to the surprisingly cool early-August day. There was almost no humidity, the clear and sunny afternoon was perfect. And it took all of ten minutes sitting in front of the Peter Pan statue in Carl Schurz Park to realize that we'd become those insufferable people who were all cuddly on a park bench.

With my entire back leaning into his chest while I enjoyed an ice cream cone, we were downright nauseatingly cute. Normally I hated that kind of outward public display, but today I didn't even care. I was having a nice time.

And Austin had this way of pulling every anxiety out of my head. I could relax.

"You don't want one?" I took a long, purposefully long, lick up the mountain of chocolate chip cookie dough ice cream.

His cheek twitched when he looked down at me as I teased him. "No, but I'm enjoying the view."

Talking to him this morning, and then everything we did after, felt like the assurance I needed. That residual worry that I was losing something became invisible over the last few weeks. He wasn't asking me for anything and that was so incredibly freeing.

I ran my teeth over my lower lip. "Just wait till later."

He smiled brightly and pressed a quick kiss on my head. It was strangely intimate, like a tiny display that I could relax, hell, I could fall asleep here if I wanted and he'd be there when I woke up.

I took another glob of ice cream in my mouth and enjoyed the sounds of the park. The distant sounds of traffic, the very present sound of birds sloshing around the sides of the fountain.

Another few silent minutes passed, and I leaned my head back onto his shoulder with a content sigh. The soft, cuddly afterglow we'd been soaking in all morning was jarred loose a few minutes later by a buzzing in my pocket.

I leaned forward and picked up the call. Austin's hand began to slide up and down my back.

"Hey, Isa," Selena said before I could answer. "I got the *Voulez* piece ahead of print."

"Oh." My voice curved up. "How is it?"

"Amazing. I'm hardly in it."

I laughed. "What do you mean?"

"Your *boyfriend* is a prince. He sort of charmed Malcolm, and about a quarter of the piece is on him. Some of it on the locations," Selena listed off. "Almost nothing on me or Henry. It's everything I was hoping for: we gave *Voulez Magazine* an exclusive that I'm hardly in and I got a wedding free of press. Please thank him for me."

I looked over my shoulder and winked at Austin. His eyebrows jumped curiously. "Oh, I will."

"One thing." Selena's voice peaked. "There is a picture of you
two. You look great. I wanted to get your okay before I approve
it, so I'm emailing you the piece now."

"Okay." I nodded.

"I have to go but let me know if it's okay with you. Love you."
The phone clicked off.

I swiped to my email and waited a few seconds. My phone
buzzed again.

Austin sat forward. "Everything okay?"

His palm continued to move slowly up and down my back.

"It's the article," I told him, opening the file and scrolling
through the three-page spread. Selena had highlighted a section about him and us. It was two paragraphs. "You're in it."

"Really?" He looked over my shoulder. "Is it good?"

Two paragraphs about him and it was almost completely
about the foundation.

"Yeah, it's great," I answered a little disbelievingly. He managed to steal the spotlight away from the bride and groom as
planned but also shine some light on the foundation. All while
doubting he could.

Austin's eyes scanned the article. "Selena's okay with this?"

"That you stole her thunder?" I laughed lightly. "She'll probably send you a gift basket."

"Or maybe buy me something at an auction," he teased,
reading on. "Wow."

When he was mentioned in the article, it practically mooned

over him. It featured the current state of the foundation, but also the eventual plans for it. How it started and, hopefully, its future.

The deep, relieved sigh he took warmed my shoulder.

"This sounds great." His eyes moved along the screen, reading as I did.

His eyes stopped at the same sentence mine did seconds later.

While accompanying his girlfriend to a wedding abroad, the honorable Austin Cade used the time to not only consider his second act but also advocate for the same charity he's championed since his early years on London's . . .

My eyes rolled over the four words "while accompanying his *girlfriend*" three times. Something in my stomach fluttered at the idea of being *his*. And him being mine.

He looked at me but didn't say anything. The warm breeze rustled in the silence between us. "I think it's perfect."

Being completely wrapped up in him felt easy. My mind quieted. I spent so much of my day in noise. Beeping from ventilators and vital monitors in surgery. The constant, coordinated communication between surgeons, nurses, anesthesiologists, and everyone else in an OR. The messy bustle of the post-op floor. Sitting here, with him, was a reprieve.

"Yeah?" he asked cautiously, like he was sure I would have seen that word and run.

"Mm-hmm, great picture of us, too." I tapped the side of the phone. "Yeah, although Malcolm may need a reminder that you're taken."

Austin's chest rumbled with a quiet chuckle.

He'd told me this morning he didn't want to wreck my plans, and I believed him because Austin didn't say things he didn't mean.

What I couldn't get myself to believe was this new feeling. The seductive warmth in my chest, one that made me *want* to divert my plans because the little life we were carving out together was becoming terrifyingly close to perfect.

A kind of perfect that was rare and fragile. I wanted to—had to—keep steady, because one misstep and it could shatter.

I swallowed against a suddenly dry throat.

Because if that happened, I'd break along with it.

Chapter 36
AUSTIN

Clouds hung over the Manhattan skyline, casting Jesse's office in a dreary gray. I leaned forward and paged through a proposal by my old club.

A week after reading the *Voulez* article that would come out tomorrow, Jesse was over the moon, happy with the press interest, practically beaming with the two contracts sitting in front of me. Everything was going according to plan.

Today we agreed I wouldn't extend my contract with the New York Lightning even if offered, and then we began discussing my next steps since it would expire at the end of this upcoming season. But I still had to break the news I wasn't going to be taking up either of the offers to coach.

"Now, we can figure out which team would . . ." Jesse tapped his fingers against his desk. His voice faded out as I glanced at my phone.

Isa was busy this week and I hadn't really seen much of her. She hadn't texted yet, but that wasn't uncommon. She was usually in surgeries all day.

"Austin." Jesse's stern bellow from across his desk snapped me back to what we were talking about.

"Yeah." I blinked back to where I was. Sitting in his office while we went through options.

"We need to make a decision on a team sooner rather than later, that way we can capitalize on the *Voulez* article coming out and get some press around your next move." Jesse paged through the offers again. "I think Farnham has the best offer and you know the team—"

"I was actually thinking about here." I braced myself for what was going to be a lot of suspicion on whether this was a good idea or not.

"What?" Jesse's tone dropped. "You mean extending your contract *here*? You said you wanted to move past playing."

"I do." I shifted in my seat. The divot between his eyebrows got deeper as I took a beat and prepared to tell him worse news than me wanting to stay in the American league.

"The foundation is doing great on its own. But what about a coaching program for talent that will eventually go to play pro? They'll need training and connections," I explained for the first time in a while, feeling self-conscious, like I wasn't really qualified to speak on it. Maybe I wasn't. "There are already pretty well-established systems—academies run by different clubs that funnel into the professional leagues—that do it around the world. It's only a matter of time until it becomes something here. Instead of a club running it, it can be a private academy that works with different teams."

"No." Jesse put his hand up. When I gave him a hard look, he huffed a breath. "Come on, Austin. Be realistic."

"You said it yourself, there's good press," I defended. "And now is the time to capitalize on it."

"Yeah, for the foundation. Charity. People love helping kids." Jesse brushed off the idea. "But starting an entirely new business endeavor? Affiliate agreements, staffing, talent scouts, not to mention how you'd fund it? It's *such* a giant risk that nobody in American sports has attempted it." Jesse rounded his desk and leaned against it. "We've been stuck in American league soccer purgatory for years and you finally have a step out right in front of you, and you want to pass on it?"

I opened my mouth to defend the idea but I didn't. I got lucky once, pulled into the Premier League against astronomical odds. What was the chance it happened again?

"Austin, you have interest for coaching. Your foundation is getting attention. This is working. And you got a girlfriend out of it. You should be *happy*."

My career was more than I could have dreamed for myself, thanks in large part to him. Taking a coaching job I probably wouldn't have had access to in the future if I waited too long was the smart move. The one I should make because luck ran out.

"I am," I finally answered. "Happy, I mean."

Everything that felt possible a couple weeks ago grayed and became more realistic.

"Take a few days." He handed me the offers. "Think about it and I'm sure you'll get a clear head."

Chapter 37
ISABELLE

$\mathcal{I}$ walked onto the post-op floor, running through the exhaustive list of discharges for the day.

At the end of a grueling week—one that consisted of two nights on call and two days when I didn't see the sun because I was in the hospital for over eighteen hours—it was finally Friday. I had the weekend off.

My phone buzzed as I turned the direction of my next patient to see.

AUSTIN: I'll see you at dinner tonight.

AUSTIN: Right?

I sighed and a smile uncurled on my face on its own. After this week, I wanted to lay in his bed all weekend.

It had been a couple days since the *Voulez* article released and not much came of it.

A couple interns happened to see the magazine in one of

the waiting rooms. They were doing the same thing I used to do when I was the intern assigned to patiently wait at the OR door to be the runner for any urgent needs—paging through waiting-room magazines during the hours of overnight cases when I wasn't needed but had to be vigilant.

The interns saw it and thought it was cool. A couple other residents did, too. Everyone in my vicinity was suddenly interested in my personal life or the Premier League. Or both.

That was about it, and it didn't really bother me.

ME: Yes, I'll meet you there.

ME: I might be a little late.

I sent the texts back and tucked the phone in my pocket.

"Good morning, Mr. Anderson." I greeted him brightly. "I'm one of the surgeons on your team and your nurse told me that you haven't been able to get up and out of bed with the physical therapist?" I asked, standing in front of my workstation on wheels, where I signed off on all the juniors' notes before evening rounds. I scanned through the note Ami left; Mr. Anderson hadn't tried PT yet and that always slowed down recovery.

"Hmm?" He looked up and smiled, then pointed to the magazine in his hands. The picture of Austin and me at the wedding in the bottom corner. "Is this you?"

"Excuse me?" I looked up from my screen.

"The doctor who was in here before left this." He handed me the magazine, folded open on itself to the first page. I scanned over it and couldn't help but feel tilted. Like I was knocked off my axis. "I told Dr. Reinhold that I wanted to get back to playing soccer with my grandkids on the weekends and we got on the topic."

It pushed me another degree in the wrong direction. Topsy-turvy, I tried to remain logical. None of it mattered. None of it changed *anything* about me or my life. This was a known outcome, one that didn't surprise me so I *shouldn't* have had a reaction.

"Yup. That's me." I smiled, rolled up the magazine, and stuck it in my back pocket.

It *was* a cute picture.

But truth bubbled in my gut.

Being taken seriously as a female surgeon was tough. I didn't let people see anything other than one side of me for a reason. Everyone needed to see me as a static figure, because how else would they trust me with something as serious as surgery if I dared be human?

That was a courtesy given only to men.

"My son played soccer," Mr. Anderson said brightly. "Wait till I tell him that I met Austin Cade's girlfriend."

I blinked a couple times. Frustration tightened my jaw.

Hundreds of hours of operating experience. Walls of degrees. Stacks of research with my name as first author. And the person whose knee *I* just repaired, referred to me by the least-exceptional part of myself—the man I happened to be seeing.

After years of avoiding it, preparing myself so I'd never have to deal with what she did, I was my mom in the most unexpected way.

It was another push, a jostle that knocked my world further to the side. I was practically upside down.

"Yeah." I typed a few last things into his chart and stood. "Pretty cool. Have you been able to get up with PT today?"

"Oh." He looked at me with a sheepish smile. "No, it was a little too painful. Can you ask the doctor for something for that?"

My muscles tightened.

"I *am* the doctor, Mr. Anderson," I reminded him gently even though I had introduced myself as his surgeon. "I performed your surgery alongside Dr. Reinhold." I tried to muster all the politeness I could because he didn't mean anything by it. And even though I always made sure to introduce myself a couple times when seeing a patient, he was post-op and in pain. Maybe he didn't hear. I checked his chart. He hadn't taken most of the meds prescribed because he was nervous to take them. "And I'll write something that won't make you too sleepy."

This conversation stole all the joy from the fact that I did a phenomenal job on Mr. Anderson's case. He had a complicated athletic injury that was difficult the entire time, but I handled it like a pro. He was going to be fine. Great even, if he started his PT soon.

It wasn't a big deal, a little bruised pride.

"Oh." His eyes squinted a bit to read my hospital badge for the confirmation he needed. It wasn't the first or last time I'd walked into a room and the patient saw me as anything *but* the doctor. "Right. Thank you."

I left the room, finished my notes, and tried to focus on

everything I had left to do for the day before I could leave. But every few seconds my mind kept reminding me *this* was probably what my mom had dealt with. Or that I hadn't logged those cases yet because I'd been distracted. Then I'd hear Austin's voice teasing me about them since I didn't need them for the Winthrop fellowship. So why was it so important I finished logging them?

Maybe I was off-balance because I wasn't focused.

* * *

I stepped into my apartment exhausted. I needed to shower, change, and head out quickly because I was already late. Hanging the keys on my little doorway key rack, I took off my shoes and stepped into my place with a long sigh.

A figure on my couch shot fear through my veins and I stopped abruptly. A millisecond later, it all clicked and I was only more confused. "Dad?"

Sitting leisurely on my couch, paging through a magazine as if he were in his own home, my dad was quietly unexpected. The dim living room lights and the fading sunset bathed the entire room in an almost-ominous orange glow.

He didn't say anything, so I went on. "How did you get in?"

"How did I get into the apartment I pay for?" he scoffed, still reading the page it was open to. I took a step closer and realized he had an issue of *Voulez* in his hands. "If you'd have gotten into Harvard as an undergrad, too, maybe that question wouldn't have popped into your silly little head."

I saved the snappy retort back because he was right. My salary as a resident didn't come close to covering this place.

"Any interesting news you'd like to share, young lady?" He stood, but his attention stayed locked on the magazine.

Suddenly, I was fifteen again, having to explain why I wasn't the top of my class at Sydney-Wells when the rankings came out. I had been second but that may as well have been last.

A jitter ran through my fingers.

It had been because that was the year I got sick with a nasty stomach bug, and I had to miss a week of school. I fell behind and he never let me forget it. Second place was for *other* people.

"How did you—"

"The chief of medicine showed it to me. He asked if you planned to go abroad with him if he takes up a position coaching." My dad let out a bitter laugh. "I was about to give a lecture to incoming surgical residents and I saw this nonsense. And got *that* inane question." He threw the magazine on the table and, finally, looked at me. I was in the eye of the storm. Calm for now, but tranquil water hid the rip current. One that would drag me to hell if I didn't comply. "You didn't even make a half decent attempt to hide anything."

"I wasn't *trying* to hide anything."

His eyebrows jumped and his mocking smile taunted me. "So, you planned to one day bring this *athlete* home to meet your parents? Have you decided to become a cheerleader?" Sarcasm dripped off every word as he took a step forward. "How exciting."

He did this with everyone. Selena wasn't smart enough to be my friend. Old boyfriends weren't motivated enough. I always saw it as protectiveness over me. But now I could see it clearly for what it was: he was protecting *his* legacy.

"That's not—"

"Can the man even read?" He rolled his eyes the same way he used to when I asked if I could spend the summer at camp instead of in all those enrichment lessons with my tutor.

I knew better than to answer the actual question. "Dad, my Winthrop interview is in two days."

"Is it?" He took another two steps forward and shifted his head to the side mockingly. "Because based on this behavior, I thought you needed a reminder. Traipsing through Paris like some dilettante and . . ." His upper lip curled at the magazine on the table. "Then making sure everyone knows how unserious you are."

My heart hammered in my chest, and I tried to stay grounded even when the beats sent waves through my muscles. "I have *always* taken my career seriously."

I had a long list of regular-person milestones that bit the dust in service to it.

"If that were true, I wouldn't have had to call Charles Winthrop himself to personally request you have the opportunity to interview."

A ringing filled my ears. "What?"

"Imagine. Me having to debase myself and ask that man—a man who isn't nearly as accomplished as I am—to accept *my* daughter."

My mind reeled. "That's not possible . . ." I swallowed against an impossibly dry throat. "I wasn't a first choice, maybe, but—"

"*Maybe?*" His voice turned in a sardonic upswing. "With all the weight of my reputation behind you, you still weren't considered. Is that acceptable to you?"

"No." I looked at floor, kept a tight jaw, and didn't bother defending myself. How could I? I was so sure it was in the bag that I hadn't thought about it. And then . . . everything went foggy.

"You won't always have my coattails to ride on," he warned. "You need to make the correct choices moving forward, and I can tell you that traipsing around Europe during one of your most important residency years is not the right one."

A few heavy steps, a slammed door, and I was left in the darkness that filled the room with a reminder that I didn't want to fail, but also, it wasn't a choice either.

My body ached with the truth that I hadn't tried hard enough. What stung more was how much all of this new information highlighted something I wasn't expecting. After being the only thing I'd chased, the fellowship I'd given up everything for had been an afterthought the last few weeks.

Chapter 38

ISABELLE

*M*y mind was stuck replaying on a loop all the work-related activities I'd missed the last few weeks—optional lectures, staying late so I could maybe get some additional OR time, networking. I was acting like I'd forgotten all of my ambition.

I sat on my couch with a blank stare until the slight creak of my door opening jarred me from the daze.

I looked around the room. It was dark.

"Isa?" Austin's voice was heavy. A good heavy. A stabilizing heavy. "Are you okay?"

I blinked a few times. I looked to my side to see him walking in. Moonlight streaked over the steep cut of his jaw and sparkled in his eyes. He turned on a light, closed the door behind him, and made his way to me. "What are you doing here?" My mind moved slowly, stuck in the sludge of everything that just happened. I glanced at the clock. "It's ten." My heart fell into my stomach. "Dinner."

"It's okay." Austin sat beside me. His eyes landed on the

Voulez Magazine copy on my coffee table before moving back up to me. "You weren't answering; I got a little worried."

"I'm sorry," I blurted. My ribs ached at the mental image of him realizing I wasn't coming. "After work, I got here and I . . ." I stammered, standing up and pacing, hoping it would relieve some of the pressure building in my stomach. "I should have called you."

"Hey . . ." He followed a step behind me, grabbing a hand and pulling me into him. When I was flush against his chest, he stroked the back of my head. "It's okay."

I breathed him in and sighed. My eyes closed for an extended moment. My muscles relaxed and allowed him to support me.

That was all I wanted.

My eyes shot open, body tensed. The realization went off like a siren in my head.

That was all I wanted? In his arms, I forgot about everything else, a blissful state of amnesia that had me trading away all the things I'd previously wanted without realizing.

"I'm really sorry for missing dinner and making you worry." I spanned a hand over his chest and pushed myself back.

He didn't deserve to be stood up. I didn't deserve someone being here for me like this when I knew it would happen again. He deserved someone who could give him the type of life I was sure he wanted.

Quality time spent together during daylight hours. A family. Children. I could barely make enough time to keep a plant alive or cook myself a meal. That wasn't going to change in fellowship. And I wasn't even sure I wanted it to. I needed to dedicate time to my legacy, and kids needed so much more than a half-absent parent.

"Isa . . ." He tried to pull me back, but I took another step away.

"But I . . ." I looked down. We didn't need to wait until he eventually saw it and made the decision on his own. It was better to draw the line clearly, the one we'd blurred so much that it was gone. "You should probably go."

This was likely how it went for my mom. When she went from the Mercado who should have had an entire methodology named after her to a regular person. At first, a forgone fellowship, then a new baby who needed someone at home for a few years. Then an uphill battle to regain any of the traction she'd lost when she took time to raise me—a battle she'd lost. A soaring career cut down not in one swipe, but in a thousand tiny decisions. Like a moth to a flame, she flew too close to something alluring—a life, a family—and those wings just melted off.

"Isa," Austin pleaded calmly, taking a few steps closer. "It's just dinner. I don't care that you missed it."

"It's not just that." The foreboding that followed all day swelled. "What are we even doing?" I continued. I walked to my door and reached for the handle, unsure. "Why are we pretending this will work?"

His jaw set on edge, cemented down. I wasn't looking to strike a nerve, or maybe I was, but I hit one. Hard.

"What we've been doing the last few weeks isn't *pretending*."

"No . . . obviously not. But it doesn't . . ." I couldn't put it into words, which made me even more frustrated. "I had a plan, and the last few weeks I've let it fall to the wayside." I could hear myself not making much sense, but the stream of consciousness poured out of me. "I know who I am, and I know what I want. And I'm choosing that."

Why drag this on? I did it with Blake for years only to end up where I started. Now I was at the precipice of everything I was chasing in my career, and it didn't feel like it was supposed to. The Winthrop fellowship felt like an afterthought. And that was the problem. At the core of it all, that was what hurt.

Nothing felt like it was supposed to.

I felt too much for Austin and suddenly not enough for the interview I had in two days. One that I didn't even deserve. The clear vision I had for myself was blurry. I didn't know which direction to go. The guiding light that I ran toward for years was dimmed.

Something dimmed it. *He* dimmed it.

And I didn't have a plan for that.

Nausea worked its way up my throat.

He took a controlled breath. "What part of this"—he pointed between us—"gets in the way of your plans?"

I *had* to be the best.

If I wasn't, all I'd be was the disappointing sequel to Dr. Felix Mercado.

If I wasn't, my mom's sacrifice in her own career would be for nothing.

If I wasn't, then I proved every one of those men in surgery who assumed I couldn't hack it right, and everything I'd given up till now was for nothing.

"All of it." The words collapsed along my breath. "How can you not see that? I don't skip lectures. I don't compromise—"

"Who asked you to compromise?" he snapped, the force in his words pushing me a step back. "I sure as hell never have."

My heart threw a tantrum in my chest. I thought it might jump out of my mouth. "You make me *want* to."

That was the scary part. In the time we'd been together, the fellowship lost its luster. One day, my ambition would go so dark I'd give it up without any argument. In service to this *feeling* I had for him. And I'd be warning my own daughter not to make the same mistakes I did.

"So, you're going to pretend this didn't happen? Pretend you don't need anything, that we aren't—"

"It was never *that* serious." I tried to convince him . . . or myself. Because it had only been a few weeks, yet I'd never felt this way before.

He took a step back, let out a frustrated huff, and ran a hand through his hair.

"You know, I was wondering why you were so broken up about Blake. It didn't make sense until I saw it that night at Versailles." He closed the space between us. "He didn't break your heart, Isa. You broke *his*. And he had the audacity to recover, make a new plan, when you didn't." He ducked his head down, so I had to look at him. When I stayed silent, he went on. "What *actually* hurt you is that he couldn't stand up to the gale-force-fucking-wind that you are. And you've decided that nobody else possibly could." His razor-sharp glare softened. His voice did, too. "But I *want to*. And that scares the hell out of you."

My words got caught in my throat, pushing tears so close to the edges of my eyes that I sucked in all the air I could to keep them back. Like a screw that had been turned too many times, my heart was stripped. It couldn't deal with the fallout of one day losing him.

"Tell me I'm wrong," he whispered.

He'd reach his breaking point. He didn't see it now, but he would. One day when he wanted a family that I wasn't ready to give him or when he'd ask for something that would put a barricade in my path, and I'd *have* to knock it down.

Then either he'd be gone or he'd resent me for everything he didn't have.

And I would be broken beyond repair. Not the tiny cracks that Blake left, but shattered because I'd never felt like this before. I couldn't get used to this only to lose it.

"Blake has nothing to do with this," I spat. "I can't give you what you want and I'm not going to pretend that I can."

That's what I'd been doing the last few weeks—pretending I could *have it all*.

In actuality, I was completely untethered to my work, and my dad had to come in for the save. I didn't log those cases; I didn't think about the fellowship.

Austin was pulling back the curtain on all the other things my life could be, but I didn't have the luxury of getting distracted. I had to be focused.

He was too alluring, too bright, he cast shadows on all the things I wanted—making me wonder if I ever wanted them to begin with. What if one day my own goals went so dim that I wouldn't even care I'd given them up?

"Why can't you give us a shot?" His voice cracked.

"Because I . . ." My words faltered. In the last few weeks, I'd put the fellowship on the back burner because he made me want to put my time in other things—in him. I'd never done that before, and we were only a few weeks in. What would a few months or years do to me if I felt like this now? How deep in love would I be then? How much would I be willing to sacrifice to never feel what would be the insurmountable pain of losing him? "I need to protect myself."

"From me?" Disbelief drew out the last syllable.

I shook my head.

"From everything you make me want," I whispered. I looked at the floor but braced my entire body, so it came out strong and together, despite how my willpower was disintegrating. "Please go home, Austin."

Austin took a step back.

He laughed humorlessly to himself. "If you were half as smart as you think you are, you'd realize that the only person standing in your way is you."

The words sank into my skin like pushpins.

I knew that. But if I didn't keep a vise grip on my goals, then maybe I'd let someone convince me to let them go. And then I'd lose myself.

For the second time that night, the door slammed shut and I stood there alone.

Chapter 39
AUSTIN

*T*he next day, I couldn't be alone. I did my normal training and had the rest of the day alone with my thoughts.

That was awful. So, I went to help Zoya since her catering business had been taking off and she could always use a hand. And whenever I was there, she usually put me to work.

"What's going on, Austin?" Zoya called from beside me. Inside the demonstration kitchen at the largest countertop, Zoya was preparing for her next job. Lined up in front of her was a grid of neatly cut puff pastry shells. She leaned over and carefully scooped filling into each.

I tried to make mine neat and tidy, but I completed about one for every seven she did. "What if I don't get so lucky this time?"

"Don't worry, I'm not using the ones you make for the event." Zoya waved me off, focusing on the work in front of her. "I gave you that dough for the same reason I give it to Jo. To keep you busy."

"Not the food," I clarified, although I was a little offended.

Mine weren't nearly as messy as Jo's were. "With the foundation and all of that."

Zoya stood up straight. She blinked a few times, set the bowl of filling aside, and gave her hands a quick wash before walking over to me without a word.

Her hand smacked against the back of my head.

"What does that mean?" Zoya's engagement ring and wedding band on her finger were the culprits for the sudden ringing in my ear.

"Ow." I rubbed the back of my head. It took Zoya two years to take them off and suddenly they were back on. Probably something I should check in on. "You're wearing your rings again?"

"Don't deflect. It's just habit," she defended, closing her palm into a fist as if that did anything to hide them. She was annoyed, so I wasn't going to ask. At least not right now. "What do mean by 'What if you're not so lucky?'"

"Jesse's not a big fan of the training facility idea. Thinks it's another wrong turn."

"Okay . . ." she said in a long, suspicious drawl. "So what? You were expecting that. And his opinion hasn't stopped you before, remember? He wasn't a fan of the original move back here, anyway."

"And he was right," I pointed out. "My career playing the game is essentially over."

"Because you *want* it to be." She put both hands on her hips. "Right?"

"Yeah." That was one thing I was positive about. I was ready to move on, and maybe if I hadn't come back I'd have had a few decent years in the Premier League, but it would have been to the same end. I think I was always going to come back here.

"So, what's changed?"

"What if I don't get so lucky this time?" I repeated.

I finally had some direction; I was so sure about it. But Jesse's reaction mixed with Isa shutting down completely made me want to cut and run. Go to something I knew would work. Hide from the uncertainty.

"Lucky?" Zoya's face scrunched. "I don't mean this to sound like a put-down, but what part of your life was lucky?"

Was she serious?

"All of it?" I answered, a little confused.

"Oh, you mean the foster kid part? The no family part? The dead best friend part? Which one of those were you *lucky* to have?" Irritation laced the line of questions.

My mouth hung open because this Zoya, the brutally honest one who ran Theo's start-up, hadn't really been around the last few years.

She let out a frustrated huff. She paced a few steps forward, then a couple back. "It used to drive Theo crazy when you did that."

"Did what?"

"Reduce all your success to a series of lucky breaks," she answered, still pacing back and forth. "The humble Austin Cade."

"That's a bad thing?" I wiped my hands with the towel since clearly I was never actually helping.

"No, but it's also undercutting everything you've managed to accomplish." She paced until she rounded the counter completely. She pointed at the barstools on the other end, motioning for me to sit. "You earned your success as much as you happened upon it. And if you can't figure something out for your plans, um, hello?" She waved her hand with her mouth hung open patronizingly. "You know I'd help you." She made a loud thump on her seat. "What's with you?"

I pushed my palms into my eyes, tired. "Nothing."

Zoya walked over to one of the large industrial fridges and pulled out a pitcher of lemonade like a bribe to get me to talk.

"You need to stop treating me like your kid," I mumbled. This was what she always did with Joseen when she was being stubborn.

"Then stop acting like my kid," she said in a singsong voice, shutting the fridge, and grabbing a couple glasses. She poured two and handed me one. With a deep sigh, she sat back down and swiveled forward in her chair. "Do you know why I lean on you so much with Jo?"

"Because Jo can be a lot."

"Well, duh." She rolled her eyes. "But sometimes I felt like maybe you needed it."

"*Me?*" Disbelief pulled on my tone.

Joseen Mistry was shooting my blood pressure up to unsafe levels because Zoya thought *I* needed help? I thought she could use some time off and maybe restart her personal life. I was hoping the last few times I watched Jo were cover for her doing just that.

Zoya cocked her head and crinkled her brow. "Oh, save the widow pity. Yes, *you.*"

"It's not widow pity," I defended.

If I felt as empty as I did on occasion without my best friend around, I could only imagine what she must have felt. I thought being helpful might give her a chance to find something to fill that space like I kept trying to do.

"Theo was my best friend. My husband. My business partner. My everything." She looked straight ahead. "But after all the grief and the sadness, I started finding my way into a new life." She turned back to face me. "You need to do that, too."

"I did."

"No, you kept the foundation going, spent every waking minute when you weren't playing with Joseen being absolutely a shell of a person for three years. Got injured and . . ." She threw her hands up. "This is the happiest I've seen you. Actually happy. Not that pretend thing you do when Joseen is around. And now, suddenly, after practically shitting sunshine that day you asked for help with your ideas, you're waffling over them?"

"I'm trying to be practical."

"No, you're not." She cocked her head to the side, her eyes narrowed. "You're scared of something. And you're running from it."

I looked away because she was right. When I didn't answer, she went on.

"And let's say I believe your excuse that it's practicality. Remember that I sold SolTech and started a catering service. Sometimes practicality is a prison." She laughed out loud. "You're more than just the kid with impressive footwork and a killer cross kick. And, for the last couple weeks, it seemed like you were finally understanding that."

The last few weeks had felt like the morning after a storm.

Part of me was so drawn to Isa because she didn't care for the sport. She wasn't impressed by it; we almost never talked about it. We talked about everything else. And despite the fact that she was clearly leaps and bounds smarter than me, I never felt anything other than intrigued by her.

Like, in her presence, I was Austin.

Not the foster kid without a family.

Not the practically illiterate kid who could barely pass eighth grade.

Not the American Footballer.

Just Austin. Her light was all the spotlight I ever wanted again.

"I guess you're right." I smiled. Zoya *was* right, I was running from something, because even though Isa wasn't the reason I was staying, I'd already started imagining what our days could look like together.

Last night pulled the rug out from under me and I wanted to get as far away from that feeling as I could.

"I'm honored to be the Mistry that you run things by." She swiveled in her chair again. "But you're more than capable of making the decision. Do it because you want it, not because you think it's something you *should* do. Or because you think it gives something back to Theo. Do it because it's your next dream."

"Yeah . . ." I trailed off. Feeling confident was so easy when I was playing. All of it came so incredibly naturally that I sort of assumed it was the only thing in the world I'd be good at. It seemed like a fair trade given everything professional play gave me. "Thanks for the pep talk."

She nodded. "Can we talk about the real reason you're being so angsty? Because I know Jesse has a way of getting in your head, but I have a feeling it's something else . . ." she ventured. "Or is your psyche a little too battered right now?"

"Not today."

The argument was still fresh, and I wanted to get whatever I was feeling figured out before I talked to anyone. For now, Isa clearly needed some space, and this time I was going to give it to her.

"Fine." She topped off both glasses. "Tomorrow it is."

Chapter 40

ISABELLE

*T*wo days after my dad dropped by to remind me of the interview that I—apparently—didn't even deserve, I was in Boston for the Winthrop fellowship interview.

Walking alongside Charles Winthrop in the large atrium at the Boston Medical Center's lobby, I felt almost like I was having an out-of-body experience. Sunlight streamed through the wall of windows on one side. The clean and clinical lobby sparkled as morning faded to a bright afternoon.

I took a deep inhale. This was what I'd wanted for so long.

I expected it to feel different. I was supposed to be nervous, but I wasn't. I was a natural.

I expected that I'd feel something similar to coming home. A feeling of a final puzzle piece falling into place. But I didn't. This felt like every other interview or hurdle I had to clear. And when I looked at it like that, suddenly it lost all of its luster.

"And after the fellowships, most of our fellows go on to practice and continue critical research . . ." Charles Winthrop went on with closing the interview. Three hours of interviews with all the people I'd spent the last few years working myself into the ground to impress, and it was great. I was happy. Happy with an asterisk because I was wondering if there was somewhere else I could have been happier. "The path to quite a legacy."

Hearing those words—ones I'd heard in some manner or another over the past decade—was like the lights coming on after a movie. The world created in front of me disappeared and reality came back into view.

Charles Winthrop finished the final tour, shook my hand, and smiled proudly. "Thank you for coming, Dr. Mercado."

It took all of fifteen minutes into my first interview for the Winthrop fellowship for the realization to be unavoidable. The one that had sprouted in the last few weeks and blossomed into something so obvious I couldn't ignore it anymore.

I didn't *want* this.

I wanted my own name. I wanted to make my mark, and I'd always assumed this was how I would do it. I'd beat my dad at his own game and become the Dr. Mercado referenced in all the textbooks.

But I wasn't going to find it here. I was only going to spend my life in some bizarre competition with my dad, telling myself it's a better career than one lost in the mix of life like my mom's. As if those were the only two options. Because for a long time, they were the only ones I let myself see.

"Thank you for having me." I mustered all the polite excitement I could and shook his hand. Even if my father ensured I had this interview, it was my own successes that made me a competitor for this spot. I would at least revel in that.

* * *

I took the next train back to New York and went straight to the same place I always spent my afternoons when I had some time off.

I needed to talk to Austin. But first I needed an actual idea of what I wanted because everything felt so blurry. The idea of letting go of Winthrop was already scary enough. But at least I knew it didn't feel right, and it wasn't that I was being blinded by my feelings for Austin; if anything, he'd taken my view from portrait to panoramic.

And I hated how I spoke to him. Maybe I just needed Selena to talk some sense into me and make me feel like less of a monster.

"I was wondering when this was going to happen." Selena licked the salt off the rim of her zero-proof margarita mocktail. "I was hoping it wouldn't."

She put the glass back down.

Selena's house on the Upper East Side was massive. There was an outdoor terrace that ran the entire length of the back of the house, enclosed by a towering brick wall. On summer nights we either opted for the first-floor terrace or one of the balconies where the skyline could be seen.

We used to have margaritas on nights when I wasn't on call. When she moved in with Henry, our margarita nights continued, and Henry worked late or made himself scarce so we could have some time together.

"What do you mean?" I stirred my *alcoholic* margarita, because after the argument with Austin a couple nights ago, I needed something to take the edge off. Tonight was the first night I wasn't preparing for an interview or working and I could relax.

When I got there, I told Selena I was thinking about something else post-residency. I had a year till then; I could go into practice or I could choose a different fellowship. It put me under a daunting timetable, but I already had one in mind.

"With Blake, you started that one fight." Selena leaned forward to scoop some guacamole on a chip and crunched it loudly. "I was there that night, for dinner, when he visited and suggested you consider UCSF after your training." She let out a long sigh. "Instead of telling him it hurt you that you had to be the one to make a sacrifice for your relationship, I think you started an argument about the ranking systems for residency programs."

I took a long sip from my straw.

That night, I'd felt like he was trying to push me into a corner. At the time, all I knew was that I was compromising, and I didn't want to.

"So . . . what did Austin ask for that you can't give him?" Selena pushed her straw around her glass.

My heart rattled against my ribs.

"Nothing." I looked down at my glass. He didn't want anything from me. He wanted me to open up and be with him in any way I was able and that was all. "He's been great and it's making me realize . . . I guess I never thought about what it would be like to *not* go after the Winthrop fellowship . . ." I *pft*ed out a breath.

"You're reconsidering what you want because someone may have shown you all that you *can* have." Selena put into words what I was stumbling over.

"Yeah, some *man*." I scoffed. "This isn't a cheesy Christmas movie, and I am *not* giving up my plans for a guy."

Selena's face brightened with a deep and airy laugh. "Did he ask you to?"

"No, but he makes me want to," I answered. And I was scared where it would end. I'd mapped out the trajectory of my entire career. What other plans would I end up diverting for a life with him? My mom had deviated from her plans for her relationship, and she couldn't undo that. What if I let go of my timeline for Austin and I ended up regretting it? "And even if I never have to give anything up, what if he does for me? What if he gives up a life *he* wants?"

I couldn't live with that.

I didn't know what my future would look like anymore, but I did know that motherhood came at a price for high-achieving women. I saw it with my own mom. I didn't know if I wanted children, but I never wanted to put myself in a position where I'd close the door on a career opportunity forever. Maybe I was selfish, but I wanted to focus on *my* life. Nobody ever faulted a man for doing that.

"Love is hard. I don't know if I can add another challenge to my life," I added.

"Love isn't hard." Selena paused contemplatively. "Life is hard. Love makes shouldering everything life will throw at you *easier*. If that's not the case, then it isn't love."

"What do you mean?" I scratched my head, confused. I looked at my margarita, then Selena. "Did I have too many of these?"

Selena laughed.

"I meant what I said. Love *isn't* hard. It just needs a little investment," Selena explained. "You found something . . . someone." She tiptoed around her words like she was walking a field of land mines. "That makes you *want* to compromise, and I get why that's scary. But when that happens, they don't feel like compromises or sacrifices anymore, because they're not. They're an investment in your own happiness."

"What if it's five years down the line and I keep *investing*, but I've changed my whole life around for our relationship?" I swallowed against that visceral fear. "What if I can't get it back?"

Selena cocked her head to the side. "Look, Isa, if you're this spooked at making a change, I can't imagine you're going to do anything drastic. And I'd like to point out"—she raised her hand—"I'm here in case you do have a bout of love-related amnesia."

I sat there under the heavy weight of her words, feeling like a child for not having come to all of this on my own, but also worried because that wasn't all of it.

"What if we get a few years down and then he realizes I can't give him what he wants?" My mind filled with how adorable he was with Jo. What if I couldn't make the time for a family? I still wasn't sure if I wanted one. "Like kids."

Losing Austin now hurt. If I fell even deeper than I was now, that heartache would completely devastate me. But holding on to him, only for him realize later I was offering a life that was less than what he wanted, was just as bad.

"Does he know that you may not want to have kids?" she asked.

"Yes."

This was a lot. Too heavy for only having known him this long, but at the same time it felt like a conversation we needed to have because everything with him felt like that.

Heavy. Stable.

Selena sighed and pushed her lips to the side of her face in thought. "Do you think he's an idiot?"

Taken aback, my body froze for a moment. "Of course not."

"Then did you stop to consider that he's already thought of that and wants a life with you more?" Selena grabbed another chip and loudly crunched it. "Did you ever stop and think he doesn't see a different kind of family as a sacrifice, rather an investment?"

Austin would thrive at fatherhood. Like how I'd be great in the Winthrop fellowship. Losing out on either felt like a loss. And I couldn't be the reason someone else didn't get what they wanted out of life. I already had that sinking feeling I stole that joy from my mom. I couldn't steal it from him, too.

"Either way, it feels like a waste of perfectly good potential," I admitted.

"Isa . . ." Selena's voice lowered. "You sound like your dad."

I barked a laugh, startling Selena. She was right, and I guessed the irony was kind of funny. "I spent so long avoiding becoming my mother, I didn't see this coming."

"What good is potential if you're stuck doing something you don't want with it?" Selena's serious face lit with a loving smile. "And don't forget, you've made sacrifices for me. Skipped interesting cases when I needed you that year when everything went to shit with the press. You didn't take a single day off for over a year so you could be present at the wedding. Did that feel like giving something up?"

"Of course not."

"Why?"

"Because I love you."

Selena's eyebrows lifted in victory. "See? They may seem like sacrifices on the outside but when you're in it, they're investments. And only you get to decide what's worth investing in."

My throat bobbed.

I wanted to hug Selena for being there for me and yell at her for being right at the same time. Instead, I took a deep breath and tried to keep every emotion that rushed through my veins in check. "Jeez, don't get so serious. It's just a guy."

"You like him."

"More than I thought I would," I admitted quietly. Regret ratcheted up my throat, clogging it a bit. "And then I screwed it all up."

I spiraled because he had the audacity to encourage me to do what I *wanted* over anything else. He was invested in *me* while I was invested in some idea of what my future should look like.

"Make it right. Apologize," she said plainly, simply. Because it was simple. With Austin, everything was what it seemed. "But before you do, I think you should talk to Blake."

I winced. "Really?"

She sighed.

"I think you need closure." Selena turned her glass on the table and looked down at it instead of looking at me, like she was bracing to say something she knew I wouldn't like.

"Clear up whatever residual resentment or anger you've been holding on to and let it go. Not for him, but for Austin. Don't start a relationship with him while still feeling anything other than indifference for your ex."

I nodded and now that I had an idea of what I wanted to do to fix things, I could finally relax a bit. I hoped Austin understood and didn't scare easily.

Chapter 41
AUSTIN

*F*our days—not that I was counting—since Isa decided that *this* was too much.

And while I wanted to see her, I was still a little angry. We hadn't been together all that long, but the speed and ferocity with which she could shut down everything that happened between us was painful. Like it meant nothing, even though I knew that wasn't true. There was something else going on and she was scared. Instead of coming to me, she lashed out, and I could see it happening but was powerless to stop it.

Nothing would change until she wanted it to, so I gave her some space.

Zoya and I walked out of the Dawn Capital building in Lower Manhattan. The streets were filled with the normal morning shuffle of people moving quickly, cars honking, vendors chatting. All the sounds of the city.

"You straightened out everything with Jesse?" Zoya asked.

For the first time in years, she was in a suit again. Originally, I was a little worried to ask for her help with this since Zoya had found a new normal running her kitchen. It had been years since she'd used her MBA in a C-suite as the head of a company, and the last time she had it was to run Theo's start-up.

But she seemed almost excited to be there. And the meetings went great.

We had capital. A lot of it.

Dawn Capital agreed to donate millions to the foundation through their charitable arm but they also agreed to invest in the academy. That meant everything that had felt far-fetched and nearly impossible for so long could happen. It wasn't just big for me, it was pretty unheard of in American sports, so it would be news once the final papers were signed.

Just early enough that we beat the salty humidity that hung over the summer morning, it was pleasant as Zoya and I walked a few blocks to the car.

"Yeah. I'm going to meet Jesse next week," I told her. Jesse wasn't a fan of a career route outside of coaching, and I was probably still in some hot water with the management firm. But I'd finally found a direction I was excited to go in. I wasn't giving it up now. "I think he'll be more accepting once he sees this."

"Even if he's not"—we stopped at a corner, waiting for the light—"you don't owe him anything."

"I know, *Mom.*" I rolled my eyes, unserious. I checked my phone, wondering if Isa had texted.

She clearly needed to work shit out for herself, and I wasn't going to push what I wanted on her. When—if—she was ready, I'd be here. Waiting.

"Why don't you call her and tell her what just happened?"

Zoya suggested as we crossed the street to the next block. "She'll be happy for you."

"I will," I answered curtly, tucking my phone back in my pocket.

With the prolonged silence, Zoya pushed again.

"So . . ." she tried again. "What's going on with Isa?"

"Nothing."

"Look." She stopped at the next street corner, taking a few steps to the side to get out of the way of fast-walking commuters on their way into work. I did the same. "I didn't bring it up at the kitchen because I knew there was a lot going on, but you can't let it fall apart when you're clearly—"

"We're in different places. She's got a lot going on and I . . ." I tried to explain. Every step we took forward was hard-fought but the backslides were too easy for her. "Maybe it was never something that was supposed to last."

"Why is that?"

"We're different people."

She huffed a breath. "What does that mean?"

"This may surprise you, but I'm *trying*," I defended. "I'm not sure she wants me to."

Zoya's mouth twisted to the side in thought.

"It doesn't surprise me." She smiled softly, patting my cheek, motherly. "That reporter had it right, the Honorable Cade. You've always been a good guy, the kind I would trust with my own friends."

"Oh, I know." I rolled my eyes since Zoya had attempted to set me up with a few of them over the past couple years.

"But . . . sometimes moving forward can be a little scary,"

she admitted. Her eyes darted around the street like if she looked at me she'd let me know something she wasn't ready to talk about. "Letting go of everything in your past doesn't mean you're hung up on it. Sometimes that hesitance is a little bit of fear. The present is safer than the future because you can control one of those."

Zoya was speaking like it was from experience.

"So, I should wait her out?" I concluded, which made this whole conversation pointless because that was exactly what I was doing.

"I can't speak for her, but self-sufficient and successful probably means she knows what she wants and doesn't want," Zoya began. "Sometimes all you need is someone who's willing to let you spin out so you can recalibrate on your own. Let her know you're there for her."

"Is that what this mystery guy did?"

"What?" Her eyes went wide and her smile dropped.

Zoya wasn't wearing her rings today, which was odd because it was sort of a big step for her when she took them off the first time. And now they were off again.

"Zoya . . ." I drawled. "Do you like a boy?"

Her lips formed a line. "I'm not answering that question."

"Why?" I crossed my arms. "We still have two blocks and a drive filled with traffic for me to bother you."

Being that Theo had been my best friend, and she was like my sister, it felt a little weird to encourage her to date. But it had been three years. He'd want her to be happy.

"Shut up." She turned and looked at the traffic light, her foot tapping on the curb like she was ready to move.

Chapter 42

ISABELLE

I had to fix things with Austin. Because he was my future. No matter how scared I was, that wasn't going to stop being true.

But Selena was right, so a few days after the Winthrop interview, Blake agreed to meet me. I walked along the stone path to where I asked Blake to meet: in front of the Peter Pan statue. It felt oddly symbolic.

I took a seat and waited for him. The warm summer breeze was a gentle reminder of all the ways I let myself fall into something that was easy rather than try for something that wasn't. Blake and I twisted ourselves into pretzels to fix something that wasn't going to work in the present day. Our version of Neverland was the empty shell of a relationship I'd carried for too long.

We'd both grown up but the remnants of what we always promised each other didn't.

When I saw him, wearing a neatly pressed shirt and pants in the summer warmth, I smiled.

"Thanks for meeting me." I stood from the bench when he approached.

I needed to tie off this thing with Blake neatly, because he may have made the wounds, but Austin was paying for them. And I didn't want him to.

Blake shifted awkwardly, his arms opened for a hug before pulling them back to his sides. "Yeah." He looked at the bench and took a seat. I took one next to him.

Then we both sat silent, staring at the statue like it was a game of chicken.

Except, this time, I think we were both a little too scared to confront each other. We didn't really fight, which was why it never really ended, at least not for me. When we did argue, it felt like the world coming down. Because it sort of was. Our backup plans, the lifeboat we'd made for ourselves—each other—sank a long time ago.

"I wanted to explain. About Francesca," he began. "Without all the verbal jabs this time."

"Before you do, I wanted to say I'm sorry," I said quickly before I could lose my nerve. Owning up to what I blamed him for even though I was at fault here, too. "You were right. I chose."

Thin lines sank into his forehead.

"It was me," I went on. "I thought choosing you meant giving up me."

He rubbed his fingers back and forth along his forehead. He was . . . confused? Maybe shocked. I don't think I actually apologized for that, for pinning it all on him when I'd made my choices a long time ago.

"I made it seem that way," Blake added curtly. "Always asking for you to make the change. Honestly, I never really considered it from your point of view. I blamed you for finding reasons to end us."

I looked ahead again. "And you don't have to explain about Francesca. It's not my business."

"I owe you an explanation. I'm sorry I didn't tell you sooner." He raked a hand through his hair. "It's just . . . with Francesca, I don't have to worry about competing priorities. No feeling like I'm being pulled in another direction. My work takes priority, and that's fine with her."

A part of me wanted to yell at him for being selfish, but then I realized how hypocritical that would be. They were happy. Or whatever it was they were. It worked for them, so I had no business judging. But whatever it was, I didn't want that. Hearing him say it now made me realize exactly how idiotic I'd been. I wanted what my best friend had. A love that was complex and a man who pushed me to be better, because sometimes I stood in my own way out of fear.

But that guy had never been Blake. It was my own fault for not seeing it sooner. "That's great. I'm happy for you."

"I know you're judging me." He gripped the bottom of the bench and looked at the ground.

"I'm not." I put both hands up.

"You are." He looked up.

"Maybe a little." I winced. "You sound a little selfish," I added. I couldn't help it. "Sorry."

"It works for us." He drifted off and I turned my head to see a small smile cresting along his jaw. "But I *am* happy. I'm happy for you, too."

I smiled. "I'm glad."

He nodded and stood. With a deep breath, he took two steps, but a part of me had to know.

"Did I break your heart?" I called after him.

He turned. With a slack jaw, he took the two steps back and sat down.

"Yeah." His chest heaved with that one heavy syllable. "You fucking destroyed it, Isa." He ran a hand down the side of his face, looking around the park like he was trying to imagine us in it together, now. And finding it to be an impossible task. "I kept telling myself, 'One more try.' Or 'This time she'll see it's for us.'" His tongue rolled from one cheek to the other. "It never happened."

"I'm sorry," I said resolutely. "*Not* for choosing myself but for blaming you for doing the same."

He shrugged. "It wasn't meant to be."

I was selfish when I needed to be. So was he.

And in that moment, I was thankful we were. Because seeing him again made me ache, but remembering the look on Austin's face when I told him to go—that felt insurmountable.

"No, it wasn't." I rolled my shoulders back. I wanted this to end nicely because I *did* want him to be happy. That was probably why trying to make him jealous at the wedding didn't feel like I wanted it to. At the end of the day, I didn't love him, but I also didn't hate him. "Can I have a plus-one to your wedding?" I joked.

His tense stare forward broke with a chuckle. Then a rolling laugh. A loud one.

I blinked a couple times in disbelief. What I said wasn't *that* funny. It took a second to make sure those weren't sobs, but they weren't.

He doubled over with laughter.

"Are you having a mental breakdown?"

"Fuck, maybe." He ran his hand down his face and sat up. "How did we get here?"

Before we dated, years ago, we were friends. Then dating muddled it, and the amity was secondary to hurt feelings and hurt pride.

"Maladaptive people pleasing?"

He paused and looked at me like I'd just proved the theory of relativity. He started laughing again. "Yeah . . . I'm getting married. You became a surgeon."

"Congratulations, by the way." My chest began to shake with a few chuckles. His marginally psychotic laughter was contagious. "Where are you registered?"

We stayed like that, in the same park we always used to come to together. The same one where we made promises that—in truth—neither of us had any plans to keep. But they were a security blanket.

"You know, when I asked you if it was serious with Austin, it wasn't because I was jealous," he said into the quiet. I looked at him incredulously. "I mean . . ." He let out a resigned exhale. "I was a little jealous. I get engaged, so Isa has to one-up me by dating the guy I idolized."

I shrugged. "I don't like to lose."

"I asked you if it was serious because you never looked at me like you look at him."

"What do you mean?"

"You look at him . . . I can't explain it." He looked up at the sky, searching his memory. "You looked like you weren't planning what you want to say next. You looked like you were . . . listening."

My heart dipped. "He's . . ."

"Yeah." Blake agreed into the silence when I didn't finish my thought. "I can tell."

Austin let me be myself without condition. He liked me as I was now, and I knew, down to my bones, he'd like the person who would change with time. Because I wasn't static or simple; I was a kaleidoscope of different things. And he liked every possibility.

My ribs ached and emotion welled in the back of my throat.

A realization came into focus . . . he loved me.

"I hope it works out." I stood and began to turn to walk in the opposite direction but stopped. "For both of us, I mean."

Blake represented a part of my past and an idyllic future that couldn't ever exist in reality. Closing this chapter was long overdue. The misguided hope and the hurt feelings. All of it.

He smiled a half smile. "Yeah, I do, too."

Chapter 43
AUSTIN

On a bright, muggy Saturday morning, I walked onto one of the large grassy portions of Central Park where people often picnicked or played a sport.

After everything got settled with the foundation's funding a few days ago, I was supposed to go to the community center in Brookyln today to start plans on staffing both the community center and training faculty.

But Isa called, asked that I meet her here, and having played games my entire life, I wasn't going to play them with her.

I took a few more steps, and next to a picnic bench was Isa, hard at work. Her hair was pulled into a bun and she had on *my* jersey with a pair of shorts underneath. She was setting something up. With a book held open in one hand and a palmful of red marking flags in another, Isa pushed a flag into the ground, stood, read some more, took a few steps forward, and repeated the process. Next to my feet just below the bench at the picnic table were a few soccer balls.

"Isa," I called. My nerves lifted.

She was *here*, which meant she was trying.

She sprang up and her focus lifted to me. "Hi."

My heart started to race. For some reason all I could think about was that once I was up close, I'd be able to see the golden flecks that lined her dark brown eyes. "What is this?"

Isa looked at all the flags she'd stuck in the ground in two parallel lines, glanced at the book, closed it, and held it to her chest. Chewing on her lip, she closed the distance between us, shy a few steps. "You owe me lessons, remember?"

I looked around again. The soccer balls in the corner, a recreational soccer net at the end of the flagged area. .

The gesture rattled between my ribs.

"I owe *Selena* lessons," I teased, because she was nervous, and I didn't like seeing Isa as anything other than happy. So, I wanted to make her comfortable.

She was wrong. She got scared and lashed out. It hurt us both. But here she was doing . . . something, and it was sweet. And Isa, for all her strength, wasn't good at being vulnerable.

She held the book to her chest. "She bought them for me."

The gentle banter poked holes in the apprehension that hung in the air.

"Because you have that little crush on me?"

She shook her head. "It's a big one."

Finally closing all the space between us, my hands cautiously slid along her hips. I didn't pull her in just yet. "Isa, what is this?"

"I have four weeks of lessons." She ran her hands over my chest. Now I yanked her close, reveling in the feeling of her. "I just wanted to *show* you that . . ."

Her throat shifted with a hard swallow. Years of armor would take time to remove.

"Isa?" I lifted her chin with my index finger.

"I'm sorry." Her eyes stayed fixed on mine. "I got scared. I've never wanted to compromise before. It felt like losing something. And if I wasn't losing something, then you were, and suddenly it felt like I had to end it before we both got hurt." She looked down. "I'm sorry. You were right. I was scared and I do want this. Us."

I managed to—unknowingly—get the upper hand on her. As far as I could tell, only one other person had done that, and the last time it happened, she lost her balance.

And for someone like Isa, a person who was steadfast, that was probably the scariest part of it.

"I know," I told her.

My fingers slipped around the nape of her neck. My heart thumped a little faster in my chest. A skitter ran across my nerves knowing we still needed to talk about what happened but aching to kiss her. It would have to wait.

She hummed and her body relaxed against mine.

"Is this a grand gesture?" I asked. "I might need grander . . ."

A curve slid up the side of her mouth. A fleeting spark in her eye faded as swiftly as it lit.

"For so long . . ." she started to explain and took a step back. My hands fell back to my sides as I let her get her bearings. "I thought compromise meant abandoning what I wanted. So, I never wanted to compromise for anyone."

I waited for a second to let that hang in the air because it seemed like that explanation was just as important for her to hear as it was for me.

"I'll never make you choose, Isa."

When I started to get to know her, I thought Isa was fiercely independent because of Blake and her pride. But all this time it was the fear that she might be boxed into a corner she couldn't get out of. Independence meant being able to maneuver however she wanted.

"I know." She blinked a couple times. Taking my hands in hers, she nodded. "Listen, Austin. I know there are a lot of things you probably want . . . like a family. And, eventually, when I'm ready for all of that, I'm not sure what it'll look like."

"Okay," I answered cautiously.

"If that's what you want—"

"Isa, I have a family. And I, of all people, understand they can look different than a cookie-cutter one."

"I mean kids," she blurted bluntly. A little impatient, refusing to skirt around it, for the sake of efficiency or to get a point across. The most "Isa" way to do it. "If I can make space for properly raising children within all the goals I have for my career, I want them. But if I can't . . ." Her weight shifted between her feet. Her voice wavered. "Then I'm not going to have them."

"If you want kids, we'll have them," I told her seriously, a little surprised that she brought up something so committed. It made me even more sure that her pushing me away was all fear, not much else. I dipped my head a little so she had to look me in the eyes. "And if not . . . then I guess I can kiss you *anywhere* I want."

She shook with a reluctant laugh. "Austin, I'm serious."

"So am I." I put my hands back on her hips and pulled her to me. "Listen, Isa. I want this. I like that you're a little bit of an egomaniac. Or that you're so sure of yourself that you won't let anything get in the way of your dreams. It's inspiring and sexy as hell."

Her lips tilted up. "My life is never convenient."

I shrugged. "Mine is these days."

"I'm still figuring out the whole work-life balance thing. And—for a while at least—work is going to win."

"I'm professionally trained to get a lot done in just ninety minutes," I shot back calmly. "I'm not worried."

"I'm high-maintenance. It's not a bad thing. I like being at the top of my game," she added. Her hands slid up my chest and her eyes met mine. "That requires time and energy. I'm always going to be my best . . . that's not going to change."

"Good."

She looked down. "I know that sometimes . . . I'm too much."

"For who?" I whispered. "Because, Isa, I can't get enough."

She nodded. "Sometimes I run from things that scare me."

My heart dipped.

I leaned my head against hers. "Don't worry. I'll catch you."

"I pushed you away." Her throat bobbed. "I'm sorry."

"Don't do it again." I dropped a quick kiss on her lips, finding it impossible not to. The fact was, I was a goner when it came to Isa. She could try to push me away, but I had a feeling she'd never be able to push me so far we couldn't find our way back. "Talk to me instead."

She nodded and tilted her head up, rocking to her tiptoes and brushing her lips against mine. This time, I pressed my lips against hers soundly.

Her warmth seeped into my bones, embedding itself so deep that she'd always be a part of me. A tiny moan from her and both my hands moved from along her face to her waist to her hips. The kiss deepened and we stood there, lost in each other.

"We should start the lesson," I whispered, pulling away and reminding myself that we were in public.

She pulled away slowly. "Before we do . . ." She took half a step back. "I need to tell you something."

"Yeah?"

"I . . ." Her brow crinkled, she twisted her fingers. "I saw Blake. I called him. Only for closure so I never have to think about him again."

My chest tightened. I didn't love that.

"Okay." I weaved my fingers into hers. "Thanks for telling me."

Her eyes narrowed at the corners. "You're not annoyed?"

"Because you saw your ex? No." I yanked her close. "That's the thing, Isa. No man is ever competing against some other guy for you. I'm competing with the life you're building for yourself. Because unless I can add to it, I don't deserve to be part of it."

Her chin wobbled.

"While we're on the subject," I told her more firmly. She needed to hear this because I wasn't having this argument again. "I *know* I can add to it. You need to let me and trust that I will."

This time, she put both hands on my cheeks and dragged me down to her lips.

I wrapped my arms around her waist again, feeling every inch of her relax in my arms, and we kissed deeply in the park. It was all I could ever want, her feeling completely herself exactly where she belonged.

Chapter 44
ISABELLE

$\mathcal{I}$ was never more aware of my posture than when I was sitting in my childhood home. Today it was even more pronounced because I was going to give them some news they weren't going to like.

A couple weeks after the interview, I took the train to DC early Saturday morning to have lunch with my parents. They were both traveling the next day, which provided me an out for leaving directly after lunch in case the news didn't go over well, and I suspected it wouldn't.

"There's someone we'd like to introduce you to." My dad cut into his fish and took a bite. He didn't wait for me to ask what he meant; he kept going. "He's a Harvard man, graduated law school there a few years ago. Now he's working with Senator Alders, and his own political career will likely follow," my dad continued; his deep voice took command of the formal dining room like it was guarding the exits. "Numerous accolades from the firm he works at. His father is a lawyer as well. His name is Alexander Ray."

"I'm already seeing someone," I said curtly, not looking up

from my dinner. He hadn't even acknowledged his *visit*. "And I didn't ask for his résumé first, by the way."

My dad's eyebrows jumped. His chest filled with air slowly. He looked at my mom expectantly. When she didn't say anything, he put his fork down with a frustrated huff.

"Carolina," my dad addressed my mom.

He always had my mom deliver bad news because he thought I was purposefully obstinate when it came to getting advice or information in general from him.

"Isa," my mom said warmly. "You're finally finishing residency; you can look to the next steps and now you'll have time to consider them seriously."

The ladder only got taller because I never stopped to think about when I was done climbing. I was happy with where I was, and I was happy with my choices.

"I *am* taking my next steps seriously." I put my utensils down. I wasn't very hungry anyway and I needed to rip this bandage off. "In fact, I turned down the Winthrop fellowship. I spoke to Dr. Reinhold, and he invited me to interview for the sports medicine fellowship. I have a few items I need to complete before it's official, but I'm starting next fall."

Turning down the fellowship felt like finishing one of those insane reformer Pilates classes Selena did.

Sheer relief.

My father's eyes flashed. He abruptly threw his napkin on the table, pushed himself back, and walked away. "Carolina, talk to her."

"Felix," my mom called as he stomped down the hallway. She pinched the bridge of her nose. "You two."

"Mom." I turned to her apologetically because her voice was wrapped in what sounded like genuine concern, which was ridiculous given how low the stakes were. "I can't do this anymore."

"Isa."

I pushed myself back from the table, itching to get up and walk away. But I didn't. I stayed there, pushed myself back toward the table, and forced myself to deal with a conversation that made me nervous.

"I can't keep chasing a goal with every breath I have if it's not what I want," I explained.

"Suddenly you don't want this?" she questioned pointedly. Behind the sharpness in her tone there was something softer. Hurt or disappointment—either way it was more painful than if she were upset.

A silence dropped over us, the kind I tried to avoid. It was the silence that twelve-year-old Isa had hated because it was always the one proceeded by a lecture on how important every single decision I made was to my future. No room for missteps.

I couldn't pin it all on my parents, though. A lot of the pressure was internal. Because girl power. And girl bossing. And being the doctor that society always wanted you to marry. Those words were like gospel to me, internalized until it felt like I *had* to be infallible. Any imperfection was failure.

That mentality provided me the success I enjoyed today but it also stole any grace I could give myself to be human.

"I came here to tell you that I love my job, but I'm not accepting the Winthrop fellowship," I repeated firmly, summoning the courage to look her in the eyes and the determination to sit in the silence for as long as I needed to make sure they knew the decision would stick. "I found something else I enjoy doing. I don't care about the legacy as much as I do my happiness."

Another stifling silence hung over us. Inside this one, I watched as my mom's eyes moved along in thought. Her face softened and she nodded.

At that table, after my dad got annoyed with me and walked off, I was a kid again.

Since we were there, I thought I may as well ask the question I was always too scared to, mostly because I wasn't sure I wanted the answer. "Do you regret having me?"

A part of me always figured I held her back. All my drive to be like my dad was because I didn't want to end up like her. Because she got stuck being the mom while my dad got to be *everything* else.

"Isa." My mom pushed back in her seat and sat up rigidly straight like she'd just been electrocuted. She shook her head disbelievingly. "Why would you—

"You're so invested in my career, it always felt like it was because you had to give up parts of yours." I finally managed to verbalize the thought that crept in the back of my mind for years. "Like I was your redemption."

I tried so hard to be self-sufficient so *nobody* could pin their unhappiness on me. It was only when I saw my mom's shoulders relax, the corners of her mouth drop, and her chest round forward with a deep exhale that I realized nobody ever had.

"I'm at the place in my career where you changed yours," I added.

I didn't need to remind her or myself because I saw it in

the way she looked at me the last year. Like she was nervous; something akin to a new mom watching her child take their first few steps. Waiting, hoping, praying they wouldn't fall.

"No. Never," she answered firmly, but her chin wobbled. She stood from her seat at the far side of the table and sat down next to me. She put her hand on mine. I looked down because the glassiness in her eyes was surely going to bring on tears in mine. "Isabelle, look at me."

I did and sucked in a deep breath, hoping the vacuum would suck back the mistiness in my eyes.

"I need you to understand and know that all of my choices were *my* choices." She grasped my chin tightly. "I have never regretted raising my remarkable daughter."

I nodded. She let go of my chin and tried not to look down. "Not even when it kept you from all that Dad got to do for his life?"

I had violin recitals and debate team and Model UN. My mom was around for almost all of it. She took days off, cut her OR schedule short, passed up conferences because she didn't want me to look out into the crowd and not see her.

"In those moments, I wondered about the road not taken," she admitted. "And we didn't have any more children because I needed to be back at work. I *needed* it. But Isa, of all the achievements I've made—because they may not be as well publicized as your father's, but they are there—you have always been my greatest." Her voice cracked and every syllable resonated in my chest. She looked me square in the eye as her tears smeared her mascara. "My joy, my pride, my reason for being from the day you were born."

I nodded again, wiping the few tears that dared defy direct orders from my brain.

"I pushed you because . . ." She took a deep breath to reset some of the emotion in the room. "Well . . . I guess I wanted to save you from ever having this conversation with your own daughter one day. I never wanted that shadow for you."

"If you could change—"

"No," she interrupted sternly. "I wanted you to have the freedom to choose anything. I'm sorry that it became pushing you in a direction, making you believe there's only one outcome."

I wanted a life. A full one. One where I enjoyed my work but had other passions to get to after work was done. I didn't want to burn the candle on both ends like the Winthrop fellowship was known to do. I wanted to do something I loved and go home to people I loved.

That choice wasn't the weakness I'd thought it was. If anything, it was the strength in knowing ambition doesn't just disappear when life takes a turn you weren't expecting, it simply flows in a new direction.

I nodded.

"I'm not doing the Winthrop fellowship, Mom." This time it was more of a question. I told her and my dad as my own person making my own choices.

Now I wanted to know what she thought.

She smiled. "Institutional validation is wonderful but hollow. Why do you think your father chases a new award every few months?"

I never thought of it like that. In contrast to my dad, my mom was steadfast. Not much shook her confidence. I was re-

alizing now that it was because she was her own vibrant person
outside of work.

"And remember, you can have a family if you want one . . .
one day," she added cautiously. "Moms aren't the only ones who
can be the primary parent. Women aren't the only ones capable
of raising children."

I smiled. The image of Austin patiently teaching Jo filled
my eyes. I wasn't sure when I'd be ready for that, but there was
lightness with knowing I didn't need to know yet.

"I love you, Mom," I croaked.

"And don't worry about your father." She pulled me into a
hug so tight I felt the bottom of her rings on my ribs. "He's so
hard on you in front of you, thinking it'll make you tough. Give
it some time. Focus on you. When he realizes that you've made
your decision, he'll also realize just how much you take after
him."

"Yeah?"

"Yes," she cooed, stroking my hair like she had when I was
a kid. "Now . . . will you tell me about this young man sometime?"

"He's, like, sort of old," I blurted.

My mom pushed my shoulders back, her eyes wide. "How
old?"

"Like eight years older than me . . ."

"*Dios*, Isa." She shook her head and let out a sigh. "Nobody
can ever accuse you of being dishonest."

Chapter 45
ISABELLE

$\mathcal{I}$ took the train back to Manhattan a couple hours later and managed to make it back by early evening.

Austin told me he'd come over to my place once I got back and we could have a quiet night in with a movie.

With my last year of residency in full swing with the summer puttering out and his final season with the team starting soon, we were sort of nesting—relaxing with each other before schedules got a little crazy.

Instead of waiting for him to come over, I went straight to his place and, as though he had been expecting me, the door was unlocked.

"Hey," he called when he heard the door open and close.

I smiled because he probably knew I'd come straight here. We had settled back into a place we were in right before the argument, except now it didn't feel like the terrifying precipice at the top of a roller coaster before I fell.

Now it felt like the opposite; a hammock's supportive embrace keeping me from hitting the ground. All the time. I felt safe and I never realized how nice it was to simply expect someone was looking out for your happiness.

"I thought I was meeting you later," he added over the sound of dishes clanking in the kitchen.

I liked his place, and I didn't want to wait to see him.

"I missed you," I called back, loudly and unabashedly, not feeling the need to hide behind anything, because it was true. And more than that, I wanted him to know.

The hallway opened up to his kitchen on one side, overlooking the giant living space and the view of Lower Manhattan.

"How was it?" He threw the kitchen towel over his shoulder, and I made my way to him in front of the stove.

"Good." My voice went up an octave unexpectedly.

He grinned. Before I left, I'd been a little nervous and I didn't hide it well. "Oh yeah?"

"Yeah. They weren't ecstatic about me choosing Dr. Reinhold's fellowship, but my mom understood."

"And your dad?"

I shrugged. "He'll come around."

"You sure that's not why you came here?" His eyes searched mine to make sure I was okay.

My heart dipped. "I'm sure."

He put both arms around me and pulled me into a soft kiss. "Or maybe you were hungry and knew I'd be making you something for tonight?"

"No, *that's* a delightful side effect." I smiled as he pulled away. "I missed you and I like your place."

It felt like a home. Warm and cozy.

I had a feeling Austin knew that without my saying it, as evidenced by the fact that he had left the door unlocked for me, like he'd expected me to change my plans after seeing my dad.

He grinned. "I love hearing that." He turned and walked back to the stove when a few sizzles got a bit louder. "Wanna help?"

I peeked over his shoulder. "No, you seem to have it covered."

I leaned over the stove with no real desire to actually cook. Besides, it looked like it was about done anyway. I was enjoying watching the process.

We settled on the couch after dinner with a couple glasses of wine.

"What do you want to watch?" Austin leaned forward and picked up the remote.

"How about a match?" I suggested. Austin had a bunch he wanted to watch saved on his TV. "I should learn the sport to make those lessons worthwhile."

My job was learning the movements likely to cause injury and then operating on them, so this was helpful, but we lived in the era of 4K game film. I could just as easily see the mechanism of injury as many times as I needed with perfect clarity. And the fellowship offered rotations in all types of sports, not just soccer. But my boyfriend was sort of a big deal in that particular sport, and I wanted to love the thing he loved.

He looked down at me with raised eyebrows. "Really?"

"Yes, I *want* to learn."

"We should probably start with the rules." Austin leaned forward and reached under the coffee table.

"Okay . . ."

He pulled a book from the second shelf underneath the coffee table. It was the book I bought to figure out how to start learning the game, the one I'd used to set up that little kicking practice lane in the park. The title, in bold black font against a bright-yellow background, was *Soccer for Dummies*. Except Austin had taken a Sharpie to DUMMIES, crossed it out, and written SURGEONS.

"I wanted to make sure we didn't bruise that ego." He kissed my forehead.

I ran my fingers over the Sharpie line.

I laughed quietly.

I'd told myself for years I'd be able to achieve my way into happiness, all on my own. I was so sure letting someone in during that process would get in the way.

Then, I'd found Austin. A man who was strong enough to listen to what I needed and brave enough to act on it. Because I was a force, and I needed someone who could not only withstand it but revel in it.

Turned out, I *could* have it all. Not one or the other. All of it.

"Okay." I flipped through the book, then back to the beginning with the rules. I handed Austin the remote. "Teach me something."

Epilogue

Two Years Later

AUSTIN

J stepped down the hallway back into the living room to find a panicked Isa moving around the room frantically. Her dark curls bounced in every direction.

"Esme is there—" Isa pointed to the small playpen in the middle of our place. She looked behind the couch, then back up to Esme, who peacefully played with her stuffed elephant in the playpen. "But Aisha . . ." Isa raked a hand through her hair, looking right past me even though I was holding Aisha. "Oh my God."

We got the little playpen out anytime Selena or Henry brought the twins over, which was almost never because Selena had a tough time leaving her daughters and Henry was an over-protective maniac.

They were one-year-olds with a fully outfitted security

detail. When they did come here, we had two guards stationed outside our door.

"She's right here." I held little Aisha in my arms as she giggled one of those tiny baby giggles that made me sure babies understood a lot more than we gave them credit for. She'd wandered down the hall a few feet when I got her. "She was headed to the bathroom, I think."

Isa's eyes darted around in thought and her skin paled. "She could have drowned."

"In an empty bathtub? In the quarter second she would have been in there alone before I got her?"

Esme was a calm baby who never pushed any boundaries. Her sister, Aisha, was practically an escape artist: rambunctious and a handful.

Isa pulled Aisha out of my arms and hugged the one-year-old snugly, rocking her in either direction. "I'm so sorry," she whispered into Aisha's cheek before pressing a long kiss against it. The adorable little psycho in her arms giggled again as Isa walked over to the playpen and put her beside her sister.

"Hey." I put my hands on Isa's shoulders as she stood in front of the two, watching them play. I could practically see her mind go to terrible places. "You're worried because you care."

Not because she was incapable, which was what I was sure she was thinking. Isa loved spending time with them, and she prepared for taking care of them on her own like she would for an exam. Not that she needed to—she was a natural, albeit a little anxious.

"Yeah, I know." She let out a relieved sigh. "Let's not tell

Henry that happened." Isa wrapped her arms around my waist and leaned into me.

"Deal." A laugh shook my shoulders.

The twins went back to playing with the pile of toys we had for them and Isa plopped down on the couch. She watched them intently for a few more seconds before relaxing a bit and leaning back.

"I can't leave them." Isa smiled and looked over to me. I looped an arm around her shoulders and pulled her in. "We're staying."

"You sure?"

Isa had graduated from her fellowship a few weeks ago and had three job offers. One to stay on here and work with a championship-winning basketball team, or head to Boston or Philadelphia for their respective teams.

"Philadelphia is a little too close to my parents." Isa counted off on her hand.

She and her dad had made their peace, in their own bizarre way. He'd told her he was proud of her exactly twice, and now they spent their monthly family dinners casually rattling off research or difficult cases they'd completed.

It often devolved to one-upmanship, but they were both willing to give the other their due. And they seemed to bond over it, so I wasn't questioning it.

"And Boston?"

"It's not Manhattan." She sighed and looked out the window. "The twins and Jo. They're here."

I smiled. Isa had been turning the idea over in her head for months. She was taking the summer off to relax after years of nonstop work but was stalled on where she'd start in the fall. There were logistics to consider for me, but I'd figure it out once she did.

"So, we're staying?"

"I reserve the right to change my mind," she said with an upward inflection, like it was question.

"I never mind when you change plans." I lifted her hand, and her engagement ring sparkled on her hand, sitting next to the wedding band we added the night after I slid the engagement ring on her finger. "You know that."

Last summer I took Isa to Paris for our anniversary, and I proposed. It was only sort of a surprise for her. Since she was easily spooked, I had Selena sneak a few hints it might happen into conversation to get an idea of Isa's reaction.

It was good one.

After she said yes, we celebrated in the same Ritz suite we were in the year before. The next morning, Isa started making a timeline while we were in bed for wedding planning. After twenty minutes, she realized she didn't want to wait. She was—in her words—not going to put off what she wanted. She suggested we elope. So, we did.

That night.

"This way nothing has to change with the academy," Isa added now.

We had all the things we needed to scout talent, and the facility opened its doors to its first class that past spring. It would be a while before it was profitable, but for now I got to teach a sport I loved to the next generation of kids who'd play it. I was living my own dream both inside and outside these walls.

"I'd figure it out," I told her for the hundredth time. "No matter where we were."

"I know." Isa rolled her head back in a faux, exaggerated huff. "And the twins and Jo need to have cool Aunt Isa close by as they grow up."

I smiled and *didn't* remind her that while she liked to think she was the fun one, she was also the one who tried to put helmets on the twins before putting them in a stroller, convinced they might be hurt.

Instead of pointing that out, I basked in the present, a home she filled with brightness, and a sharp wit. A future spent with a woman I'd never get tired of watching as she chased her dreams.

ACKNOWLEDGMENTS

*T*o my readers, thank you. Without your love and support, Isa's story would still be sitting on my laptop instead of these pages. Thank you.

To my wonderful husband, writing this story was made sweeter because you and I got to nerd out about the particulars of surgery. The story about appendicitis might sound familiar (*wink*). I love you.

Kimberly and Aimee, thank you for continuously supporting my work and my career in whichever direction I choose to navigate it in.

Julia, thank you for the care you take in all my stories.

Shaye and Linds, you already know.